THE
UNASSUMING
CURATOR

OTHER BOOKS AND AUDIOBOOKS
BY SIAN ANN BESSEY

GEORGIAN GENTLEMEN SERIES
The Noble Smuggler
An Uncommon Earl
An Alleged Rogue
An Unfamiliar Duke
The Unassuming Curator

CONTEMPORARY
Forgotten Notes
Cover of Darkness
Deception
You Came for Me
The Insider
The Gem Thief

HISTORICAL
Within the Dark Hills
One Last Spring
To Win a Lady's Heart
For Castle and Crown
The Heart of the Rebellion
The Call of the Sea

FALCON POINT SERIES
Heirs of Falcon Point
The Danger with Diamonds

KIDS ON A MISSION SERIES
Escape from Germany
Uprising in Samoa
Ambushed in Africa

CHILDREN'S
A Family Is Forever
Teddy Bear, Blankie, and a Prayer

ANTHOLOGIES AND BOOKLETS
The Perfect Gift
A Hopeful Christmas
No Strangers at Christmas

THE UNASSUMING CURATOR

A HISTORICAL ROMANCE

FROM THE BEST-SELLING AUTHOR OF THE GEORGIAN GENTLEMEN SERIES

SIAN ANN BESSEY

Covenant Communications, Inc.

Cover image: © Lee Avison / Trevillion Images. Background image: © Vecteezy.
Interior image: © Ekaterinavasilevskaya1 / Dreamstime.com

Cover design by Emily Remington
Cover design copyright © 2023 by Covenant Communications, Inc.

Published by Covenant Communications, Inc.
American Fork, Utah

Library of Congress Cataloging-in-Publication Data

Name: Sian Ann Bessey
Title: The Unassuming Curator / Sian Ann Bessey
Description: American Fork, UT : Covenant Communications, Inc. [2023]
Identifiers: Library of Congress Control Number 2022944919 | ISBN 978-1-52442-313-1
LC record available at https://lccn.loc.gov/2022944919

Printed in the United States of America
First Printing: April 2023

29 28 27 26 25 24 23   10 9 8 7 6 5 4 3 2 1

PRAISE FOR THE UNASSUMING CURATOR

"The first couple of chapters of *The Unassuming Curator* drew me in whole-heartedly. I knew this would be a compelling historical romance. With an edgy dilemma, Sian Ann Bessey applies all the elements of a good romance: intriguing characters, a mysterious plot, hidden dangers, and excellent writing. The author skillfully unfolds layers of deceit and emotion that tie the characters together. With a twist, new events change the fate of Emily and Henry. I found the characters well-developed and lively. I liked the way the author kept me guessing who would end up with Henry. I highly recommend this novel for its intelligent characters and romantic elegance. I am looking forward to reading more in the series."

—Readers' Favorite five-star review

"Prepare to fall in love with both of Bessey's main characters. They are noble, witty, and uncommonly intelligent but down-to-earth. This novel had all the musts of a Georgian-period historical romance—likable characters, well-researched history, some suspense, witty repartee, quirky side-characters, a London season, balls, and—most importantly—a romance that builds from friendship to love in a beautifully believable way."

—Laura Rupper, author of *The Sergeant and the Girl Next Door*

"You can safely assume that *The Unassuming Curator* is completely charming. Henry Buckland is digging up a red campion flower when he meets Miss Emily Norton, a young lady who knows all about gardening. Both leads are extremely likable and their relationship grows consistently, like a flower. I also enjoyed learning about the history of being color blind. This is a lovely, sweet romance that is a must for any historical fiction collector."

—Samatha Hastings, author of *Secret of the Sonnets*

Other Praise for Sian Ann Bessey

"Historical fiction at its finest!"

—Esther Hatch, award-winning author of A Proper Scandal series

"A dream come true for lovers of history. An absolute joy for anyone who treasures a beautifully told story."

—Sarah M. Eden, *USA Today* best-selling author

Every time I hold a newly published book in my hands, I am reminded of the many people at Covenant who work so hard on my behalf. I will be forever grateful to each of them. A single page isn't big enough to list them all, but I would like to dedicate this book to a truly remarkable group of unsung heroes. Thank you for all you do.

Blair Leishman
audio engineer, who records every audiobook with phenomenal quality.

Christina Marcano
graphics manager, who orchestrates book, marketing, and sales design needs for every author and ensures Covenant has some of the best covers in the market.

Crystal Bray
marking project manager, who makes sure the stores are stocked and laid out in a way that features authors and new releases in the best possible way.

Jessica Bybee
public relations representative, who juggles more things than should be humanly possible and does it with efficiency and grace.

Jill Badell
director of retail, who trains and manages all store employees to ensure they are representing and selling Covenant's books in the best possible way.

LeAnn Holt
front desk receptionist, who greets each visitor to Covenant with a friendly face and offers a helpful hand to every author who enters the office.

Mark Jorgensen
warehouse worker, who has been with Covenant for more years than I can count. Covenant might actually fall apart without him.

Mark Ware
production manager, who finds presses for every single book Covenant produces or reprints. He is the reason the physical copies of my books exist.

Rob Snider
warehouse manager, who coordinates and manages every shipment of books to every store.

Tracy Bentley
business affairs specialist, who successfully keeps track of more numbers and documents than I can comprehend and has shown me extraordinary kindness.

CHAPTER 1

Berkshire, England 1790

HENRY BUCKLAND DID NOT HAVE time for a detour. He was expected in London by day's end, and Lord Claridge, the chair of the British Museum's board of trustees, would be most disgruntled if he arrived late. Unfortunately for the venerable gentleman, Henry's incentive to linger in the country lane was equally compelling. After all, if one had the good fortune to stumble upon a perfect red campion specimen, it simply should not be ignored.

With another brief glance at the lowering sun, Henry's gaze moved from the charcoal sketch in the book on his knee to the spindly plant fighting for space in the hedgerow before him. His rapidly drawn illustration had captured the shape of the leaves and petals well enough. If he added a brief written description, cataloging should be easy enough to do when he reached London—as long as the flowers maintained their vibrant hue long enough for his colleague Nicholas Fernsby to confirm his representation of the color.

Setting his sketchbook on the ground, Henry studied the small flower in the afternoon light, attempting to gauge its hue against the green foliage of the hawthorn bush. For as long as he could remember, he had struggled to ascertain the difference between certain colors. Reds appeared brownish-green, pinks were a shade of gray, and when located beside each other, purples merged with blue. He'd learned to ignore the childhood teasing when he'd been unable to discern a piece of clothing or furniture by its color, but it was difficult to disregard the problem when he was called upon to identify plant specimens.

He reached into his satchel and withdrew a small trowel and linen bag. Henry was well aware that not many gentlemen traveled with such unusual items, but he was rarely without them. As a botanist and one of three curators at the British Museum, he was constantly on the lookout for new material to add to the museum's growing collection of dried flowers. More often than not—like today—he came upon them unexpectedly, and he had long since learned that it paid to be prepared.

Henry eyed the plant critically. How would most people describe the color of the delicate petals?

"What are you, little flower?" he muttered.

"It's a red campion."

At the sound of the female voice, Henry scrambled to his feet and turned to face a petite young lady. "I beg your pardon?"

Her yellow gown was cinched at her small waist and swished gently as she stepped toward him. Dark curls peeked out from beneath her straw bonnet, and when she raised her head, her equally dark eyes met his.

"The flower," she said, pointing to the plant he'd sketched. "It's a red campion."

He nodded. "It is, indeed."

A furrow appeared along her brow. "If you already knew what it was called, why did you ask?"

Henry stifled a sigh. No matter that he'd assumed he was alone on the narrow lane leading from the country inn, he should have known better than to verbalize his question.

"I believe you may have been misled by what you overheard," he said. "I was speculating on the flower's color rather than its name."

"Pink," she said, the crease along her forehead deepening. "Surely that is obvious."

With so insistent a response, perhaps he would not need Fernsby's input on the matter after all. He grasped at the silver lining to this awkward conversation and attempted to redirect it slightly. "You would think so, would you not? But why would someone name a pink flower 'red campion'? It seems to me that it was a rather dastardly act."

It took only a moment for a slight uptick in the corner of her mouth to appear, and he knew that she'd picked up on his jesting.

"One might even say that it is as reprehensible as calling the pink and white blooms in the flower beds of many English homes by the name Spanish Bluebells," she said.

He chuckled. It seemed that the young lady could claim some wit along with a respectable knowledge of local flora. Had she been taught by a governess? She did not wear the clothing of a servant, and yet, she appeared to be unaccompanied. He glanced at the empty lane. Not more than ten yards away, the narrow road bent slightly, soon after to join the main thoroughfare to London.

The hedgerow hid all but the chimneys of The Rose and Crown Inn that stood at the intersection of the two roads. Henry had stopped there on his way to London to rest his horse and stretch his legs. It was possible that she was doing the same, but that did not explain why she was currently alone.

He was still determining whether it would be impolite to ask when she spoke again.

"Are you intending to dig up the red campion?"

With a start, Henry realized he was still holding his trowel. "As a matter of fact, I am."

"It seems a shame to deprive others of the splash of color it affords in the hedgerow."

Henry stared at her. She was in earnest. "There are plenty of red campion flowers to be had along the lane," he said.

"Do you intend to dig them up too?"

"Not at all. I require only one plant for my work."

He saw the flicker of interest enter her brown eyes moments before the sound of running feet reached them, and the lad Henry had seen at the inn's stables appeared around the bend.

"Beggin' yer pardon, miss," the boy panted. "'Is lordship sent me t' find you."

"Oh dear. Is he ready to leave?"

"I believe so, miss."

"Please tell him I will join him immediately."

"Yes, miss." The lad pivoted and started back the way he'd come.

The young lady turned to Henry once more. "It appears that I must go. I wish you well with your digging, sir."

He inclined his head. "And I wish you well on your journey."

"I confess, meeting a collector of red campions along the way has set this trip apart from all others." The genuine warmth of her smile caught him off guard. "Good day to you."

She did not wait for a response. Instead, she hurried after the stableboy and was quickly lost to view around the bend.

Henry stood for a moment, watching the spot where she'd disappeared. Who was she? And who was the nobleman who waited for her? Not the young lady's husband, certainly, or else the stableboy would have greeted her with a title. A father, perhaps. Or a guardian? And why would a titled gentleman allow a young lady to roam a country lane alone?

The quiet road offered Henry no answers. Shaking his head at his own foolishness, he knelt beside the hedge and began loosening the dirt around the red campion plant with his trowel. The young lady and her escort were of no concern to him, and he had no time to waste. Reaching London before Lord Claridge left the museum may now be an unattainable goal, but arriving first thing in the morning remained a possibility.

Emily Norton slowed her steps as she approached the waiting carriage. She did not need to see the look on her brother, Adam's, face to know she should not have strayed so far. Up until a month ago, her erstwhile governess and companion, Miss Glover, would have been at her side. But Miss Glover had recently left the household to live in a small cottage near the sea in Cornwall.

Everyone at Dunsbourne Manor—most especially, Emily—hoped the change in climate would relieve the worsening discomfort in the elderly lady's joints, but Miss Glover's removal had left an unexpectedly large void that not even Emily's new sister-in-law, Phoebe, had been able to completely fill. Phoebe was Emily's dearest friend, but as the mistress of Dunsbourne Manor, she had to divide her time far more than Miss Glover ever had, and over the last few weeks, Emily had become used to wandering the gardens and orchard at Dunsbourne Manor on her own. She should have known that such freedom was not acceptable at an unfamiliar inn.

Clasping her hands together, she met Adam's disapproving gaze. "Forgive me for keeping you waiting."

"When you told me you wished to take some air after our meal, I thought you would stay within sight of the carriage," Adam said.

She caught the censure in his tone even though the words remained unspoken. "I did not go far. Just around the bend to see the wildflowers."

"You are eighteen years of age, Emily. Surely you are too old to be collecting wildflowers."

Emily was tempted to tell him there was a gentleman digging up red campions a little farther down the lane who was most certainly older than she was, but she did not think such information would be especially politic at present.

"I should not have gone without speaking to you first," she said.

He released a frustrated sigh. "You do not need my permission to take a walk, Em, but I cannot have you going about without a companion. Especially when we reach London."

"I know."

He must have sensed her contrition, for his expression softened. "You're not the only one who'd rather be outside than sitting inside a carriage or a parlor."

She managed a small smile. "I know that too."

Though the Dunsbourne orchards had turned sufficient profit over the last two years for Adam to hire additional help, he chose to spend much of his time working alongside his gardener among the apple trees. If it weren't for his overriding sense of duty to introduce Emily into London Society, he would be there still.

"Come," he said, offering her his hand.

She stepped into the carriage. Phoebe was already inside and gave Emily an understanding look as she took the seat across from her.

"We may be hard pressed to find Adam an orchard in the center of town, but there are parks aplenty," Phoebe said. "You will love the spring flowers at Hyde Park. I daresay they will be in full bloom within a fortnight."

"I agree." Adam had followed Emily into the carriage and sat beside his wife. "And I have no doubt Lady Millward will happily provide a servant to accompany you, should you ever wish to go somewhere while I am working or Phoebe is resting."

The carriage lurched into motion, and Emily nodded. She'd been looking forward to seeing the sights of London almost as much as she'd been dreading her launch into Society. Their original departure date had been delayed for months: first, by the late apple harvest, and second, by concerns over Phoebe's health. Only the joyful discovery that her prolonged illness was due to the fact that she was expecting a baby had offset Phoebe's disappointment at postponing their arrival in London.

Despite her need for rest and her uneasy stomach, however, Phoebe had continued to tutor Emily in the niceties of high Society. Emily now knew the steps of every dance and the rules of comportment at musical evenings and the theater. She'd learned what were considered acceptable topics of conversation with a lady or a gentleman, and she'd gained sufficient knowledge of current fashions to enter a social setting with confidence. And yet, the mere thought of being the subject of attention at one large event after another caused her stomach to roil. She knew full well that the country balls she'd attended over the last eighteen months were hardly a match for the ones held in London. And those events had been trying enough.

She forced her thoughts elsewhere. "What type of occupation would require someone to collect red campion?" she asked.

Adam blinked. "Red campion?"

"Yes," Emily said. "Why would one gather it?"

Phoebe glanced at her husband's bewildered expression and came to his rescue. "For a flower arrangement, perhaps."

It was the most obvious answer, but it didn't explain the trowel or a need for the plant's roots. Emily wrinkled her nose in concentration. Surely she'd learned something about the wildflower in one of the many books she'd pored over in the Dunsbourne Manor library.

"If I remember correctly, the flower itself is known to be mildly toxic," she said.

"Then you may disregard my suggestion," Phoebe said.

"What of the leaves or the root?" Adam asked.

"It seems to me that the root can be used as an ingredient in soap," Emily said thoughtfully.

"Well, there you are, then." Phoebe smiled. "That must be it."

"Yes, I suppose so." Soap making seemed a very odd occupation for a gentleman. Then again, digging up flowers in a hedgerow was not exactly commonplace.

"Why do you wish to know?" Adam was looking at her curiously.

"There were several red campions in the hedgerow near the inn," Emily said, mentally scrambling for a reasonable response. "One of them looked to have been dug up." That was surely true by now.

Adam shrugged. "I would imagine the damage was done by an animal of some sort."

"Then let us hope it was not foolish enough to eat the flowers," Phoebe said.

With a soft chuckle, Adam took his wife's hand. "Alternatively, there may be a hedgehog or a badger in this neighborhood with a remarkably clean mouth."

Emily smiled. Watching Adam's tenderness with Phoebe warmed her heart. And she would far rather picture the wild animals of Berkshire wandering the countryside with gleaming white teeth than contemplate members of the *ton* working their way around a London ballroom.

Releasing a tense breath, she leaned back against the seat cushion and studied the countryside through the window. Tiny yellow and white daisies dotted the green fields, and a cluster of wild crocuses grew at the base of a grove of trees. She watched for red campion but saw none. Perhaps the plant was not as ubiquitous as she'd originally thought.

In the distance, a row of gray stone houses came into view. The buildings were a poignant reminder that they would soon be leaving the countryside behind. Emily squared her shoulders. She would feign courage until she could truly claim it as her own. And if she was very fortunate, Lady Millward's library might include a book about wildflowers that she could borrow. Her spirits lifted. With a good book in hand, she could escape almost anything.

Chapter 2

Henry approached the stairs leading to the large doors of Montagu House. Behind him, the wide drive stretched out between rectangular mani-cured lawns and tidy rows of well-pruned shrubs. Strategically placed gravel paths guided guests from the courtyard to the front of the elegant french-style building and the entrance of the British Museum. A pigeon cooed loudly from atop the head of one of the garden's stone statues, and Henry paused his ascent to check his pocket watch.

This blissful early-morning calm would not last long. Very soon, those wish-ing to view the museum's various collections would begin arriving at Montagu House, and all semblance of peace would be gone.

"Good morning, Rutherford." Henry greeted the middle-aged porter as he entered.

"Welcome back, Mr. Buckland," Rutherford said, inclining his head politely. "I trust your journey went well."

"Well enough to please the board of trustees, I believe." He raised an eye-brow. There was no use putting off the inevitable. "I assume the chair came looking for me yesterday."

"He did, sir."

Lord Claridge was nothing if not predictable. His displeasure at discover-ing that Henry had yet to return was a certainty.

"You are the epitome of protocol, Rutherford, but the truth might prepare me better. How badly was he muttering?"

"Not nearly so loudly as when the Roman coins exhibit was delayed, sir."

If the porter had been attempting reassurance, he'd failed miserably. Claridge had all but had steam coming from his ears over the coin fiasco.

"I certainly hope not. I may be one day late in bringing him news of the Grenville collection, but I trust he will find that the wait was worthwhile."

The porter nodded knowingly. "Where will we be needing to find space this time?"

"The manuscript saloon."

"I daresay that's just as well. Mr. Watts will likely find all sorts of things for the museum on his travels, but I don't suppose many of them will be books."

Henry could not fault Rutherford's logic. Weeks ago, the British Museum's director, Mr. Watts, had set sail for the South Seas in search of more artifacts, the likes of which Captain James Cook and other explorers had brought back from their voyages. Seeing as the items currently on display from those far-off isles included such things as spears, knives, and shields used by the indigenous people, along with wood carvings and an assortment of remarkable seashells, it was unlikely that many of the pieces Mr. Watts chose to ship to the museum would end up in the reading room.

"I'm sure you are right," Henry said. "But in the meantime, I'd best inform Mr. Townsend that Lady Grenville's extensive collection of books will likely arrive within the fortnight."

"I imagine he'll be glad of the warning," Rutherford said, stepping back a pace. "I believe you will find him in the manuscript saloon, sir."

"Thank you, Rutherford." Henry offered him a nod of appreciation and crossed the ornate entrance hall with purposeful strides.

Montagu House had undergone extensive renovations after it had been purchased to house the British Museum's first collections. The original exhibition gallery and reading room opened in 1759 and had now grown to include literary and natural history exhibits that filled the entire building. Henry's area of expertise kept him primarily on the upper story with the natural history collections, but Mr. Townsend's domain was the vast compilation of literature on the ground floor.

Passing the grand staircase and the full-sized stuffed giraffe and bear standing on either side of it, Henry entered the large room. Arched windows ran the length of one wall, offering ample light and a view of the flower garden and terrace beyond. The other three walls were lined with bookshelves that ran from the floor to the vaulted ceiling. Four tall stepladders stood in various locations beside the shelving units, and half a dozen solid desks were piled with tomes and loose papers. Few chairs were to be seen—this was, after all, the manuscript saloon rather than a reading room—but upon one of the chairs, a white-wigged gentleman was sitting, poring over a scroll of paper on the table before him.

At the sound of Henry's footsteps on the marble-tiled floor, the gentleman looked up.

"Ah, Buckland," he said. "You have returned."

"I have." Henry offered him a polite smile.

Mr. George Townsend was at least thirty years Henry's senior and had been working at the museum for about that long. To the best of Henry's knowledge, the gentleman had never married but had devoted his life to the acquisition of books and documents for the museum's library. His knowledge of all things literary was unparalleled. Unfortunately, the same could not be said for his sartorial taste. No matter the day or the season, he dressed in black. Indeed, he might have been mistaken for a clergyman had it not been for his rather extravagant, lacy cravats.

"Was Lady Grenville's butterfly display all it was touted to be?" Townsend asked.

"She has a few notable species within the exhibit," Henry hedged. Having traveled all the way to Oxfordshire at the duchess's request, it would not do to openly criticize the mediocre collection. Particularly as she was so determined to have it on display at the museum.

"I am glad to hear it." The older man's attention returned to the scroll on the desk.

"Her compilation of original manuscripts, however, was significantly more impressive."

Townsend's head bobbed up instantly. "Manuscripts, you say?"

"Yes. She owns some rather marvelous illuminated books and prints created by someone by the name of William Blake."

Townsend stroked his stubbly chin thoughtfully. "I've heard of the fellow. Considers himself a bit of a visionary. Can't see it myself, but if his work has caught the eye of Lady Grenville, it will undoubtedly do the same for others." He paused. "Is she willing to part with them?"

"She has determined to donate a generous portion of her library to the museum. I believe Blake's relief etchings are up for negotiation."

Townsend frowned. "The trustees should have had me speak with her when they received her offer of a donation."

Henry did not bother to remind him that the books Lady Grenville wished to donate were an appendage to the butterfly collection, something that was fully within his purview. "When I make my report, I shall suggest that you be the one to contact her about the relief etchings and manuscripts," Henry said.

If passing further negotiations over to Townsend saved Henry from having to endure another tea with Lady Grenville and her prize Persian cat, so much the better. He suppressed a shudder. The duchess had kept him conversing in her drawing room for almost three hours, and he'd left the manor with his breeches and coat covered in cat hair.

"Most wise," Townsend said. "It would not do to make an error simply because one is inexperienced."

Henry recognized the cut. Townsend hardly bothered to veil them, but after having made his mark at Cambridge before coming to work at the museum last year at Mr. Watts's specific request, Henry refused to apologize for his lack of experience in acquiring books.

"Welcome back, Buckland."

The familiar voice at the door to the manuscript saloon was a welcome interruption. Henry turned to see Nicholas Fernsby enter. Fernsby was a few years older than Henry. Having studied painting in Paris for three years, the gentleman considered himself a skilled artist. He oversaw the art collection at the museum, and his clothing reflected his penchant for anything colorful. Today's ensemble included turquoise breeches and coat, a brown-and-yellow striped vest, and a white shirt that sported the most voluminous cravat Henry had ever seen.

"I see you're steadfastly maintaining your lack of punctuality, Fernsby," Townsend said. He had even less patience with the flamboyant curator than he did with Henry.

"I prefer to consider it fashionably late," Fernsby said. "Although, if I'd truly wished to make a grand entrance, I would have waited until there were some guests in the building."

"I would remind you that this is the British Museum, not the theater," Townsend said.

Fernsby raised his eyebrows. "By Jove, Townsend, that's a capital notion."

The wrinkles in the older gentleman's forehead deepened. "What idea is that?"

"Why, to build a theater in the museum." Ignoring Townsend's look of horror, Fernsby continued. "It's really quite brilliant. A simple stage at one end of the manuscript saloon where a small group of players acts out the plays housed in the museum."

Townsend opened his mouth, closed it, and then opened it again.

Henry did not need to identify the color flooding the gentleman's cheeks to know that it did not omen well. "We'd best be about our work, I think, Fernsby," he said, starting for the door and hoping his colleague would have the good sense to follow. "Good day, Townsend. I shall write to the trustees regarding Lady Grenville's donation today."

He did not wait for a response. Thankfully, it appeared that Fernsby chose not to either. The sound of his footsteps echoed Henry's into the entrance hall.

"In fairness," Fernsby's voice held a hint of humor, "the idea did have some merit."

Henry stopped at the foot of the grand staircase and waited for Fernsby to join him. "On a scale of one to ten, I would place the suggestion at a one."

Fernsby grinned. "Ever the scientist."

Henry leveled him with a long-suffering look. "Do you need a scientist to remind you of what happens when a spark lands upon kindling?"

Fernsby's chuckle followed them up the stairs. "I've missed you, Buckland. Especially yesterday, when I was required to take your tours."

"Yes, I'm sorry about that. I did try to get back in time." He paused. He didn't need to defend a work-related absence to Fernsby. "I was only gone a little more than a week."

"It was altogether too quiet for too long. Townsend and I scarcely exchanged a word the whole time."

It was Henry's turn to grin. "Perhaps there is a glimmer of common sense in you after all."

They walked the length of the landing, passing the room that showcased Sir Hans Sloane's collection and the gallery of antiquity before reaching Henry's office. He inserted the key into the lock and opened the door. The air was chill, but the books, inkwell, and quills lying on the table were just as he'd left them. Two chairs, a glass-fronted bookcase, and a workbench made up the remainder of the furniture. Scientific equipment lined the windowsill, and on one corner of the workbench sat a pitcher of water, a bowl, and his microscope.

"Did you gather more samples?" Fernsby asked.

"I did." Henry slid his satchel's strap over his head, enthusiasm for his work bubbling within him. "I stumbled upon a cluster of crested cow-wheat in a woodland area not far from Grenville Manor and the first red campion of the season outside an inn in Berkshire."

"Do you need any help with the colors?"

Asking the person who oversaw art at the museum to describe the exact hue of his flowers' petals had been such a natural request that Fernsby had accepted it without question.

"I'll come and find you if I do," Henry said. "I've been told that pink is a reliable description for the red campion."

"Sounds right," Fernsby said.

Henry shook his head helplessly. Why couldn't people refer to the flower by its Latin name? *Silene dioica* was a perfectly pronounceable appellation and not nearly so misleading as red campion. Pushing aside his uncharacteristic grumpiness, he unwrapped the limp plants and carefully set them on the workbench. With their shared confidence in color identification, Fernsby and the young lady on the lane would have undoubtedly gotten along very well.

Emily descended the staircase in Lady Millward's townhouse. Morning light was streaming in through the narrow windows on either side of the dark front door, spilling over the polished marble floor of the entry below. There was no sign of the butler who had met them at the door the evening before, but the faint chink of china and murmur of voices told her that others in the household were already at breakfast.

Hurrying down the last few stairs, she reached the hall in time to hear the cogs in the longcase clock whirr and the chimes begin. Ten o'clock. She grimaced. After the long drive from Berkshire, the comfortable bed in the beautifully appointed guest bedchamber she'd been assigned to use during her stay had been most welcome. She'd slept well. But arising so late on her first day in London would surely not recommend her well to Phoebe's aunt, Lady Millward.

Upon their arrival last night, Phoebe's exhaustion had shown on her face, and Lady Millward had declared that all conversation between them was to be postponed until everyone had rested. Phoebe's relief had been obvious. As had Adam's. He had assisted Phoebe to her bedchamber without delay, and Emily had followed in their wake, secretly glad of the reprieve from socializing with a virtual stranger for one more night.

Lady Millward was not exactly a stranger, of course. The lady had attended Adam and Phoebe's wedding, and Emily had spoken to her briefly several months later when she'd visited Phoebe's parents at their house near Dunsbourne Manor. But they had never exchanged more than polite pleasantries, and although Phoebe had always spoken fondly of her aunt, Emily was still not quite sure what to make of the lady whose personality exuded as much flamboyance as Miss Glover's did restraint.

Adam's voice reached her from an open door on her left. This must be the dining room. Squaring her shoulders, she ran her hands down her peach-colored gown, took a deep breath, and walked in.

Pale-blue wallpaper covered the walls. Paintings of various sizes and compositions added additional splashes of color. Three large windows looked out upon a small garden and were currently shedding light on a large, highly polished dining table in the center of the room. A dozen chairs surrounded the table, two of which were currently occupied.

"Ah, Miss Norton! I am so glad you are come." Lady Millward offered her a welcoming smile as Adam came to his feet. "How did you sleep?"

"Very well, thank you, my lady. The bed, the bedchamber, everything is lovely."

Lady Millward's smile widened, and Emily made the interesting observation that the many lines on the lady's face suggested that smiling was something she engaged in rather often.

"How very kind of you," Lady Millward said. She gestured toward a sideboard laden with dishes, from which emanated the glorious smells of sausages and freshly baked bread. "Please help yourself to some food and join us. Your brother has just begun telling me about the latest developments in the Dunsbourne Manor orchards."

"You are in for a rather long conversation, I fear," Emily said. "The list of improvements Adam has implemented over the last year is extensive."

Lady Millward looked to Adam, humor in her eyes. "Either your sister is exceptionally proud of what you have accomplished, Lord Dunsbourne, or else she is attempting to warn me of impending boredom."

Adam chuckled. "I daresay she might own to a little of both."

The tension in Emily's shoulders eased a fraction. If Adam was comfortable with Lady Millward's teasing, perhaps the older lady was not quite so formidable as Emily had feared.

"How is Phoebe this morning?" Emily asked.

Adam's expression softened. "She rested well and intends to join us shortly."

"I am glad to hear it."

Mindful that Adam would remain standing until she had taken her seat, Emily moved to the sideboard and quickly filled a plate. As she approached the table, a footman appeared to withdraw a chair for her. She sat, and Adam did the same.

"If you are fond of drinking chocolate, Miss Norton, I would recommend you try some this morning," Lady Millward said. "I have yet to ascertain exactly what my cook does to make it froth so well, but I have told her she must keep doing it."

"I should be happy to taste it," Emily said.

Lady Millward directed a nod at the footman, who promptly fetched a large floral teapot from the sideboard and began filling a matching teacup with the chocolatey brew. Emily's surprise must have shown on her face because Lady Millward offered her a knowing smile.

"A lesson in not judging by appearance, Miss Norton," she said. "Rather important as you enter London Society for the first time, I think. Not all teapots contain tea. Not all ladies behave benevolently. And not all gentlemen embrace the virtues they are purported to uphold."

Phoebe had already warned Emily of the same. Hearing Lady Millward repeat the counsel did little to assuage Emily's anxiety over what lay ahead.

"How does one navigate Society if it is so full of counterfeits?" she asked.

"You place great confidence in the opinion of your distrustful brother," Adam said.

"That is certainly one way," Lady Millward agreed. "A protective glowering baron standing at your side can do much to ward off undesirables."

"As a matter of fact, I have already experienced that phenomenon," Emily said, offering Adam a stern look. "Unfortunately, said baron tends to dissuade every gentleman from approaching, not merely the undesirables."

Lady Millward raised her teacup to her lips but was not able to completely hide her smile. She took a sip of her drinking chocolate before lowering the cup again. "If I may be so bold," she said, "might I suggest that although an elderly viscountess is not nearly so forbidding as a young baron, she can be similarly helpful."

"So, I believe," Adam said. "In fact, I did hear rumor that you were a rather valuable ally to Lord Bloxley during his and Lady Bloxley's courtship."

Emily caught the glint of humor in his eyes and sensed a story behind his words. "What did you do?" she asked.

Lady Millward brushed off her question with a wave of her hand. "That is a tale for another day, my dear. Today, we must focus on your situation."

Her situation. Emily forced down the piece of bread roll she'd just placed in her mouth. She was an orphan, who, up until two years ago, had had no experience in Society whatsoever. When she'd reached the age of sixteen, Adam had taken her to her very first dinner party, but it had only been after Phoebe had entered their lives that Emily had begun to develop the skills necessary to navigate the turbulent waters of Society. Unfortunately, she knew full well that a mastery of basic dance steps and an awareness of today's fashions hardly meant she was ready to face the *ton*.

"I scarcely know where to begin," she said. "I think it likely that I will need assistance with everything that lies ahead."

"Do not sell yourself short, Miss Norton," Lady Millward said. "Already, I can tell that you are a delight. You shall be a welcome addition to the assemblies of London."

"I own that I am somewhat biased," Adam said, "but you have the right of it, Lady Millward. Emily is uncommonly intelligent and yet never considers herself above anyone else."

"A rare quality, indeed," Lady Millward said. "Tell me, my dear, what is it that consumes most of your time and attention? Where do your interests lie?"

"My interests?" How could Emily possibly narrow down her varied interests to only one or two?

"Yes," Lady Millward said. "At your age, Phoebe's passion lay in fashion. Her sister, Jane's, was in art. What is yours?"

"I believe I would have to say that it is reading," Emily said. "Reading consumes the better part of my time."

Lady Millward nodded encouragingly. "And do you have a favorite novelist or poet?"

Emily had read the works of many novelists and poets, but none of them had captured her heart or imagination the way her favorite books in the Dunsbourne library had done. If Lady Millward truly wished to know where her passion lay, Emily would need to be fully honest with her. "I appreciate the writing of many skilled authors, my lady," she said, "but, in truth, my passion lies elsewhere. I love reading about the world—about far-off lands, animals, plants, rivers, and mountain ranges."

Lady Millward raised her eyebrows and Emily's heart sank. She'd seen similar expressions of disbelief followed by disapproval amongst members of Berkshire's gentry. "My former companion, Miss Glover, taught me to knit," she added, attempting to infuse her voice with the same level of enthusiasm she'd exhibited for reading. Knitting was not the musical talent most young ladies aspired to, but it was surely more ladylike than studying world geography and biology. "I have spent significant time improving my skill and can now create a reasonably well-shaped scarf."

"Is that so?" Lady Millward said. "How remarkably refreshing."

Emily blinked. She caught Adam's eye. He was doing an admirable job at hiding his surprise at the older lady's response.

"R . . . refreshing, my lady?" Emily said.

"Absolutely. Knitting a scarf would seem a very practical use of one's time. And I, for one, am excessively tired of hearing young ladies attempt to sing higher or play the pianoforte with greater gusto than anyone else in the room. I believe our social gatherings would be far more interesting if we spent time discussing the latest expedition to the Alps or the migratory patterns of African elephants."

Emily attempted to gather her wits. "I . . . I am very glad you think so."

Lady Millward dipped a teaspoon into her drinking chocolate and stirred it absently. "Do elephant herds relocate on a regular basis? I'm not sure that I have ever considered the subject before."

"According to Mr. Conrad Gesner's book, *Historiae Animalium*, they do."

"Well, I have learned something new today." Lady Millward's expression cleared. "I look forward to your enlightening me further, Miss Norton."

Emily's smile was instant, as was the bubble of hope that rose within her.

"I would be happy to discuss such subjects with you, my lady. Although, I think it fair to say that you have a great deal more to teach me than I can teach you."

Lady Millward took another sip of her beverage and studied Emily over the top of her teacup. "Lord Dunsbourne," she said, setting the cup down on the saucer, "your sister and I are going to get along very well." She gave a satisfied nod, and her voluminously coiffured white hair wobbled. "Very well, indeed."

"I was quite sure that you would, Aunt Millward." Phoebe's voice reached them from the doorway, instantly drawing everyone's attention. Adam rose to greet her, kissing her cheek softly as she took the chair beside him. "I hope you have not decided upon the best way to launch Emily into Society without me."

Emily recognized Phoebe's teasing tone, but Lady Millward was completely unperturbed.

"We should begin with something intimate, I think. It never hurts to allow a small group of people to meet someone rather special first. The privileged like being treated as such." The older lady's thoughtful look evaporated. "I have it. Lord and Lady Farwell are holding a dinner party tonight. It will be just the thing. The Farwells are sufficiently well connected that they will have invited people of consequence. And with a limited number of guests, it will be impossible for Miss Norton to go unnoticed."

Emily's stomach churned. Truth be told, she would rather blend into the furnishings and quietly observe others than be the center of attention.

"That sounds ideal," Adam said. "But do you think Lord and Lady Farwell will be open to including us in their party at such short notice?"

Lady Millward smiled knowingly. "Familial connections can offer one a rather useful advantage, my lord. Lady Leonora Farwell is my late husband's sister. We have remained close despite his having been gone for many years. I have no doubt she will be eager to see Phoebe again and also to meet you and your sister."

Emily stared at her breakfast plate. If her stomach behaved so traitorously over nothing more than a conversation of what was to come this evening, she was doomed.

CHAPTER 3

THE HACKNEY TURNED ONTO BERKELEY Square, its wheels slowing as it approached Benning House. Inside the carriage, Henry withdrew his pocket watch and glanced at it. Twenty minutes. It was not long, but his valet, Felix, had managed the job in less. If Henry could only reach his bedchamber without being accosted by his mother, his valet was perfectly capable of transforming him from a museum curator to a member of the nobility before his parents' guests arrived. He shifted to the edge of his seat and prepared for a speedy exit.

The carriage had barely come to a stop before his feet were on the pavement. He tossed a coin to the startled driver and hurried up the stairs to the townhouse's front door. The butler, Akers, must have been watching for him because the door opened the moment Henry reached the top step.

"Good evening, Mr. Buckland," Akers said, inclining his head as he moved aside to allow him entry.

"Good evening, Akers." Henry handed the man his hat. "Is the coast clear?"

The butler's expression remained unchanged, but his voice lowered slightly. "I believe your father is in his study, sir. Lord Benning arrived about an hour ago. To the best of my knowledge, he and your mother are upstairs still."

Henry grinned. There'd been several times since he'd started his job at the British Museum that he had given serious consideration to renting rooms closer to his workplace, but it was hard to turn his back on the benefits of living in his family's townhouse. A loyal butler was certainly one of those perks, and since Henry's parents and brother, Benedict, were only in London for a few weeks of the year, Henry liked to think that he claimed a greater measure of that loyalty.

"You're a good man, Akers," Henry said.

The butler accepted his comment with a small bow. "We have had this same conversation a time or two, sir. I have come to expect it."

Henry's grin widened. "Let us hope that Felix is equally well prepared."

"I daresay he is, sir."

The longcase clock in the hall chimed the quarter hour. He had only fifteen minutes remaining to him. Crossing the entry at a brisk walk, he took the stairs two at a time, arriving on the landing before the chime fully faded. He reached the door to his bedchamber and opened it just as another door farther down the passage opened. As the sound of his mother's voice talking to her maid reached him, Henry stepped into his room and closed the door behind him.

Felix set Henry's dinner jacket on the back of the chair and turned to face him. "Welcome home, sir."

"Thank you, Felix." Henry glanced at the clothing laid out across the bed. "It looks like you are ready for me."

"Yes, sir. Lady Farwell gave me to understand that tonight's dinner is to be an elegant affair, so I thought perhaps your cream-colored breeches with the burgundy-and-cream embroidered waistcoat."

Trusting in his valet's superior perception of colors, Henry tugged his cravat loose. "Yes. That will do very well."

After a long day at the museum, entertaining his mother's guests was not the way he would wish to spend the evening, but she had made him promise that he would be in attendance, so he had left his office with his cataloging incomplete in order to keep his word.

He reached for the clean shirt Felix held out to him.

Thankfully, as the second son of Lord and Lady Farwell, Henry was not the primary target of Society matrons with eligible daughters, but he was often called upon to round out the numbers at functions.

"Did you happen to hear who is attending this evening's dinner party?" Henry asked.

"Not officially, sir."

"Unofficially, then." The servants talked. There was no point in hiding it.

"I did hear mention of the Dowager Lady Pendleton," Felix said.

Henry froze, his arm halfway into his sleeve. "'You heard mention,' as in the lady issued a horrible threat that has now blown over, or 'you heard mention,' as in she is actually expected at Benning House within the next ten minutes?"

Felix cleared his throat uncomfortably. "Given that Cook is in rather a flap over her jelly not setting as firmly as it should, I would assume the latter."

"Blast it all!" Henry pushed his hand through his cuff with more force than was necessary. "Whatever possessed my mother to allow that awful woman back into the house? The last time she was here, she reduced two maids to tears with her biting tongue."

"I believe she requested an invitation, sir."

Henry stared at him. The dowager marchioness was known for being rude, but to demand a place at his parents' table seemed beyond even her assertiveness. "Why?"

Felix helped Henry into his waistcoat and reached for the crisp white cravat lying across the back of a nearby chair. "I cannot say for certain, sir."

Henry gave him an exasperated look. "Then tell me without certainty. Deuce take it, Felix, you've been my valet for eight years. I am well aware of your sense of propriety and confidentiality, and I am most grateful for it. But at this precise moment, I should like to hear the servants' gossip. If I am to be required to spend the evening with the Dowager Lady Pendleton, I should like to know why."

"It is my understanding that she is not coming alone, sir." Felix straightened Henry's cravat and held out his jacket. "She will be accompanied by Lord and Lady Pendleton and their daughter, Lady Aurelia."

Lady Aurelia. The name conjured up a memory of a tall young lady whose eager and continual chatter at the Overtons' ball a fortnight ago had encouraged a circle of gossip-hungry young ladies and discouraged the approach of most gentlemen.

"What do you know of Lady Aurelia?" Henry asked, shrugging into his jacket and wishing he'd paid more attention at the handful of social functions he'd attended since his parents had arrived in Town.

Felix brushed a piece of lint off one sleeve. "I believe this is her first Season in London, and the dowager marchioness wished to facilitate an introduction."

Henry groaned. Everything made perfect sense now. Not only would his mother wish to avoid offending the overbearing Dowager Lady Pendleton by denying her request, but she was also unabashedly anxious to have her sons marry well. The daughter of the Marquess Pendleton would surely be an advantageous match for the future Viscount Farwell.

"Is Ben halfway to Gloucestershire already?"

"To the best of my knowledge, sir, no one has called for the carriage."

Henry spared a moment for a brief glance in the mirror. As far as outward appearances were concerned, he would pass muster. "I'd best go and join the poor fellow, then," he said. "It sounds like he's in need of an ally."

Emily exited the carriage and studied the townhouse before her. Four rows of white-framed, multipaned windows punctuated the tall, redbrick walls. White stones surrounded the front door in a welcoming arch, and window boxes hung beneath the windows on the first floor. The sun had yet to fully set, but candles flickered on the ground floor windowsills, turning the glass golden.

"How nice to have a townhome that looks out upon a small green," Phoebe said, coming to stand beside her. "It brings a hint of the country to a house in the city."

"Yes," Emily said. She'd noticed the tree-lined path cutting through the grassy area on the other side of the road as they'd turned the corner. "What is the name of this little park, Lady Millward?"

When the older lady did not immediately respond, Emily turned to see that her attention was on the people approaching Benning House ahead of them. An elderly lady, her gray hair ratted even higher than Lady Millward's, walked on the arm of a tall gentleman. She carried a cane in her other hand but held herself with the stiff assurance of a woman of means. Behind them were two more ladies, each dressed exquisitely, with a light dusting of powder on their light-brown coiffeurs.

Emily watched them enter the house before glancing back at Lady Millward. She was frowning. "Is something the matter, Lady Millward?"

Her frown instantly disappeared. "Nothing that we cannot conquer, my dear."

It was not exactly the reassurance Emily had been expecting. "So, there is something?"

"You are too perceptive by half, Miss Norton." The older lady slipped her arm through Emily's, and they followed Adam and Phoebe down the pavement. "It appears that one of the other guests tonight is the Dowager Lady Pendleton."

"Is she someone I should know?"

"She would certainly think so."

Emily gave her an anxious look. "Perhaps some additional information on the lady might be beneficial."

Lady Millward appeared thoughtful. "You may be right." She glanced at Adam and Phoebe. They had reached Benning House's doorsteps and would be at the front door momentarily. "As time is of the essence, I shall be brief. Suffice it to say that the Dowager Lady Pendleton has made it her life's work to secure the most illustrious marital matches for her son and five daughters.

"Several years ago, she married off her youngest daughter, Marian, to the Duke of Tinslow, and Society breathed a collective sigh of relief that the dowager marchioness's primary motivation for intimidating others into subjection existed no longer. Unfortunately, no one considered the rise of the next generation of Pendleton young ladies. Her oldest granddaughter had her coming out this year, and by all accounts, the Dowager Lady Pendleton will not rest until she has secured a match for her also."

"I see," Emily said. "So am I to assume, therefore, that at least one eligible, titled gentleman will be in attendance at tonight's dinner party?"

"I believe that is a distinct possibility. And I am not sure who deserves our pity more, the gentleman in question or the dowager marchioness."

Emily offered her a puzzled look. "Why would the dowager marchioness be in need of our pity?"

A hint of mischief danced in Lady Millward's eyes. "Miss Norton, I have found that there are two kinds of gentlemen in the world: those who give way under pressure and those who are strengthened by it. If the dowager marchioness has not already discovered this truth for herself, I believe my nephews will help her realize it tonight."

Emily smiled. It was her first real smile since she'd entered the carriage this evening, and it felt rather marvelous. The Dowager Lady Pendleton's machinations had nothing whatsoever to do with her. And if a gentleman was to be the target of attention this evening, there was far less likelihood that anyone would take notice of Emily—or of her discomfort. The knot of nervousness that had settled in her stomach during breakfast eased a fraction. Perhaps she would survive her first foray into London Society after all.

The butler greeted them politely, and upon their entering the house, he handed off their hats and outerwear to two footmen and led them to an open door on the left.

"Lady Millward, Lord and Lady Dunsbourne, and Miss Norton," he announced.

The guests who'd arrived before them moved farther into the room and a middle-aged couple standing at the doorway turned to greet them.

"How lovely to see you, Bea!" An attractive woman in a stunning lilac gown reached out to take Lady Millward's hands in a heartwarming show of genuine affection.

"Thank you, Leonora. It has been far too long." Lady Millward turned to the gentleman wearing a green jacket and cream-colored breeches standing beside her. "Good evening, Charles."

"Beatrice." The gentleman bowed courteously, but his smile was welcoming. "We are very happy to have you join us." His gaze moved to Emily and

Phoebe before settling on Adam, and Lady Millward immediately made the introductions.

"Charles, may I present Lord Dunsbourne, my niece, Lady Dunsbourne, and Lord Dunsbourne's sister, Miss Norton. They are newly arrived in London from Berkshire." She gestured toward the older couple. "Our host and hostess this evening, Lord and Lady Farwell."

The gentlemen greeted each other with a polite nod.

"Welcome to Benning House," Lady Farwell said.

"Thank you, my lady," Phoebe said. "We appreciate your willingness to include us in your party at such short notice."

"Our pleasure." Lady Farwell smiled, but her husband was eyeing Adam curiously.

"I say, Dunsbourne. Are you the gentleman producing that rather splendid cider I've been hearing about?"

"I am, my lord."

"Well now, I should very much like to hear more about your operation. We have a large country estate in Gloucestershire ourselves. Excellent grazing land, but I have wondered about introducing some fruit trees."

"A worthwhile investment, my lord," Adam said. "Have you considered what variety of trees you might plant?"

"Oh dear," Lady Farwell whispered to Phoebe. "I think our husbands may be lost to us for the time being."

Phoebe laughed lightly. "So it would seem. What are your interests, my lady?"

When Lady Farwell launched into a description of some new furnishings she had recently acquired, Lady Millward tapped Emily's arm. "Come, Miss Norton," she said softly. "Unless you wish to offer your input on the advantages of velvet curtains over silk, I suggest we allow Phoebe and Leonora to continue this conversation without us."

Making a mental note to locate a book on fabrics in the near future, Emily followed Lady Millward farther into the room.

Lady Farwell's penchant for decorating was immediately apparent. Chairs upholstered in gold fabric sat on either side of an elegant green sofa boasting cushions with gold tassels. More chairs were positioned near the windows. These were upholstered in blue and matched the heavy curtains. Candles flickered in brass candelabras on two end tables and the mantelpiece, the light picking up the colors of the flowers in the vase near the pianoforte and the multicolored rugs on the highly polished wood floor.

"What a lovely room," Emily said, pausing to take in the art hanging on the robin-egg-blue walls.

"Leonora's flair for beautifying a house is undeniable," Lady Millward said. "She is fortunate that Charles has the means to keep up with her purchases."

"Yes, I suppose she is." The furniture at Dunsbourne Manor would appear very shabby in comparison to these pieces, but Emily experienced a moment of longing for the faded red armchair in the drawing room at home where she was wont to curl up and read. No matter their elegance, these chairs lacked the worn look that spoke of familiarity and coziness. "Do you think Lady Farwell takes comfort into consideration as well as style and color?"

"A worthy question," Lady Millward said. "One that I believe my nephews can likely answer after we offer ourselves as reinforcements."

"Reinforcements?"

"Indeed." Lady Millward's eyes sparkled. "The Dowager Lady Pendleton has them in her sights. Knowing Benedict and Henry as I do, it is unlikely that we will be needed, but I rather hope that we will."

CHAPTER 4

THE DOWAGER LADY PENDLETON HAD taken very little time to complete her deliberate appraisal of the room and its occupants. From his position at Benedict's side, Henry had watched her gaze pass over his mother's elegant new sofa, the elaborate flower arrangement, old Lord Basingstoke and his son, Colonel Eastberry, to hover on him. He'd felt her brief assessment before her attention had shifted to his brother.

"Lord Benning!" she said, her wide silk skirts billowing as she neared them. "A word, if you please."

Henry lowered the arm he'd been resting on the mantel. "Brace yourself," he whispered. "She's coming in with guns blazing."

"The lady may be accused of many things," Benedict muttered, "but feeble, she is not."

"Nor subtle."

Benedict's lips twitched. "No. Definitely not subtle."

The elderly lady came to a stop before them, and both gentlemen bowed.

"Good evening, my lady," Benedict said. "Welcome to Benning House."

Setting her cane before her, she placed both hands on it and acknowledged his greeting with a slight inclination of her head. "Thank you, my lord. I am glad of the opportunity to renew my friendship with your dear mother."

Given that the Dowager Lady Pendleton had entered the room after having exchanged little more than a few brief words with their mother, Henry doubted their supposed friendship had experienced much renewing as of yet.

"I am sure she is delighted that you are come," Benedict said.

"Yes, of course."

The sentiment was expected, it seemed. Henry suppressed the urge to raise his eyes to the ceiling, knowing full well what was to come next.

"My granddaughter, Lady Aurelia, has spoken of little else since we received your mother's kind invitation," she said. "I must say, it came as quite a shock to learn that she has yet to be formally introduced to you, my lord. After all, she has been in London since the start of the Season."

"Not so surprising as you may think, my lady," Benedict said, choosing to ignore her implied censure. "I have been required to return to Gloucestershire multiple times over the last many weeks. Indeed, I will be leaving Town again within a day or two."

It was the first Henry had heard of the trip, but he couldn't fault Benedict for contriving one. His brother was not one to ignore his parliamentary or social obligations, but the Dowager Lady Pendleton's maneuverings fell firmly outside both of those spheres. If he wished to avoid any expectation for future interaction, Henry was quite happy to assist him. "My brother takes his responsibility of overseeing the working of his land and the lives of his tenants very seriously, my lady," he said. "Unfortunately, the current parliamentary session is a difficult time for him to be in London, as it corresponds with lambing and calving season in Gloucestershire."

"Nevertheless, I am quite sure Lord Benning has a steward to take care of such things," she countered.

"Oh, he does," Henry said. "And a mighty good one, at that. But he has often said that there is nothing quite so satisfying as being in the barn when the young animals first make their appearance."

The elderly lady offered him a disbelieving look, her aquiline nose wrinkling with distaste as the swish of skirts heralded the arrival of another guest.

"Have a care for the Dowager Lady Pendleton's sensitivities, gentlemen. I am quite sure she has no desire to hear of Benedict's experiences delivering lambs."

At the sound of the familiar voice, Henry's lips broke into a wide smile. Aunt Millward. The lady was a breath of fresh air in a room full of stuffiness, and there was no one he would rather have join them this evening. He turned to face their new guest as Benedict greeted her with a polite bow.

"Good evening, Aunt Millward," Benedict said.

Henry followed suit. "Good evening, Aunt."

"Good evening to you both," Aunt Millward said. "And to you, my lady."

The Dowager Lady Pendleton barely acknowledged her greeting. The meddling woman's previously skeptical expression had now become aghast. "Is it true, my lord? Do you regularly take upon yourself the work of a farm laborer?"

Benedict was doing an outstanding job of maintaining a solemn facade.

"If my spending time in the barn when my animals are in distress qualifies me for that appellation, then I am most certainly guilty as charged."

The dowager marchioness raised her cane and took a step back. "You realize that such behavior is highly irregular and is not something that would be looked upon favorably by many within the *ton*."

"As you say, my lady," Benedict said, inclining his head in polite agreement. "But such is the price to be paid by a country gentleman, I fear."

"Indeed." The Dowager Lady Pendleton set down her cane again and leaned upon it. "If you will excuse me, gentlemen, Lady Millward, I must ensure that Lady Aurelia is properly introduced to the other guests." She swung around, all but running into someone standing directly behind her.

"I beg your pardon, my lady." A dark-haired young lady wearing a white gown stumbled back a pace.

The Dowager Lady Pendleton eyed her with irritation. "I do not believe we have met."

"No, my lady."

Henry glanced at the newcomer, blinked, and looked again. Color had infused the young lady's cheeks, but there was no mistaking her familiar profile. Notwithstanding the fact that he had spoken to her less than two days ago, he could offer no introduction.

"Miss Norton," Aunt Millward said. "May I present the Dowager Lady Pendleton and my nephews, Lord Benning and Mr. Henry Buckland. Miss Norton is Lord Dunsbourne's sister and sister-in-law to my niece, Lady Dunsbourne."

Henry's mind raced. He knew very little about Aunt Millward's extended family, but he had met her brother's daughters once, a few years past. The older one had married Lord Bloxley, he remembered. The niece she was referring to now must be the younger one.

Yet to face the two gentlemen, Miss Norton dropped into a curtsy. "I am honored to meet you, my lady."

"Yes. Quite." The older lady's expression was inscrutable. "Lord Dunsbourne's sister, you say?"

"Yes, my lady."

"I knew your mother. News of her death came as a great shock."

"Her passing was unexpected." Regret tinged Miss Norton's voice. "She died soon after my birth, but I have heard that she was a remarkable woman."

"She was."

The two words were the closest Henry had ever heard the Dowager Lady Pendleton come to issuing a compliment, but he sensed Miss Norton's discomfort and felt it his duty to alleviate it. "How long do you plan to be in London, Miss Norton?" It was not the most engaging of questions, but given the shock he'd just received in seeing the young lady from the country lane standing in his drawing room, he considered it a praiseworthy accomplishment.

She turned from the Dowager Lady Pendleton to face him for the first time, and the color that had tinted her cheeks moments before drained away.

Chapter 5

It was the red campion collector. Emily was sure of it. The gentleman was dressed far more finely than he had been when he'd been digging flowers from the hedgerow, but there was no mistaking his hazel eyes and strong jawline. And if he was half as intelligent as those eyes suggested, he had recognized her. She battled a new wave of dismay. Obstructing the Dowager Lady Pendleton had been a wretched beginning to the evening. To have the esteemed lady recall Emily's mother's noteworthiness in the face of Emily's bumbling had stung. But if those attending her first dinner engagement in London were to learn that she wandered country lanes unchaperoned, her mortification would be complete. Not to mention the disappointment she would be to Adam.

The few seconds these thoughts took to circle her head were filled with silence, and with a start, she realized that everyone was awaiting her response to Mr. Buckland's question. How long was she to be in London? At this precise moment, one day more seemed too many. "I . . . I believe my brother and sister-in-law hope to stay until Season's end," she managed.

"To arrive so late in the Season would seem very imprudent." It appeared that the Dowager Lady Pendleton had yet to take her leave. "Surely they are aware that the grandest balls were held weeks ago."

"I am sure they are, my lady. But it was not possible for us to leave Berkshire earlier in the Season."

"Lord Dunsbourne is a man after your own heart, Benedict," Lady Millward said. "He works alongside his men in his orchard to produce a very fine apple cider."

Lord Benning raised his eyebrows. "Is that so? I shall have to speak with him. Father and I were recently discussing the merits of introducing fruit trees to the grounds at Farwell Hall."

"If you wish to be part of that conversation, you'd best join them right away," Lady Millward said. "Your father and Lord Dunsbourne were discussing apple varieties when we left them."

Lord Benning's enthusiastic response was instant. "An excellent suggestion, Aunt."

Seemingly oblivious to the Dowager Lady Pendleton's stormy look, Lady Millward took the gentleman's arm. "Come. I shall take it upon myself to introduce you."

It seemed that Lord Benning needed no further persuading, and as he and Lady Millward stepped away from the small group, the Dowager Lady Pendleton uttered a disparaging humph and started across the room in the opposite direction.

"I fear that the Dowager Lady Pendleton may be a little put out," Emily said.

"So it would seem," Mr. Buckland concurred.

She turned to see humor dancing in the gentleman's eyes. "That does not concern you?"

"On the contrary, Miss Norton. I am most relieved."

Lady Millward's voice reached her. She was making introductions.

"I get the distinct impression that your aunt is rather adept at rescue missions."

Mr. Buckland laughed. It was a warm sound that released Emily's full smile.

"That, she is, Miss Norton." He glanced at his brother, who was now talking animatedly with Adam. "By the time you joined us, Benedict and I had done a decent job of planting a seed of doubt over Benedict's suitability as a match for Lady Aurelia, but only Aunt Millward could have nurtured the seed so quickly and so magnificently."

As glad as she was that Lady Millward had come to the aid of her nephew, Emily could not help but feel for the young lady on the other end of this equation. "What of Lady Aurelia?" she asked. "Will she be crushed by Lord Benning's lack of interest in pursuing her?"

The humor left Mr. Buckland's face. "You are good to think of her. She is to be pitied, certainly. Not because Benedict refuses to fall in with her grandmother's machinations but, rather, because her grandmother will not cease her meddling. The Dowager Lady Pendleton cares little for the interests or feelings of her offspring. Her focus is purely on the titles and wealth they may acquire through marriage."

"That is unfortunate." A wave of gratitude for Adam and his gentle support swept over her. And with it came a renewed desire to spare him the details of her recent misstep. She mustered her courage, knowing that she must speak now, before the opportunity was gone. "Mr. Buckland. About our previous meeting . . ."

The gentleman had uncommonly expressive eyes, and currently, they were shining with an odd mixture of curiosity and expectancy. "Yes, Miss Norton?"

"I . . . uh . . . I wondered if perhaps we could refrain from sharing the details with anyone else."

"You wish people to assume that this is the first time we have ever set eyes upon each other?" he said.

"Yes." She clasped her hands together. "It would be better, don't you think?" She had a sinking feeling that she could see humor glinting in his eyes now.

"I'm not sure that I fully understand why that would be so."

Mentally revising her earlier guess that Mr. Buckland was an intelligent individual, Emily's fingers tightened their grip. Honesty was surely her best policy, even if it meant admitting to her unsophistication in front of a relative stranger. "No matter that I wished to stretch my legs after having been in the carriage for some time, I should not have wandered a country lane unaccompanied. My brother was quick to point out my error when I returned to the carriage, and I am determined to do better, but . . ." She swallowed. "I did not tell him that I had met anyone on my ramble. I . . . I thought it better to spare him any unnecessary concern."

Mr. Buckland smiled. "A worthy goal, Miss Norton. A gentleman holding a trowel was hardly a threat worth mentioning."

"Then, you agree?" She clung to the hope he'd offered her. "You are willing to act as though we have only now met?"

"Unless my memory has failed me completely, we were introduced only a few minutes ago, Miss Norton."

"You are right." Relief brought a smile to her face.

"I am glad to hear it. Although, I confess, Benedict and I have never before taken someone we know so little into our confidence."

Emily recognized his unspoken request. "You have nothing to fear on that score, sir. My silence was assured the moment Lady Millward asked me to accompany her on her mission of reinforcement."

"Did she call it that?"

"She did, although she was somewhat vague with regard to the details of said mission."

He chuckled. "My aunt is a worthy ally and is remarkably good at thinking on her feet."

"I am beginning to see that."

"Have you been acquainted—"

"My lords, ladies, and gentlemen." A sonorous voice interrupted Mr. Buckland's question and cut through the hum of conversation in the room. Emily swung around to see the butler standing stiffly at the door. He inclined his head to acknowledge those in the room before continuing. "Dinner is served."

Mr. Buckland offered her an apologetic look. "Forgive me, Miss Norton. It seems that I must find my dinner partner."

"Yes, of course," Emily said, experiencing an unexpected pang of regret. She'd given no thought as to who'd been assigned to escort her into dinner, but it appeared it was not to be Mr. Buckland.

He bowed. "It was very nice to meet you."

Already, he had put their past encounter behind him.

Emily bobbed a curtsy. "The pleasure was all mine, sir." She met his eyes. They were filled with warmth and gave her the courage to speak again—to voice the question that had consumed her since she'd left him on the lane in Berkshire. "Before you go, may I ask why you were digging up the red campion plant?"

"I am the curator over the natural history compilation at the British Museum. We boast a large collection of dried plants and flowers, but many are in need of replacement. I have learned to be prepared for those moments when one stumbles upon a perfect specimen."

Emily stared at him. A curator at the British Museum. Never in her wildest dreams could she have conceived of so thrilling and fascinating an occupation. "How marvelous!" she breathed.

His eyebrows came together, and he studied her quizzically. "You truly believe that?"

"Absolutely. Don't you?"

"Yes," he said, finally stepping away. "As a matter of fact, I do."

Compared to Benedict, Henry considered himself fortunate. He was seated at the table between the younger Lady Pendleton and Aunt Millward. Benedict, poor fellow, was sandwiched between the Dowager Lady Pendleton and Lady Aurelia. The Dowager Lady Pendleton was all but ignoring Benedict, choosing to converse almost exclusively with their mother, who was seated across the table. Lady Aurelia appeared more than happy to make up for her grandmother's neglect, however, and had been regaling Benedict with tales of all the balls she'd attended since arriving in London. Her constant chatter, punctuated by giggles, had scarcely stopped long enough for her to put food in her mouth, and if the level of concentration Benedict was giving to cutting his brussels sprouts was any indication, he had reached his limit.

Thankfully, Henry had been spared making small talk with Lady Pendleton because she'd spent most of the meal discussing the shocking lack of reliable hired help with Lord Basingstoke. Aunt Millward had been blissfully content to focus on her meal and had allowed Henry the same luxury. Indeed, it would have been a perfect scenario had it not been for the conversation occurring at the far end of the table.

Henry stabbed a piece of carrot as Colonel Eastberry launched into a third story about yet another personal encounter with an Indian elephant.

"The herd had trampled the local fellow's crop of sugarcane by the time we arrived," Eastberry said. "Shocking what such enormous creatures can destroy in a matter of minutes."

"Poor man," Miss Norton said. "It must have been devastating."

"You would think so, wouldn't you? But the Indians are a resilient lot. Once we'd cleared the elephants out of the area, they were back in the fields, attempting to save what they could."

"I suppose they would know how to salvage cuttings from the damaged canes to propagate more."

Eastberry's brows came together. "Why, yes, I daresay they would."

"Were there many calves in the herd?" Miss Norton asked.

Henry stabbed another carrot. Lud. How many other young ladies in England knew that sugarcane grew from cuttings or that baby elephants were called calves? The well-decorated military gentleman may be accustomed to having an audience, but Henry doubted that he'd ever had one so genuinely interested or surprisingly knowledgeable as Miss Norton

"Four or five young ones, if memory serves," Eastberry said. "And at least ten extremely large adults."

"Unless the calves were traveling with a herd of males, they were not *all* extremely large," Henry muttered.

"A valid point," Aunt Millward said.

Henry eyed his aunt over the rim of the glass in his hand. "You were not supposed to hear that."

"My dear boy, the comments not meant for one's ears are the most interesting and enlightening comments of all."

"Undoubtedly," he said dryly.

She took a small bite of the roast duck on her plate and studied the couple at the end of the table thoughtfully. "Tell me, Henry, what do you think of Colonel Eastberry?"

The fair-haired gentleman in question was smiling at something Miss Norton was saying, the brass buttons on his officer's dress uniform gleaming in the candlelight.

"By all accounts, he's given admirable service to the Crown and has left his mark on the East India Company," Henry said, attempting to shrug off his inexplicable irritation. "Despite his propensity for exaggeration, he seems an honorable fellow."

"Indeed. And Miss Norton? What are your first impressions of her?"

"She is remarkably well versed on the subjects of sugarcane and elephants." He took a sip of wine and lowered his glass. "And wildflowers."

"I must have missed the floral portion of her conversation with Colonel Eastberry," Aunt Millward said. "But if that is the case, I would imagine that you and Miss Norton would have a great deal in common."

"It's possible." Henry refused to admit that the same thought had already occurred to him. It had taken him a full ten minutes to process Miss Norton's unaffected wonder upon learning of his chosen career. He was far more used to reactions that fell somewhere along the mild-interest to total-perplexity spectrum.

"Perhaps you should engage her in conversation," Aunt Millward prodded.

"There is no need for that. Quite apart from the fact that it would require talking across half the length of the table, Eastberry is entertaining the lady perfectly well."

She raised an eyebrow. "Too well, perhaps?"

Henry stifled a sigh. "I am sure Benedict is most grateful for your assistance this evening, Aunt, but I do not have the same need for your oversight."

"Hm." She appeared disturbingly unconvinced.

"Aunt Millward, I mean it."

"Very well," she said, turning her attention back to her meal. "But if I do not receive complimentary tickets for entrance into the British Museum within the next few days, you shall hear from me."

"You wish to acquire tickets to the museum?" He did nothing to hide his surprise. "I distinctly remember you visiting the most recent exhibit last month."

"I did. But Miss Norton has seen none of the collections, and I rather think she would enjoy perusing them."

He could not argue with that, and his aunt seemed to know it.

Setting down her knife and fork, she gave him a penetrating look. "Henry, since you claim to need no assistance when it comes to socializing with young ladies, I shall simply submit an observation for your consideration: Miss Norton appears to be uncommonly curious about the world around her. Colonel Eastberry has spent time in India—has ridden an elephant, even—but unless Miss Norton boards the next ship bound for Calcutta, she cannot personally experience those things. You, on the other hand, have full access to the treasures housed at the British Museum. Those are wonders she can see and feel for herself—if someone were sufficiently considerate to provide her with a ticket."

At the far end of the table, Eastberry had diverted the conversation from elephant herds to mango fruit.

"If there is a genteel way to eat them, I have yet to learn it," he said. "The juice simply cannot be contained."

"But you consider eating them worth the mess they produce?" Miss Norton asked.

"Without question," Eastberry replied. "Mangos are most assuredly the most delicious fruit I have ever tasted. And when it comes to exotic foods, I have sampled more than my fair share."

Henry reached for the poached pear on the plate before him. It was no mango, but it happened to be his favorite dessert, and he wasn't going to allow Eastberry and Miss Norton's discussion to dilute his enjoyment of the dish. He cut into it, his spoon clinking noisily against the china beneath. Eastberry glanced his way. So did Miss Norton. She met his eyes and smiled. He managed a brief nod before Eastberry claimed her attention again.

"A trip to the British Museum is always a good idea when one is visiting London," Henry said, knowing full well that his aunt was listening even though his attention was on his food. "I will have four tickets delivered to your town-house tomorrow."

"Splendid," she said, sounding abnormally pleased. "I shall look forward to having another opportunity to view shards of broken pottery, dead flowers, and ancient coins."

Henry shook his head helplessly but was unable to prevent a soft chuckle from escaping. Aunt Millward was incorrigible.

CHAPTER 6

RAIN WAS POURING DOWN THE windows. Emily lowered the book she'd been reading, set it on her knee, and gazed through the wet panes at the blurry view of Lady Millward's small garden. After an evening of socializing, she'd not been sorry to wake up to the sound of rain. London's cold, damp weather was a far cry from the heat and humidity described in the volume about India that she'd discovered in the townhouse's modest library this morning, but there was something wonderfully soothing about reading in the comfort of a deep armchair beside the fire.

Colonel Eastberry's vivid descriptions of India had fascinated her, and she'd left the Farwells' dinner party eager to learn more about the far-off land. But now that she was seated in the quiet drawing room with reading material in hand, she was finding it unusually difficult to concentrate. The book's descriptive passages of the Bombay and Madras presidencies were seemingly no match for the images and snippets of conversations from the previous evening that kept invading her thoughts.

Her initial run-in with the Dowager Lady Pendleton had had the potential to completely ruin the evening, but entering the house with Lady Millward at her side had made all the difference. Not only had Lady Millward given her fair warning of the elderly stateswoman's disposition, but she'd also made Emily an ally. And by so doing, Emily had immediately become Lord Benning's and Mr. Buckland's ally too.

She smiled at the memory of the Dowager Lady Pendleton's horrified expression upon learning of Lord Benning's partiality for farm labor. If she had any idea how Adam spent most of his time or how many hours Emily gathered apples during harvests, she likely would shun them both. As it was, after their initial meeting, the dowager had limited her interaction with Emily to a cursory question about Emily's musical talent followed by a full explanation of Lady Aurelia's proficiency on the pianoforte.

Despite her grandmother's newfound reservations, Lady Aurelia had attached herself to Lord Benning at every available moment from the time they'd sat down together at dinner to the moment her family had exited Benning House. The gentleman had been the epitome of civility, but even Emily—with her limited experience among strangers—had caught an occasional glimpse of strain on his face.

She'd recognized a similar emotion in Mr. Buckland's expression at the dinner table. Although why he would feel that way when he was seated beside Lady Millward, she could not fathom. Emily had been grateful to be seated beside Colonel Eastberry. For the entire meal, he'd maintained an interesting monologue with very little need for her to contribute more than a few comments and a question or two. But in her heart of hearts, Emily knew that if the choice had been hers, she would have preferred to sit beside Mr. Buckland.

She ran her fingers absently over the open pages. She was not sure what caused her to marvel the most: that the gentleman she'd seen collecting red campion on her recent journey was in attendance at her first dinner party in London, that he was willing to fully overlook her earlier impropriety, or that he was a curator at the British Museum. Her fingers stilled, and she sighed. A red campion plant was surely one of the most prosaic items on display at so distinguished an institution. What would it be like to have daily access to an untold number of treasures from around the world?

A knock on the townhouse's front door brought Emily out of her musing. The sound of the butler's solid footsteps followed, and then voices. The door closed, and the butler's footsteps faded away. A messenger rather than a caller, it would seem. Emily glanced out of the window again. With today's inclement weather, the absence of visitors was hardly surprising.

Picking up her book once more, she turned to the next page. Monkeys. Surely those intriguing creatures would capture her attention.

She had managed only two paragraphs when the door to the small library opened and Lady Millward walked in.

"Ah! I thought I might find you here." The older lady smiled. "Have you found something new to read?"

"Yes." Emily held up the book. "It's about India. I haven't got very far yet, but I'm learning a great deal." She hesitated. "Thank you for allowing me access to your library."

Lady Millward's gaze ran across the bookshelves lining one wall. "My husband was a great reader, but I fear it is an interest I cannot claim. Since his passing, these books and this room have been somewhat neglected. I am glad to see them being enjoyed once more."

Phoebe had told Emily that Lord Millward had died when she was very young, so Emily knew his passing was not a recent loss for the older lady, but she guessed that since they'd had no children, being widowed at a relatively young age had made for many years of loneliness. It was a condition Emily knew all too well.

"My mother died soon after my birth, and since Adam is significantly older than I am, he was away at school or university most of my growing-up years. I think I turned to books for companionship."

Lady Millward circled the end table and took a seat on the armchair across from the one Emily was using. "And along the way, you learned all sorts of things," she said.

Emily smiled. "Yes, I suppose I did." She sobered as memories of Adam's concern over some of her topics of study resurfaced. "Perhaps the study of wild animals or distant lands is not considered suitable reading for a well-bred young lady, but I find it so much more interesting than stitchery or practicing the pianoforte or . . . or knitting."

"I think it is time that I let you in on a secret, Miss Norton." Lady Millward leaned forward in her chair. "I have never enjoyed those things either."

"Truly?"

"Truly." Lady Millward was most definite. "There is little so tedious as unpicking embroidery or banging at the same notes over and over again."

Warmth filled Emily's chest. She could not remember a time when her unconventional interests had been so validated, and to have the endorsement come from a well-respected lady of title and means was all the more heartening. "What do you enjoy doing, my lady?"

Lady Millward contemplated the question a moment. "I'm afraid I cannot claim true proficiency in anything particularly literary, musical, or creative. But I do consider myself a good judge of character, and I take great delight in mentoring those individuals whom I feel I can assist by virtue of my position in Society or my life experience."

"Such as your bolstering of Lord Benning's stance last night."

Lady Millward's blue eyes sparkled with something that looked remarkably like mischief. "I believe the Dowager Lady Pendleton's expression when I mentioned Benedict's involvement with the lambing made up for all the times I've been forced to listen to her recite the names of her ancestors who have married into royalty."

Emily bit her lip to prevent a giggle from emerging. "Is the list extensive?"

Lady Millward groaned. "To hear her tell it, it's a wonder the king hasn't taken upon himself the name Pendleton."

There was no holding back Emily's laughter now. "Lady Millward," she said. "You are quite marvelous."

"As are you, my dear. In fact, as we are so obviously well-suited companions, I think it time that we dispense with formalities. You are like a sister to Phoebe, so I think it only fitting that you address me as Aunt Millward."

There was nothing Emily would like better, but she had no desire to add *presumptuous* to her list of oddities in the minds of other members of the *ton*. "Is . . . is that entirely proper?"

Lady Millward brushed away her concern with a flick of her wrist. "Since Lord Bloxley has designated me an honorary aunt and has no qualms about using that appellation in public, I think we are safe."

Emily's smile was immediate. "Then I should be honored to do the same. And I would very much like it if you would call me Emily."

"With pleasure," the older lady said. "And now that we have that behind us, let me share my news." She raised her other hand, and for the first time, Emily noticed that she held several pieces of paper. "A courier from the British Museum arrived not long ago."

Emily's heart rate quickened. "The British Museum?"

"Yes. It seems that Henry has managed to procure four tickets to tour the collections this Thursday and has offered them to us."

"We . . . we can tour the collections this Thursday?" Emily said, her voice catching. "I had thought that it would be impossible to gain admittance during the short time we are to be in London. Adam was told that those wishing to visit the museum were having to wait weeks to obtain tickets."

"Is that so? Well, there we are. I daresay it pays to have one of the curators for a nephew."

"Yes," Emily said with bemusement. "Yes, I suppose it does."

Aunt Millward smiled. "Am I to assume that you would like to go?"

"Oh, very much!" The words came out in a rush.

"Wonderful. Then, I shall seek out Phoebe and your brother to see if they wish to join us." Aunt Millward rose, and clutching the book to her chest, Emily also came to her feet.

"I must write to Mr. Buckland to thank him for his kindness."

"Why don't you simply tell him in person?" Aunt Millward said.

"Will we see him there?"

"I certainly hope so." Aunt Millward had already reached the door. "He knows that I will not countenance any other tour guide."

The chatter of voices penetrated the closed door of Henry's office. He raised his gaze from the paperwork on the table before him and reached for his pocket watch as the voices and footsteps faded down the passage. The museum's visitors were undoubtedly headed to the gallery of antiquity with Fernsby, which meant that if Henry did not hurry, he would not reach the lobby in time to greet the next group.

Setting down his quill, he reached for the jacket he'd draped across the back of the chair. Conducting guided tours was a mixed blessing. He enjoyed sharing the unique collections with others—especially those who'd never seen the items housed at the British Museum before—but the tours took him away from the work he truly loved. No matter if it was the botanical collections, the ethnographic materials, natural minerals, or other antiquities, he was at his happiest when he was fully immersed in human history and the wonders of the natural world.

He donned his jacket and exited the room. The half dozen fossils he had yet to catalog would have to wait another hour, but he would finish that group today, even if it meant being late for dinner.

Locking the door behind him, he returned his thoughts to his parents' dinner party the night before. Benedict had survived virtually unscathed. Aunt Millward's presence had been an unforeseen boon, and Miss Norton's had been an unanticipated pleasure. His surprise at seeing her in his parents' drawing room had redoubled when he'd learned of her connection to his aunt. Discovering that it was her love of the outdoors and a natural curiosity for what might lie around the next bend that had drawn Miss Norton down the Berkshire lane unaccompanied had piqued his interest. Both were motivations he could understand—and they were as rare in a well-dressed young lady as they were refreshing.

Eastberry had taken full advantage of her obvious interest in those things. The gentleman had barely stopped talking about his exploits in India long enough to eat his meal. Lingering remnants of Henry's irritation over Eastberry's poorly disguised bragging brought Henry's brows together. Henry did not know Miss Norton well enough to ascertain how much the colonel had turned her head with his stories, but he had a feeling his aunt was right about the young lady's desire to experience the world around her firsthand. And Henry had an absurdly strong desire to be the one to facilitate her next adventure.

He started down the stairs. Already, people were gathering in the lobby. Henry did not know whether Aunt Millward was truly unaware that tickets for the museum tours were extremely difficult to procure, or if she simply faced that hindrance the same way she out-maneuvered the Dowager Lady Pendleton— with confidence and aplomb. A smile tugged at his lips. Whatever her system, it worked. He had rearranged his schedule to accommodate one more tour on Thursday and had already sent the tickets to her townhouse.

"Buckland!"

At the sound of his name, Henry scanned the floor below. A tall, thin gentleman crossed the lobby, heading for the stairs. The regular click, click, click of his cane hitting the marble tile echoed off the vaulted ceiling, adding a feel of urgency to his brisk pace. Henry hurried down the few remaining stairs. It would not do to keep the chair of the museum's board of trustees waiting a second time.

"Good afternoon, Lord Claridge." Henry reached the ground floor and bowed.

"And to you, Buckland." He pointed toward the manuscript saloon. "A word, if you wouldn't mind."

A gust of cold air swirled around their ankles as the front door opened and closed to admit two more people.

"Of course, my lord." It would appear that Henry was going to be late for his tour group after all. "I apologize that I was not here the last time you visited. My meeting with Lady Grenville took longer than I'd anticipated."

"So, I imagine."

On the upper floor, Fernsby's voice reached them, directing those who were coming to the end of their time in the museum to the stairs. Henry opted to remain silent and follow Lord Claridge into the quiet room. The wooden chair in the far corner was occupied by a gentleman studying the pages of a huge tome. Across from him, Townsend was reshelving books.

Townsend looked up as they walked in. "Lord Claridge." He inclined his head, set down the books on the nearest table, and moved closer. "It's an honor to have you here, my lord."

"Thank you, Townsend." The gentleman waved his hand in the vague direction of the bookshelves. "Don't let me disturb you. I need to speak with Buckland and could hardly hear myself think over the people gathered in the lobby."

"I understand, my lord." Townsend may have grasped Lord Claridge's meaning, but his clipped tone suggested that he was not happy about it. "It can be excessively loud at this time of day."

"Quite."

Townsend made no move, but Lord Claridge was no longer looking at him. He raised a piece of paper in his hand. "I received a letter from Lady Grenville's solicitor today, Buckland."

Henry tensed. When he'd left Lady Grenville's home, she'd given him a verbal assurance that the items they had discussed would soon find their way to the museum. Had she changed her mind or added some outrageous stipulations?

"He wrote to tell me of Lady Grenville's desire to make an extensive dona-tion to the museum," Lord Claridge continued. "I must say, it came as a most welcome surprise. The viscountess's butterfly collection is one thing; her exten-sive collection of books and manuscripts is quite another."

Relief flooded Henry. Lady Grenville had not reneged upon her promise after all. "I am happy to know that she has contacted her solicitor regarding the matter, my lord."

"Agreed. Involving solicitors will undoubtedly make the transfer of own-ership much smoother." He waggled the paper. "I believe you can expect Lady Grenville's contribution within the fortnight."

Before Henry could respond, Townsend cleared his throat. "If I may be so bold, my lord, may I offer my services? I feel sure that Buckland would agree that my particular expertise lends itself better to the viscountess's collection of books and manuscripts than does his."

"Good of you to offer, Townsend," Lord Claridge said. "Unfortunately, Lady Grenville has made it quite clear that she will only work with Buckland." His white eyebrows came together as he continued to address Townsend. "I seem to recall that you visited the lady with the hope of acquiring certain items several years ago, and she was unwilling to part with them."

Townsend's acknowledging nod was stiff. "I am glad to know that she has acted upon my original proposal after all this time."

Henry refrained from mentioning that it was only after he'd listened to Lady Grenville reminisce for over three hours about her husband's penchant for discovering new poets that she'd even contemplated the possibility of including those early manuscripts with her butterfly collection donation.

"It is certainly true that the subject of Lady Grenville's impressive compilation of literature has arisen several times in the past," Lord Claridge said, "but the trustees were given the distinct impression that the viscountess had no interest in donating any part of it before now. They will be gratified to hear of her change of heart." He patted Henry's arm. "All credit to you for that, Buckland. Well done."

"Thank you, my lord."

The chair gave a pleased nod. "Yes, well, I felt it my duty to personally commend you for acquiring so large an endowment, but with that said, I'd best be on my way." He turned to leave. "Walk with me to the entrance. I have a few questions to ask before I meet with the board. Good day to you, Townsend."

"Good day, my lord." Townsend's glower followed Henry out of the reading room.

Fernsby's tour group had reached the lobby, and the noise level was considerably higher than it had been before. Regardless of the commotion, however, Henry had the distinct impression that he was better off there than in the manuscript saloon.

CHAPTER 7

EMILY WATCHED THE LONDON STREETS pass by through the window of Aunt Millward's carriage. Light rain was falling, darkening the soot-covered brick walls and creating puddles on the road. A few people hurried along the pavement, their heads lowered, and a stray dog stood at a corner, barking as the carriage rolled by. In the distance, a splash of green marked a small patch of grass surrounded by trees, and Emily experienced a pang of homesickness for the countryside around Dunsbourne Manor.

She brushed away the unexpected emotion. How could she possibly harbor melancholy in her present circumstances? Since her arrival in London, she'd taken a drive through Hyde Park and had ridden across the magnificent Westminster Bridge. She'd sat beneath the vast domed ceiling in St. Paul's Cathedral and enjoyed a cup of tea at Twinings after spending an afternoon visiting Phoebe's favorite modiste. Every outing had been eye-opening. Every outing had been a delight. But none had filled her with as much nervous anticipation as the one upon which she was currently embarked.

Closing her eyes, she pressed her hand against the boning in her corset. It did little to settle the butterflies swirling within her, but it provided a moment to collect herself. The museum would be marvelous. How could it not be? Mr. Buckland would be gracious. He had already exhibited that trait. Logic dictated that there was absolutely no reason for her disquiet. Unfortunately, logic did not seem to be influencing her current feelings.

"Are you well, Emily?"

Emily opened her eyes to see Phoebe studying her anxiously.

Her sister-in-law was sitting next to Adam on the other side of the carriage, and when she spoke, Adam turned to look at Emily too. "You do look rather pale, Em," he said.

Meeting Mr. Buckland while appearing wan was not exactly what she had hoped for when she'd donned her favorite pink floral gown this morning.

"I am well enough," she said, mustering a cheerful smile. "I think perhaps my stomach is somewhat unsettled due to the movement of the carriage over the uneven road."

"Take heart." Aunt Millward patted her hand. "You will not have to endure it much longer. Look. You can see the walls surrounding Montagu House now."

The carriage slowed, and a tall stone wall came into view. Emily set one gloved hand on the vehicle's narrow windowsill as the carriage turned onto a gravel drive. To the left, manicured hedges surrounded tidy squares of grass. To the right, the most magnificent house Emily had ever seen stretched out along the full length of the courtyard.

"Oh my." The words were little more than a whispered breath.

Aunt Millward offered her an understanding look. "It does tend to take one's breath away, doesn't it? I believe that when Ralph Montagu commissioned Robert Hooke to design the house, he wished it to be the finest in all of London." She studied it through the window. "It suffered some severe water damage before it was purchased for the museum, and from what I've been told, significant remodeling work was done to make it what you see today."

"I look forward to viewing the inside," Phoebe said, her eyes alight with interest.

Emily nodded. Phoebe would likely focus her attention on the building's design and ornamentation. For herself, Emily wished to see the items it housed.

The carriage came to a stop, and Adam alighted first. After assisting Phoebe and Aunt Millward, he reached for Emily's hand.

"Are you feeling up for this, Em?" he asked softly. "You don't have you go if you are ill."

"I would not miss it," she said. "I've been counting the days ever since Mr. Buckland sent the tickets."

"Of that I have no doubt." He gave her a teasing look. "If we lose you at one of the exhibits, I shall come back for you tomorrow."

"That's very good of you. Although, I wish I'd put a bread roll in my reticule to hold me over."

Adam chuckled. "Come," he said. "I daresay Mr. Buckland is waiting."

A porter stood beneath the portico, and as they ascended the stairs, he pushed opened the heavy door. "Welcome to the British Museum, Lady Millward," he said with a bow. "Lord and Lady Dunsbourne. Miss Norton." He bowed once more.

"Thank you, Rutherford," Aunt Millward said. "I assume my nephew is expecting us."

"Yes, my lady. I believe you will find him inside."

She gave a crisp nod and led them into the lobby.

Why Aunt Millward continued to wear the peacock feather monstrosity she fondly called her favorite hat, Henry had no idea. But it did have the advantage of making her easily recognizable. He spotted the damp plumage waving above the heads of the other guests the moment she entered the lobby. From his position near the base of the stairs, he watched Lord and Lady Dunsbourne follow after her. The elegantly dressed lady with her hand on the arm of the dark-haired gentleman turned heads as she walked by, but Henry found himself searching for someone else.

A portly gentleman wearing a tall hat moved aside, and then Henry saw her. Dark ringlets hung below her simple bonnet, and a pale-colored shawl covered her shoulders and part of her floral gown. He watched as she turned her head, a look of wonder on her face as she gazed around the vast lobby. And then her eyes met his. Her smile was hesitant at first, but when he responded with a smile of his own, hers blossomed, and his heart stuttered.

"Ah, there you are, Henry!" Aunt Millward's voice cut through the milling visitors.

Shaking off his bewildering response to Miss Norton, he stepped forward.

"Good afternoon, Aunt Millward." He bowed. "Lord and Lady Dunsbourne. Miss Norton. Welcome to the British Museum."

Dunsbourne inclined his head, and the ladies curtsied.

"We are glad to be here," Dunsbourne said. "It was good of you to send us tickets, Buckland."

"My pleasure."

"What are we to see first?" It appeared that Aunt Millward had not come to the museum to exchange small talk.

"Do you have a preference?" he asked.

She looked to her guests, her eyebrows raised in question. "Do we?"

"I should like to see everything," Miss Norton said.

"Well then." Aunt Millward's voice rang with approval. "It sounds like we'd best get started."

"Might I suggest beginning with the manuscript saloon," Henry said. "After that, we can work our way upstairs to the other rooms." Miss Norton's enthusiastic nod was all the encouragement he needed. He pointed to his left. "This way."

He pulled open the door and glanced inside. A handful of people were wandering around the large room. Townsend stood beside a nearby bookshelf, his hands behind his back, surveying the visitors with unmistakable vigilance. Henry had not spoken to the older curator since Claridge's visit. Given the expression on the man's face when the chair of the board had left, it had seemed wise to keep his distance. But there could be no avoiding the curator now.

Henry waited until his guests had entered the room before following them in and gesturing toward the closest display. Lord and Lady Dunsbourne and Miss Norton obediently stepped toward it; his aunt, however, hung back.

"Is there a reason why Mr. Townsend is eyeing you with such displeasure, Henry?"

He should have anticipated her question; very little got past Aunt Millward. Thankfully, she had kept her voice low.

"I believe he is somewhat disgruntled that an assignment he felt should have been his was given to me," he replied softly.

"Something that involved manuscripts, no doubt."

"Yes. A new acquisition from a rather prominent family."

"And your feelings on the matter?"

"He is undoubtedly more qualified to assess the papers than I am, but the lady in question has made her wishes known, and the chair of the board is determined to comply."

An understanding look flickered across her face. "Foolish man," she muttered. "If he gave half as much attention to being personable as he does to his precious books, he would procure far more of them."

And then, before Henry realized what she was about, she started across the room toward his colleague.

"Good day, Mr. Townsend." Her jovial greeting caught the attention of everyone in the room. Henry stifled a groan. He probably should have reminded his aunt that the manuscript saloon was generally considered a quiet place of study and contemplation. Then again, Aunt Millward was not known for conforming to expectations. "I am so glad you are here," she continued, not waiting for the gentleman to reply. "I must hear your opinion on William Heberden's recently published paper. My nephew has told me you are an expert on his writing."

Several others stepped a little closer to Townsend.

One of them, a gentleman Henry did not recognize, spoke up. "I, too, would be most interested to hear what you have to say. Have you, by any chance, read Heberden's work on *digitorum nodi*?"

Henry wasn't sure if the physician's writing was actually within Townsend's realm of expertise, but now was not the time to question it. He had complete faith in his aunt's ability to steer the conversation aright, so he turned his attention to Miss Norton. "Come," he said. "Let me show you one of the museum's oldest pieces of writing."

Emily stood in one of the galleries, gazing at a painting of a basket of fruit created by an Italian artist named Caravaggio. The apple on the canvas looked so like one of the Genet Moyle apples in the Dunsbourne Orchard, she could almost taste it.

She had thought nothing could top seeing the rare books and documents in the manuscript saloon, but every exhibit Mr. Buckland had shown them since had outdone the last. She'd viewed rare artwork and lithographs, Roman coins and military medals, fossils and precious stones, and trinkets from the vast continent of Asia, the tiny islands of the South Seas, and everywhere in between.

"What do you think, Miss Norton?" Aunt Millward had left the gentlemen discussing a document in the manuscript saloon to join them on their tour. "Are you as enamored by these brightly colored rocks as Phoebe appears to be?"

Phoebe laughed. They had stopped to admire the contents of a glass-fronted case that housed a stunning array of precious stones.

"You know my fondness for fabric, design, and color, Aunt. I cannot pass a display such as this without imagining these stones as part of a magnificent ensemble."

"I believe that Mr. Fernsby, our curator over art, would fully agree with you, Lady Dunsbourne," Mr. Buckland said.

"Of that I have no doubt," Aunt Millward said. "The gentleman dresses like a peacock."

The feathers on her hat waved indignantly, and Emily looked away to prevent a giggle from escaping. She caught Mr. Buckland's eye. He grinned, and she lost her battle. Raising her gloved hand to her mouth, she managed to muffle her laughter with a cough. "I beg your pardon," she said.

"Not at all," Aunt Millward responded. "I asked for your opinion and should very much like to hear it."

Her opinion? Emily swallowed, attempting to replay the recent conversation in her mind. What exactly had Aunt Millward asked before peacocks, feathers, and Mr. Buckland's smile had so fully distracted her? She sensed Mr. Buckland's movement and hazarded another glance at him. He inclined his head slightly toward the display. The colorful rocks. That was it.

"I like the display very much," she said. "Although, I believe my fascination comes from seeing the gems in their natural state rather than as imagining them in a piece of jewelry." She paused, her gaze flitting from one rock to another. "It is truly remarkable. For the most part, the vibrant luster normally associated with lapis lazuli, amethysts, and sapphires is missing. It would be easy to overlook these gemstones if one were to happen upon them on a hillside."

"And yet you are able to discern the difference in their color?" Mr. Buckland asked.

"Yes." She hesitated, meeting his eyes once more. She did not know why, but for some reason, this question was important to him. "I may struggle to identify the gems without the labels pinned beneath each sample, but I see their unique shades."

He nodded, but the lightheartedness he'd exhibited moments earlier was gone. Emily frowned. Had she said something wrong? Adam and Phoebe had stepped away to study a curious wall-hanging made of wooden beads, but she was unaccountably reluctant to join them.

"I was once told the museum also houses a remarkable collection of dried plants and flowers," she said.

The corner of his lips quirked upward again. Perhaps there was a portion of his good humor remaining after all.

"That is true," he said. "It is an ever-expanding collection."

"Is that the one you've been working on recently, Henry?" Aunt Millward asked. She leaned a little closer to Emily. "Be warned, my dear, Henry has been known to wade into ponds in perfectly good boots and climb crags that should never be scaled in search of plant specimens."

Emily recognized Aunt Millward's good-natured teasing and could not help but join in. "How very peculiar," she said. "I recently learned of a gentleman who is wont to wander country roads with a trowel in hand for that very same purpose."

At the sound of Mr. Buckland's soft chuckle, Aunt Millward tucked her arm through Emily's. "Very odd, don't you think?"

"Most certainly."

"Although relatively harmless," Aunt Millward added.

"One would hope so." Fighting back a smile, Emily dared a glance at Mr. Buckland. He was watching them, his arms folded across his chest, his eyes glinting.

"Am I to assume from this rather one-sided conversation that you ladies have no interest in seeing the museum's plant collection?"

"Now, why ever would you think that?" The peacock feathers on Aunt Millward's hat swirled in mock indignation.

"I can't imagine," Mr. Buckland said dryly.

"Truth be told, I've been looking forward to seeing what you do with the flowers you have gathered," Emily admitted.

"Do we have time?" Aunt Millward asked.

Mr. Buckland withdrew his pocket watch and glanced at it. His eyebrows lifted in surprise. "We passed the three hours allotted for your tour some time ago. I fear the museum is scheduled to close in fifteen minutes."

Emily's astonishment was immediate. Disappointment was swift to follow. How could time have passed so quickly? There was so much to experience still. "If we are not required to leave for another quarter hour, may I selfishly claim the time to see part of the botanical collection?" she asked.

"You may," he said. "Do you have a preference as to which type of plants you see?"

"English wildflowers," Emily said without hesitation. "I've been surrounded by them all my life but have never taken the opportunity to truly appreciate their beauty."

Mr. Buckland smiled. "I located a particularly good red campion specimen recently. Unfortunately, it is still in the flower press. But I believe there are sufficient other species on display to please you."

An unusual warmth filled Emily's heart, but whether it was in anticipation of seeing the wildflower collection or simply in response to Mr. Buckland's kindness, she could not tell. Nor did she especially wish to.

Chapter 8

"Thank you, Felix. That will do."

Henry's valet stepped aside to allow him a full view of the looking glass. Felix had paired Henry's brown breeches with his gold jacket and embroidered waistcoat. The white lace at his sleeves and cravat lay perfectly, and his shoes were polished to a shine. Indeed, the gentleman staring back at Henry was very well put together and was an unnerving testament to the fact that appearances could be deceiving.

Releasing a tense breath, he turned his back on his reflection and took the hat in Felix's extended hand. He was being ridiculous. Just because Miss Norton had not been far from his thoughts since she'd left the museum two days before and he would likely see her again this evening did not mean that he should be acting as though he'd never set foot in a ballroom before. He had. Many times. And he was relatively adept at dancing, mingling, and—when necessary—making himself scarce. There was no logical reason for his current discomfort, a fact that only exacerbated his frustration.

Footsteps sounded in the passage outside his bedchamber, and he heard his mother's voice. Benedict had made good on his promise to leave for Gloucestershire earlier in the week, so she'd been particularly pleased when Henry had agreed to attend the Tilsons' ball. Shaking his head at his own foolishness, he donned his hat and gathered his gloves. As much as he wished that he'd refused the invitation and could spend the evening in his office at the museum, the deed was done, and there was no benefit to be had by making his parents wait for him to appear.

Exiting his rooms, he walked to the top of the stairs. From there, he could see his parents standing in the hall below. His mother laughed softly at something his father said. His father smiled and took her hand before leaning closer to brush a light kiss across her cheek. It was a simple scene—one Henry had seen replayed countless times during his growing-up years—but this evening, for the first time, he acknowledged its rarity among married couples in Society. As the second son who bore no title, Henry had been spared the level of matchmaking Benedict was forced to endure, but with an honorable profession and property in Shropshire that provided him additional income, neither was he fully exempt from the maneuverings of the likes of the Dowager Lady Pendleton.

Squaring his shoulders, he started down the stairs. Benedict was not the only one in the family who desired a match that included the type of love their parents shared. If Henry never found it, he would simply devote his life to his work. An image of Townsend dressed in black and poring over a book late at night in the manuscript saloon entered his head, and he winced. If he came to that, he would place Felix fully in charge of his wardrobe. The man's color sense rivaled Fernsby's.

As if to validate that thought, his mother raised her head and greeted him with a smile. "You look splendid, Henry."

"Thank you, Mother." He reached the ground floor, his expression softening at her obvious pleasure. "So do you."

"She does, indeed." His father took her arm. "I shall be fending off gentlemen all evening."

Henry grinned. "Would you save me a dance, Mother?"

His father gave him a warning look, and Henry laughed. Perhaps the evening would prove more entertaining than he'd previously anticipated.

Emily entered the Tilsons' ballroom at Aunt Millward's side, with Adam and Phoebe close behind. Flickering candles illuminated the vast space, and large urns filled with flowers divided small groupings of chairs. People—more than she had ever before seen congregated in one room—lined the walls and streamed in a swirl of colored silk and lace across the dance floor.

"Goodness." She took a deep breath in a vain attempt to calm her nerves. "How ever does one navigate so large a gathering?"

Aunt Millward smiled reassuringly. "One person at a time, my dear. All it will take is a couple of well-placed introductions and you shall be well on your way."

Well on her way to what? An evening of memorizing names and faces and saying just the right thing to every stranger she met? Her feet slowed.

Phoebe stepped up beside her and linked their arms. "Remember," she said softly, "you are not alone." She cocked her head to one side. "In the short time we've been in London, you have completely won over Aunt Millward, and although I have yet to determine whether she or Adam is most protective of you, I do know they will both come to your rescue if ever you need them. As will I."

"Thank you." Emily squeezed Phoebe's arm. "I'm not really as timid as I seem. It's just that this sight . . . the number of people . . . for someone who is used to solitude, it's a little overwhelming."

"It is. But it's also exciting, and I want you to enjoy every moment of it." Phoebe's eyes sparkled. "And to that end, I will do my best to keep Adam from scaring off any potential suitors."

"You would likely need to lock him outside to accomplish that."

Tapping her chin with her forefinger, Phoebe gave the appearance of pondering Emily's suggestion carefully. "I believe that idea may have considerable merit."

"Phoebe, I have seen that scheming look before." Adam joined them, looking from one lady to the other, his eyebrow raised. "What are you up to?"

"I think she is rather hoping you will take a walk with her on the patio," Emily said.

"Now?"

Phoebe slipped her arm out from beneath Emily's and claimed Adam's. "Now would be lovely," she said. "Aunt Millward will stay with Emily."

"Yes, yes." Aunt Millward waved them away. "Off you go. Emily and I will be fine."

Adam wavered for only a moment. "In her current condition, it would probably be wise to have Phoebe out of this press for a time."

Emily smiled. "We can meet up again after you have taken some air."

He nodded and turned to guide Phoebe toward the french doors. Emily watched them go, her smile faltering. Perhaps one day there would be a gentleman in her life who loved her as deeply as Adam loved Phoebe. Perhaps. If she were very fortunate. She took another deep breath and raised her chin a fraction. Until then, she had a grand ball to navigate, and she'd best begin right away.

The ballroom was crowded. Henry paused at its entrance and allowed his gaze to traverse the room. This late in the Season, most of the people attending the ball were familiar. He focused on those standing near the refreshment table. He could not see Lord Dunsbourne's dark head above the throng, and without her signature peacock-feathered hat, Aunt Millward was going to be almost impossible to spot among all the white-haired ladies. He scanned the guests standing in clusters along the wall, and a niggle of doubt entered his mind. No one had mentioned this ball when his aunt and her guests had visited the museum two days before. It was entirely possible that they had no plans to attend. He shook the thought away. Surely after arriving in London so late in the Season, Lord and Lady Dunsbourne would not forgo this opportunity to introduce Miss Norton to Society. The Tilsons' ball was known for being one of the grandest affairs of the year.

He skimmed the crowd again. Miss Norton was so petite that his best chance of seeing her would be if she was out on the dance floor. Weaving through a group of gentlemen discussing a recent race at Ascot, he inched toward the center of the room. A few gentlemen greeted him by name, but he did not stop to join their conversation. Lady Dalrimple, standing between her two daughters, smiled encouragingly at him. He acknowledged her with a polite nod and veered away.

Old Mr. Baldwin was talking loudly to Lord Littlewood. The gentleman's rambling complaint about his gout followed Henry to the edge of the dance floor. Over the music, Lady Aurelia's distinctive laugh reached him from somewhere to his left, and for about the tenth time since Felix had handed him his hat, he questioned his decision to come.

"Good evening, Henry."

Henry swung around as his aunt arrived beside him in a cloud of green silk and ribbons.

"Aunt Millward," he said. "I wondered if you would be here."

"I have been here for the best part of an hour." She eyed him critically. "But you certainly took your time to arrive. I was beginning to think you had failed me."

"Failed you?" What on earth was she talking about? Had she sent him a message that he'd never received?

"Not me, exactly," she said. "But most certainly Miss Norton."

"Miss Norton?" Henry's concern rose. His aunt had a bevy of friends, acquaintances, and servants who would assist her should she have a need. To the best of his knowledge, Miss Norton knew almost no one in London beyond her brother and sister-in-law.

"Of course." Aunt Millward shook her head despairingly. "Honestly, Henry, if you cannot manage to do anything more than repeat whatever I say, this evening is sunk."

Henry snapped his mouth closed, catching the question "This evening is sunk?" before it rolled off his tongue.

She opened her fan and wafted warm air across her face, watching him expectantly. "Well? Are you ready to enter the fray?"

Tamping down the urge to run his fingers through his hair, Henry dug deep for an extra measure of patience. "Aunt Millward, I do not mean to be obtuse, but I fear you are going to have to explain yourself a little better than this. What exactly does Miss Norton need?"

"Look," she said, pointing to the right.

During the last few minutes, the music had ended, and couples were leaving the dance floor. Mr. and Mrs. Markham walked by. Henry had not seen them since the birth of their son six months previous. They were followed by aging Lord Bolton with newly out Miss Brownlow. Then came Lord Culham, a gentleman whose reputation as a gambler was superseded only by his notoriety as a philanderer. And on his arm was Miss Norton.

Henry stared. Tiny white pearls winked from within the dark curls piled on her head. Ringlets fell to her shoulders. Her gown, a cream-colored creation that floated with her every move was somehow both striking and unpretentious. She was, in a word, stunning. And she was being escorted across the room on the arm of the very worst kind of man.

"Why is she dancing with Culham?" Henry's question was remarkably audible given his clenched teeth.

"Because he asked her. As did Mr. Poltock, Mr. Morris, Lord Atwood, and Colonel Eastberry before him." She eyed him meaningfully. "You were not here."

At some point during this exchange, Henry had fisted his hands. Now he made a conscious effort to uncurl his fingers. Aunt Millward was right. He could not blame Culham or any of those other gentlemen for asking Miss Norton to dance. Nor could he fault her for agreeing. But what he could do was influence her next choice of partner.

"If you will excuse me, Aunt Millward," he said, "it seems that I have inadvertently neglected Miss Norton and must set things right immediately."

Above the top of her fan, his aunt's eyes crinkled. "You are excused."

Culham appeared to be taking his time returning Miss Norton to the edge of the dance floor. He was also standing too close to her for Henry's liking. Setting his jaw, Henry closed the distance between them with long, deliberate strides. There were undoubtedly other gentlemen planning to ask Miss Norton to dance as soon as Culham stepped aside. Henry would simply have to act before that occurred.

"Good evening, Miss Norton." Henry circled Culham, coming to a stop before the couple. Miss Norton's forward momentum faltered. Out of the corner of his eye, Henry caught Culham's frown, but his attention was on the young lady. He bowed, and she offered him a warm smile.

"Mr. Buckland. How lovely to see you!"

Lud. It was no wonder the gentlemen at this assembly were clamoring to dance with her. A smile like that was enough to make a man's knees weak.

"I did not realize you were acquainted with Miss Norton, Buckland." There was no mistaking Culham's irritation. Henry ignored it.

"We met before she came to London," Henry said. It was stretching the truth a little, but they had at least spoken to one another. And claiming a prior acquaintanceship with the young lady felt necessary in the face of Culham's obvious interest in Miss Norton. "Indeed, if she would do me the honor, I would like to request the pleasure of the next dance."

Culham raised an eyebrow, eyeing the short distance between them and the edge of the dance floor. If the gentleman truly cared about propriety, Henry might have felt a pang of remorse for taking Miss Norton from him before he returned her to her place among the other ladies. As it was, Henry knew that Culham had about as much respect for etiquette as an untrained puppy and was considerably more designing. The sooner Miss Norton was removed from him, the better.

"I would be delighted, Mr. Buckland," Miss Norton said.

With a poorly disguised glare directed at Henry, Culham inclined his head toward Miss Norton. "It seems that my time with you has been cut short, Miss Norton. But never fear, I shall seek you out again." He raised her hand to his lips.

"You are very kind, sir."

Culham had yet to release her hand. A small line appeared along Miss Norton's forehead, and then she tugged her hand free. Henry immediately stepped forward to offer her his arm. Relieved when she took it, he paused only long enough for Miss Norton to bob a brief curtsy to Culham before leading her away.

Chapter 9

EMILY SUPPRESSED A SHUDDER. LORD Culham had been all politeness and charm. Too much politeness and charm, in fact. Somehow, she'd managed to match his banal pleasantries and ignore his excessive compliments for the duration of the minuet, but when the music had ended and she had no longer needed to focus on the dance steps, both had become significantly harder to endure. He reminded her of the shiny apples that fell to the ground in the orchard at Dunsbourne Manor. It was only when one picked them up and turned them over that the seemingly appetizing fruit revealed its hollow interior and maybe even a maggot or two.

"Are you well, Miss Norton?"

Mr. Buckland's concerned voice shook her from her unpleasant thoughts. "Forgive me. Yes." She tightened her hold on his arm. "I have yet to thank you."

"If I have done anything worthy of your thanks, I am grateful, although I cannot think what it could possibly be."

It was probably very bad form to tell him he had saved her from spending any more time with a maggoty apple. But it was disturbingly tempting. She glanced at him, and he raised a quizzical eyebrow, the corner of his lips pulling up into a half smile.

"Are you not going to tell me? In truth, since Aunt Millward has already reproved me for being negligent this evening, I could use a feather in my cap—no matter how small or bedraggled."

She laughed and felt the tension ease from her shoulders. Here, at last, was a gentleman she could converse with about something more than the weather or the size of the assembly.

"It would have to be a rather spectacular feather to outdo the ones Lady Finchley is wearing tonight," she said.

He looked intrigued. "Is that so? What is so remarkable about Lady Finchley's headwear?"

"Aunt Millward tells me they are ostrich feathers," she said, unable to hide her wonder. "I've never seen feathers so large. Not even Aunt Millward's peacock feathers can compare."

Mr. Buckland smiled. "And are they garnering the lady all the attention she hoped?"

"I believe they must be, for she has been surrounded by guests all evening. You can see her on the left side of the ballroom now, wearing a purple gown."

He turned his head to look. "Near the large potted plant in the corner?"

Emily followed his gaze. There were at least half a dozen ladies clustered together near the miniature tree, and although two of them were dressed in shades of deep blue, not one was wearing a purple gown.

"No. She is standing closer to the refreshment table."

His attention shifted, and she saw his expression clear. "I see the feathers, and I understand your wonder. They are quite extraordinary."

"Yes."

They were almost as lavish as the older lady's purple gown, which she had considered impossible to miss. And yet, for Mr. Buckland, it had not appeared to stand out among the other gowns. Her thoughts went back to the gemstones they'd viewed at the museum a couple of days before. The amethyst had been a similar color to Lady Finchley's dress, and he had specifically asked her if she could tell it apart from the other rocks.

The musicians played the first notes of the allemande, and his hazel eyes met hers. Was it possible that Mr. Buckland experienced some kind of difficulty with his eyesight?

"Are you ready?" he asked.

She blinked and nodded. He took her hand. An unexpected frisson of awareness skittered up her arm. The music swelled, and suddenly, they were moving, stepping forward, back, circling each other, and coming together again. She forgot to count steps. There was no need. His fingers were strong, but his grip was gentle, and he guided her through the dance with a fluidity she'd never before experienced.

The music came to an end, and all around her, ladies were curtsying. Emily followed suit, her thoughts in a whirl. How had the dance finished so soon? She was not ready to end her time with Mr. Buckland. Especially if it meant that she would be forced to dance with any more gentlemen like Lord Culham.

She raised her head. He was watching her, a strange expression on his face.

"You dance beautifully, Miss Norton," he said.

"You are very kind to say so. It's a fairly recently acquired skill and one that has not come without several run-ins with rather unyielding pieces of furniture."

He chuckled and offered her his arm. "No one would ever suspect it."

As they started toward the edge of the ballroom, Emily's dread of reentering the milling throng mounted, and seemingly of their own volition, her footsteps slowed. She'd been introduced to more people than she had any hope of remembering this evening. Already, she recalled only a small fraction of their names.

"It's a bit much, isn't it?"

Mr. Buckland's quietly spoken question took her off guard. She turned to look at him. He had slackened his pace to match hers, and she saw understanding in his eyes.

"It is rather," she admitted. "I have never seen so many people in one place. I am far more used to sitting quietly by the river at Dunsbourne Manor than I am to socializing in vast groups."

"There are those who find large crowds and a long evening of dancing enlivening," he said. "But I would contend that they are fewer in number than those who consider them challenging."

"Do you really think so?" It was hard to imagine that many of the smiling ladies and gentlemen were hiding a fraction of the discomfort she had been experiencing since entering the ballroom.

"I know so," he said. "And as I am one of them, may I ask if—out of the goodness of your heart—you would be willing to facilitate my escape for a few minutes by taking the air on the patio with me?"

Emily could not contain her smile. "It would be my pleasure."

Mr. Buckland did not hesitate. Veering away from a tall, thin gentleman who seemed intent on intercepting them, he guided her past a group of chatting ladies and toward the distant french doors. An elderly gentleman returning from the refreshment table with two glasses of punch crossed their path. He greeted Mr. Buckland briefly before handing one of the glasses to a lady in purple. Lady Finchley. Even if she had not seen the fluffy ostrich feathers sway, Emily would have recognized the lady's distinctive purple gown. She frowned. The same gown Mr. Buckland had failed to identify.

They had almost reached the exit. Mr. Buckland reached for the door, and Emily marshaled her courage. "I realize that we have not known each other long, but as you are the possessor of one of my secrets, may I be so forward as to ask you a personal question?"

"Something greater than learning that I would rather be in a quiet room with a collection of rocks and dried plants than at one of London's most popular balls?" he asked.

"Seeing as I would make the same choice in a heartbeat, I do not consider that a very great secret. Besides, you have only recently attempted to convince me that yours is a popularly held opinion."

"Fair enough." He waited for her to walk out ahead of him. "What is it that you wish to ask me?"

She stepped onto the patio and breathed in the fresh air. Shadows flitted across the circles of light on the flagstones, and the murmur of voices reached her from the darkness. A breeze lifted her curls from her shoulder, the sudden drop in temperature sending a shiver down her spine.

"Miss Norton?" She heard the concern in Mr. Buckland's voice. "I cannot promise that I will be able to answer your question, but I would not have you be afraid to ask."

"You are very good." She shook her head. "I am being ridiculous. It's just that when you were unable to identify Lady Finchley by the distinctive hue of her gown, I was reminded that you asked about the color of the amethyst when we were at the museum, and I—" She sensed rather than saw him stiffen, and a ball of dread formed in her stomach. What had she done? Was satisfying her curiosity worth risking offending the gentleman who had shown her such kindness? "Forgive me. I spoke out of turn. I have nothing more to say other than to thank you for being so gracious to a young lady who has much yet to learn."

"On the contrary, Miss Norton. I am twice amazed at how educated you are on a wide variety of subjects and am particularly impressed by your observational skills. We have been in each other's company only four times, but you have detected a disability that I have successfully hidden from people who have known me all my life."

Emily's heart pounded. "Truly, sir, I did not mean to have you share something you have not told others."

His smile was strained. "Unless I am mistaken, I believe we have already entered that territory together." He took her elbow. "Come. I shall tell you what little I can."

They walked toward the stone railing. Somewhere to the right, a lady tittered, and footsteps sounded on the stone stairs. Another couple walked past them. The gentlemen exchanged polite nods. Mr. Buckland waited until they were out of earshot.

"During my years at Cambridge, I spent a great deal of time reading, examining plant specimens, and writing about them. At the end of a long day in the laboratory, I often found myself struggling to see the details on a page or sample. One of my professors wore spectacles and suggested that I might benefit from acquiring a pair."

She had not seen him wear spectacles. "Did they help?"

"Yes. Immeasurably." This time his smile was more natural. "I do not need to wear them all the time. Only when my eyes are tired. In sunlight, they would help me see each of the freckles on your nose."

That he had noticed her freckles did not bring her a similar measure of happiness, but she was glad for his success. "Your spectacles must work exceptionally well because Phoebe assures me that my freckles are very small."

"They are very small indeed," he said. "They are also most becoming."

The light evening breeze did nothing to temper the warmth that filled her cheeks. It was high time Mr. Buckland returned to the subject of his eyes rather than her freckles. "I am glad that your spectacles have enabled you to better focus, but am I to assume that they did not make everything right?"

"Yes."

The finality of that single word told Emily more about how difficult this was for him than any lengthy explanation would have. "I am sorry," she said.

"As am I." He shrugged. "It was a fleeting hope." He leaned against the railing and gazed out onto the darkened garden beyond. "For as long as I can remember, I have been unable to discern between certain colors. From my perspective, reds have a greenish hue, sometimes appearing as a dull brown. Purples and blues, when placed near each other, become indistinguishable."

As improbable as his claim seemed to be, the regret in the gentleman's voice attested to its reality. Emily was silent for a moment, allowing the implications of what he described to settle upon her. How would her life be different if she could not differentiate between the vast array of colors in fabric, in paintings, in nature?

She swiveled to face him. "The red campion," she gasped.

"I still maintain that it is misnamed," he said.

"I agree. It's pink."

"So you told me. And my colleague Mr. Fernsby concurred." He released a tight breath. "To me, it is gray."

Emily recognized his frustration and ached for him. "Does it make your work difficult?"

"Sometimes. Mr. Fernsby is an artist and is more than happy to give me the benefit of his expertise. He wears a broad color palate every day. But it is exasperating that I am forced to rely on others for something that should be so simple."

"There is nothing simple about your work at the museum," she said. "And that you do it so conscientiously despite your handicap is a credit to you."

"Is it? Sometimes I wonder if another would be better suited for my job. Someone less likely to make a grievous error in classifying new specimens."

"I do not believe that."

His smile was halfhearted. "As much as I appreciate your confidence in my abilities, you hardly know me well enough to be a fair judge."

"How many gentlemen do you know who can claim such a passion for plant collection that they carry a trowel with them wherever they go?" She hesitated. "You didn't actually bring one to the ball though, did you?"

This time, she elicited a genuine laugh from him. "Lady Tilson would have my head—or, at least, my standing in Society—if I were to dig up anything from her beloved garden. So, no, I did not bring it with me this evening. While I am in London, I tend to limit my outings with a trowel to the less populated areas of the city."

"Are there any?" Emily was genuinely surprised. Her experience thus far had been roads lined with rows upon rows of buildings, along with countless pedestrians, mounted horses, and carriages.

"Fewer than I would like, but such places do exist. There are a few wilderness-like spots in some of the parks."

Before she could press him for more information on the exact location of a patch of untamed greenery she could visit and pretend to be in the country once more, the clatter of rapid footsteps sounded on the flagstones behind her.

"Emily!"

She swung around to see Adam hurrying toward her. A rapid mental review of her situation assured her that she was doing nothing untoward. She and Mr. Buckland were standing an appropriate distance apart, were yet within the lanterns' light, and were within sight of several other people. Unfortunately, her positive assessment was not reflected on her brother's face.

He came to a stop and acknowledged Mr. Buckland with a brief nod. "I beg your pardon, Buckland. I do not mean to interrupt, but my wife has fallen ill, and your aunt has called for the carriage and is insisting upon returning home with us." He turned to Emily. "I'm sorry to cut your evening short, Em."

"Nonsense," Emily said. "I am in full agreement with Aunt Millward." She tucked her arm through Adam's. Phoebe had been horribly ill for the first four months of her pregnancy, and although she had seemed much improved over the last few weeks, it was not surprising that the extra exertion needed to prepare for the ball may have negatively affected her. "Is Phoebe suffering from the same sickness she has experienced before?"

He shook his head, and Emily caught the hint of fear in his eyes. "No. She is complaining of sharp pains."

Emily's grip on her brother's arm tightened. "Where is she now?"

"She is with her aunt in the entrance hall, awaiting the carriage."

"We must go to her." Emily faced Mr. Buckland. No explanation was necessary; he had heard her exchange with Adam. But she wished she could offer him more than this hurried farewell. She dropped into a hasty curtsy. "I apologize, sir. I hope we will have the opportunity to renew our conversation before too long."

"Of course." He bowed. "Please give my best wishes to Lady Dunsbourne. I wish you both well."

Henry stood at the stone railing as Miss Norton disappeared into the ballroom on her brother's arm. What had come over him? The young lady was uncannily observant and refreshingly open, but he had deflected questions about his inability to identify colors before. Why had he not done so when she had asked? He released a frustrated breath. He had likely shared more than he should, but there was something about Miss Norton that made the concept of dissembling abhorrent. And even though he'd not been given the opportunity to ask for her confidentiality, he knew he had it. Just as she had his.

The image of her standing alone on the country road entered his mind, and he managed a smile. Her secret indiscretion was very minor. As minor as the freckles on her nose. His smile widened, and he started for the door. Perhaps it was for the best that Miss Norton was oblivious to the charm she exuded when she wrinkled said nose. She might stop doing it.

He entered the ballroom and looked around. It may take him a while to locate his parents amid this throng, but the sooner he did so, the sooner he could talk his father into abandoning this large social event in favor of playing a game of chess before the fire at home. With Miss Norton's departure, the ball had completely lost its appeal.

Chapter 10

ADAM MADE ANOTHER CIRCUIT OF the drawing room before stopping to glare at the door that separated him from the passage and the stairs leading up to Phoebe's bedchamber. "What's taking so long?" He ran his fingers through his hair. "This is all wrong. I should be with her."

Aunt Millward handed Emily a cup of tea before pouring one for Adam. "As difficult as it is to hear, my dear Lord Dunsbourne, you are not wanted upstairs at the moment. None of us is. Dr. Thorndike is the finest physician in London. He will provide Phoebe with the best possible care."

Emily picked up her teaspoon and stirred the steaming brown liquid in the cup she was holding. The light chink of the silver spoon touching the china filled the silent room. She stopped stirring and glanced at the clock on the mantel. They'd been waiting for almost an hour already. She was not sure that Adam would last much longer before he marched up the stairs demanding to know what the doctor had discovered.

The journey from the Tilsons' house had been made as expeditiously as possible. Phoebe's soft moans had been the only sound in the carriage, and upon their arrival at Aunt Millward's home, Adam had carried her directly upstairs. Aunt Millward had sent for Dr. Thorndike, claiming that as a good friend of the family, he would respond to her request despite the lateness of the hour. She had been right. The doctor had arrived in remarkably short order and had been with Phoebe ever since.

"Have some tea, my lord," Aunt Millward said, offering Adam the newly filled cup. "You must keep up your strength, and it has been several hours since we ate."

Emily was not convinced that a cup of tea would make a marked difference in Adam's vigor, but giving him something to do other than pace would benefit them all. He was likely to wear a path in the carpet if he continued unchecked.

Perhaps he also saw the wisdom in focusing on something else because he crossed the short distance to Aunt Millward's chair and accepted the cup and saucer. "Thank you. You are very thoughtful."

"Or it is simply that I do not have the energy to pace the room, and pouring endless cups of tea keeps me from watching the clock." She eyed him meaningfully over the rim of her cup. "Thoughtful or lacking stamina. Both suppositions have merit, but I like yours better. Shall we stick with that one?"

Adam's strained expression eased a fraction. "Certainly. But regardless of convention, if Dr. Thorndike does not appear within the next five minutes, I intend to enter Phoebe's room to speak with him."

Aunt Millward took another sip of tea. "I must say, it has been my observation that more often than not, conventions are best ignored." She set her cup on her saucer. "If you go, I shall follow."

Emily was trying to determine whether three anxious family members arriving outside the bedchamber would be too much for the doctor and Phoebe when the sound of a door closing above them was immediately followed by clipped footsteps on the stairs. Adam set his teacup on the end table and had almost reached the drawing room door when Dr. Thorndike appeared.

"How is she?" Adam asked without preamble.

The doctor, who could not be much more than ten years Adam's senior, offered him a weary smile. "Her pains have subsided. I have given her some seltzer water elixir, and she is resting."

"And the baby?"

"Thankfully, the baby appears to have decided to remain where it is for the time being."

Adam ran his hand across his face, his expression of relief captured by Aunt Millward's sigh.

"I would warn you, however, my lord," the doctor continued, "Lady Dunsbourne's situation, although improved, remains precarious. I have advised her to keep to her bed for at least a fortnight. No more balls, long walks, or shopping expeditions. She may find such restrictions challenging, but for the time being, the less exertion she attempts, the better."

"Of course," Adam said.

"She shall not lift a finger." Aunt Millward made the pronouncement with such firmness Emily felt a moment of panic for Phoebe.

"Perhaps you could allow her the use of sufficient fingers to turn the pages of a book or draw a needle through fabric," she suggested. "I believe Phoebe might go slightly mad if she can do nothing but lie in bed staring at the ceiling for a fortnight."

"Quite right, Miss Norton," Dr. Thorndike said, a hint of a smile on his tired face. "She will undoubtedly be in want of some quiet activities. The exercise of a few fingers and thumbs would seem to be a good compromise."

"Marvelous," Aunt Millward said. "I shall ensure that Phoebe has whatever sewing supplies she may need. Emily, perhaps you would be good enough to choose her some books from the library."

Phoebe's favorite reading material was *The Ladies' Cabinet of Fashion* magazines, but given Aunt Millward's rather eccentric taste in headwear and wide-pannier gowns, Emily considered it unlikely that the elderly lady subscribed to anything of the sort. Indeed, she had a sinking feeling that finding Phoebe a book she might enjoy reading from the viscount's collection was going to be significantly more difficult than Aunt Millward's chosen assignment.

"I am grateful to you both," Adam said. "And to you, sir." He bowed slightly. "Coming out so late in the evening was very good of you."

"Glad to be of service, my lord. I have given Lady Dunsbourne's maid instructions to administer a cold-water bath in the morning, and I shall stop by to check on her ladyship in the afternoon."

"You have my thanks," Adam said. "And now, if you'll excuse me, I must go to my wife."

Dr. Thorndike inclined his head, and Adam made a hasty exit.

Aunt Millward raised the teapot once more. "Allow me to pour you a cup of tea before you leave, Dr. Thorndike," she said.

"That would be most welcome." He lowered himself onto one end of the red sofa and tugged at his finely cut but serviceable jacket.

"Milk and sugar?" Aunt Millward asked.

"A little of both, if you please."

Shifting the purple cushion at his elbow, Dr. Thorndike accepted the cup and saucer from Aunt Millward and relaxed against the back of the sofa. It was a simple thing, but it brought a sense of calm to an evening that had been fraught with tension. For the first time since she'd left the Tilsons' ball, Emily allowed her thoughts to move from concern for Phoebe to Mr. Buckland's stunning revelation.

She might have considered the gentleman's assertion that he could not distinguish between colors to be some kind of jest had she not witnessed how difficult an admission it had been for him. But in all her reading, she had never heard of anything like this. What could possibly cause so strange a condition?

"What news from the medical community, Dr. Thorndike?" Aunt Millward asked. "I am always anxious to hear of the advancements being made to save lives."

Emily caught the flash of surprise in the doctor's eyes. A discussion of medical advancements was not generally considered polite conversation in a drawing room, particularly if the only people present were ladies.

"I agree, my lady. Such news is most heartening." He was treading carefully, and Emily was quite sure it would not be sufficient to satisfy Aunt Millward. She was right.

"Heartening indeed," Aunt Millward said. "And most of us do not hear nearly enough of it. Tell me something you have learned recently."

Dr. Thorndike looked thoughtful. "There is a gentleman from Glasgow by the name of John Hunter who is making quite a name for himself as a surgeon. Unlike most other physicians, he maintains that the enlarging of gunshot wounds should only be done in instances when bone fragments must be removed and attributes most infections to the surgeon's unnecessary probing of the wound."

"Do you believe his claim has merit?" Aunt Millward asked.

"I do." The doctor set down his cup and saucer. "The simple fact that more people die of infection following an injury than of the injury itself tells me that we must make a fundamental change in our approach to such surgeries."

Emily glanced at Aunt Millward. She showed no sign of queasiness or distaste. Rather, her expression reflected genuine interest and thoughtful consideration. Emily hardly dared breathe for fear that these two remarkable individuals would remember that she was in the room and cease their fascinating conversation.

"Remarkable," Aunt Millward said. "Of course, it would seem to me that if one could discover the root cause of infections, it would be quite literally life changing."

"Most certainly. And I pray that one day such knowledge is ours."

"I have great hope in the future of medicine, Dr. Thorndike. With gentlemen such as you and this John Hunter continuing to pioneer new theories, we cannot help but see improvements." She turned to Emily. "Do you not think so, my dear?"

Emily startled. She should have known better than to believe Aunt Millward would countenance a silent eavesdropper. But listening to a discussion so far removed from normal drawing room conversations was different from being invited to participate. She grasped her teacup a little tighter. "With the ways our knowledge of the world keeps expanding, I imagine there is a great deal still to learn in every subject, including a better understanding of how our bodies might be healed." She paused momentarily, and then, clutching her courage as firmly as the teacup, she continued. "I learned of a most unusual ailment recently, and I wonder, Dr. Thorndike, if you might know anything regarding the condition."

The doctor raised an inquisitive eyebrow. "I am intrigued, Miss Norton. Pray, tell me more."

How did she describe something she understood so little? More importantly, how did she do so without any hint that Aunt Millward was well acquainted with the sufferer?

"I know of several ladies and gentlemen who rely upon eyeglasses to assist with their vision," she began.

Dr. Thorndike nodded. "Difficulty in focusing on small stitches or the written word, particularly in poor light, is an unfortunately common complaint."

"So, I believe." She took a deep breath. "But have you ever known difficulty with one's eyesight to impact a person's ability to discern colors?"

Aunt Millward appeared mystified.

Dr. Thorndike, on the other hand, leaned forward in his seat, and fixed her with a steady look. "I am twice intrigued, Miss Norton, for, rare though it is, I discussed this very subject with a colleague of mine only three days ago."

"Then you are familiar with it?" Hope added enthusiasm to her voice.

"Familiar, yes. An expert, not in the least. In fact, I would say that there is only one gentleman in all of England who might be considered an expert on the subject, although he may take exception to that title, as his research is very much a work in progress."

"Who is that?" Aunt Millward asked.

"His name is John Dalton. He's a chemist who hails from the Manchester area, but he has coined the phrase 'anomalous vision,' which supposedly refers to a condition that prevents a person from seeing colors as most of us see them."

"Has he also uncovered a cure for this ailment?" Emily asked.

"Not that I am aware. And the gentleman has every reason to uncover one, as I am told he suffers from the disorder himself."

"Good gracious. How alarming," Aunt Millward said. "Tell me, are all prominent scientists and physicians named John?"

Dr. Thorndike chuckled. "As my given name is Jacob, I certainly hope not, but I will grant you that several of them are."

Aunt Millward had successfully deflected the conversation onto a lighter subject. If Emily were to forcibly return it to Mr. Dalton and his anomalous vision, it would undoubtedly draw too much attention to her burning desire to know more. At present, difficult though it was, the topic was best left alone. She would leave it to Mr. Buckland to determine whether or not to reach out to the scientist from Manchester. It would be enough if she could make him feel less alone in his situation.

Dr. Thorndike glanced at the clock on the mantel and came to his feet. "I appreciate your hospitality, Lady Millward," he said, "but it is late. I must be on my way and allow you and Miss Norton to retire for the night."

Aunt Millward and Emily rose.

"We are in your debt, Dr. Thorndike," Aunt Millward said.

"Not at all. Do not hesitate to send word should Lady Dunsbourne's condition worsen, but I am hopeful that a period of respite will bring the desired results."

Aunt Millward nodded and walked with him to the drawing room door. Above the fireplace, the clock chimed the eleven o'clock hour, and like a heavy blanket, exhaustion settled upon Emily. It was too late to send a message to Mr. Buckland this evening, but she would write to him first thing tomorrow morning. And then she would fill the remainder of her day searching Aunt Millward's library for any books that might entice Phoebe to stay in bed and read.

Chapter 11

"Good morning, Rutherford." Henry greeted the British Museum's porter at the door of Montagu House.

"Good morning, sir." Rutherford reached for a small pile of correspondence on the corner of the nearby desk and handed it to Henry. "Looks to be another wet day."

"Indeed." With the amount of moisture gathering on the marble floor around Henry's sodden boots, Rutherford was stating the obvious, but after three full days of rain, the inclement weather was hard to ignore.

Holding the morning post in one hand, Henry took off his hat with the other and gave the object a slight shake. Water droplets scattered through the air. "It seems to me that we are overdue for some sunshine."

Rutherford nodded. "I wouldn't complain if the rain stopped. Keeping these floors dry has been all but impossible."

The museum had experienced a steady flow of visitors all week. In fact, if it weren't that admission was limited to ticket-holders, they probably would have been overrun by Londoners whose outdoor activities had been thwarted by the bad weather.

As he had done far too many times for comfort, Henry wondered how Miss Norton had been keeping herself amused over the last few days. He'd heard nothing of Lady Dunsbourne's condition after she and her family members had left the Tilsons' ball. Not that he'd expected to; such things were usually kept private. But he sincerely hoped her condition had improved. He did not know the family well, but he had enjoyed each of his interactions with them. And he particularly liked Miss Norton.

He started up the stairs, his thoughts centered on Miss Norton's bewitching appearance at the ball. What kind of spell had she cast upon him that had loosened his tongue so fully? No matter the childhood teasing he'd endured from peers when he'd chosen the wrong color marbles during their games or his mother's frustration when he'd repeatedly passed her an assortment of embroidery threads rather than the specific one she'd requested of him, up until four nights ago, his brother, Benedict, and his valet, Felix, were the only ones who had known the full extent of his disability. He stifled a groan. Miss Norton must think him barmy. Or at the very least, the oddest gentleman she'd ever had occasion to meet.

He reached the door of his office and withdrew the key from his waistcoat pocket. His first tour began in two hours. If he could manage to put Miss Norton and their fateful conversation at the ball behind him, he might be able to catalog the last of the late Lord Mumford's collection of Egyptian pottery before he was needed in the entrance hall.

"All right, Buckland, I've remained silent long enough. Spill it!"

Henry swung around to see Fernsby approaching along the landing. The gentleman's hair was pulled back in an extravagant yellow ribbon that matched his waistcoat. His jacket was undoubtedly some shade of red and seemed to be similar in tone to his breeches.

"Good morning to you too, Fernsby," Henry said dryly.

Fernsby grunted. "There's nothing *good* about this morning unless you're a duck or a frog. Even the worms are out on the roads protesting the continued rain."

Henry opened the door and walked in. Not surprisingly, Fernsby followed.

"Did you need something?" Henry asked, setting his letters on the table.

"Yes." Fernsby folded his arms over his sunny waistcoat. "The truth."

Tamping down his alarm, Henry took his time hanging up his wet hat and cloak. Had he made a mistake with the last batch of semiprecious stones? He'd been sure of the sapphire, but the variety of agates had caused him difficulty. "The truth about what?" There was no point in beating about the bush.

"Whatever it is that you've said or done to Townsend to put him into such a foul mood."

It was a testament to his measure of relief that Fernsby's accusation caused Henry to smile. "Has he been barking at you more than usual?"

Fernsby eyed him suspiciously. "It's more than that, and you know it. He's never cheery, I grant you, but for the best part of a fortnight, he's been especially dour. And it seems to me that you've been avoiding him."

Henry moved around the large table in the center of the room and took his seat. Half a dozen pieces of pottery lay in a tidy row in a box on his left. His quill, inkwell, and ledger stood ready at his right, but experience told him he'd get no work done until Fernsby's curiosity was satisfied. "Claridge visited the museum a week last Friday," he said.

Fernsby's eyebrows rose. "Why did I not know of it?"

"He was here for only half an hour before leaving for a board meeting. Apparently, he'd heard from Lady Grenville's solicitor. The viscountess has instructed him to draw up the papers to transfer ownership of her butterfly collection and a significant portion of her husband's compilation of literature to the museum."

"I would have thought Townsend would consider that to be excellent news. What does he have to be grumpy about?"

Henry rolled up one sleeve to protect it from the fresh ink he still hoped to apply to the next page of his ledger. "It seems that Lady Grenville has determined that the transfer of items is conditional upon her working exclusively with me. Claridge came to thank me for acquiring the endowment and to ask me to oversee the material when it arrives."

Fernsby's expression was unusually thoughtful. "And Townsend's nose was put out of joint because books and manuscripts come under his purview."

"Yes."

"Did Claridge say whether he'd heard anything from Mr. Watts?"

Puzzled by the abrupt change in subject from Townsend's displeasure to the museum director's continued absence, Henry shook his head. "No. Why?"

"We've been waiting on the shipment he promised for weeks. I just wondered if Claridge had heard of any ship sightings yet." He shrugged. "Perhaps there will be something for Townsend to focus on in those crates when they arrive."

Given that the cargo was coming from the South Seas, it was extremely unlikely that there would be much literature in the containers, but Henry would not fault Fernsby for trying to be positive. "It's possible."

"Yes." Fernsby appeared thoughtful. "If Claridge stops by to talk to you again, let me know, would you? It doesn't hurt to be prepared for Townsend's increased displeasure."

"I don't see why he'd need to speak to me a second time," Henry said. "Rutherford will take charge of any deliveries, as he always does. Once everything's unloaded, I will happily give Townsend charge over all of Lord Grenville's papers."

"An assignment he will no doubt undertake with considerable resentment if it comes through you."

"I sincerely hope not."

Fernsby snorted. "The old man should have stepped down and allowed someone younger to take the position years ago."

"His cantankerous disposition notwithstanding, it's hard to imagine any-one taking more diligent care of the manuscript saloon."

"Lady Grenville obviously thinks otherwise, and it would seem that Claridge concurs."

Henry shook his head. "Claridge has agreed to follow along with Lady Grenville's whims for the sake of the museum."

"Perhaps," Fernsby said, but he did not look fully convinced.

Henry reached for the letters he'd set on the corner of the table. If rolling up his sleeve was an insufficient clue that he was anxious to be about his work, perhaps opening today's post would encourage Fernsby to vacate his office. He glanced at the letter on the top of the pile. His name and the address of the museum were written in a decidedly feminine hand. He stilled. He'd seen a sample of Lady Grenville's penmanship once before. It had been considerably more spidery and uneven than this tidy script. But if there was any possibility that the viscountess had written to give him further instructions, he would rather not have his colleague in the room.

"If you would excuse me, Fernsby," he said. "I have to take the first tour this morning, and I should probably look through this correspondence first."

"Of course." Fernsby glanced at the letters in Henry's hand and then turned to the door. "I'll be in the art storage room, if you need me."

Henry waited until Fernsby closed the door behind him before breaking the seal on the envelope and withdrawing a single sheet of paper. His gaze fell on the signature at the bottom, and his pulse quickened. Miss Emily Norton. Why was she writing to him? Shifting slightly so the letter was in better light, he began to read.

> *Millward House,*
> *London*
> *28 March 1790*
>
> *Dear Mr. Buckland,*
>
> *My hasty departure from the Tilsons' ball prevented me from properly expressing my gratitude to you for talking to me so openly that evening and for taking me into your confidence. I wish to assure you that your trust is not misplaced; I will not divulge any particulars of our conversation to another.*

I daresay it will come as no surprise to know that the details you shared regarding your difficulty in identifying colors lingered with me long after we parted. So it was that when Dr. Jacob Thorndike—a doctor whom Aunt Millward holds in high esteem—joined us in the drawing room after having cared for Lady Dunsbourne, I took it upon myself to ask what he knew of vision impairment with regard to difficulty in detecting specific hues. To my amazement and delight, he was acquainted with the condition and told me of a gentleman named John Dalton, living in Manchester, who is currently studying this particular phenomenon.

As I pen this, I realize that even though I mentioned no names or specific reason for my interest in the malady, my actions may be construed by you as meddlesome. Please accept my apologies if you feel thus. My reason for asking Dr. Thorndike was to attempt to gain greater understanding; my purpose in now relaying his response to you is simply to offer you a glimmer of hope. You can be assured that the condition with which you suffer is not of your own making, nor are you the only one caused to bear it. Furthermore, as the disability has been identified by at least one scientist as something needing further study, it stands to reason that a cure may be discovered in the not-too-distant future. I pray this may be true and that awareness of Mr. Dalton's work will help you feel less alone.

Yours sincerely,
Miss Emily Norton

Henry sat back in his chair, his breath releasing in a rush as he attempted to sort through his swirling emotions. A burn of indignation at Miss Norton's unasked-for involvement in his very personal challenge mingled with shock that she had so fully taken his burden to heart. Acknowledgment that she had in actuality acted in his best interest was quickly followed by a flood of gratitude.

He reread Miss Norton's last line again. How had she known? He'd not spoken of the isolation he'd often experienced facing a world that looked different to him than it did to everyone else. He was sure of it. It was something he rarely admitted even to himself. And this John Dalton? Was it possible that he could give Henry answers to the questions he'd had since childhood? Hope rose within him. He would write to the gentleman in Manchester today, and as soon as the rain stopped, he would pay a visit to Miss Norton.

He stood and walked to the window, gazing down at the museum's grounds through the water-streaked glass. The rain had washed clean the city's sooty air and had turned the vegetation a deep green. The manicured lawn and hedges appeared almost as verdant as their untamed counterparts in the countryside. Almost. As he pondered that observation, a singular idea settled upon him. He would go to Aunt Millward's house to see Miss Norton, but he would not stay for the usual cup of tea and a biscuit. He would invite the young lady to go on an outing with him. An outing as unique as she was.

CHAPTER 12

"There," Phoebe said. "That was the last stitch." A beam of sunlight danced across the polished wood floor, reflecting off the scissors in her hand as she snipped at a thread and held up the tiny linen slip for Emily to see. "What do you think?"

Emily set aside the book she'd been reading and rose from the chair beside Phoebe's bed.

"Oh, Phoebe." She reached for the infant-sized garment to admire the row of miniature yellow ducklings Phoebe had embroidered around the neckline and across the yoke. "I could never make anything nearly so beautiful."

Phoebe smiled. "Well, I have yet to master the art of knitting, so you may make the baby a hat instead."

"And if it turns out as well as the scarves I've made in the past, it will likely fit Adam."

Phoebe laughed, and with a smile, Emily handed her back the slip. After five days free of the frightening pains she'd experienced at the Tilsons' ball, the fear that had shone in Phoebe's eyes had been replaced by hope.

"It's a good thing I enjoy embroidery so well. I might have gone mad if I'd had to lie here with nothing more than a pile of the late Lord Millward's books."

It was Emily's turn to laugh. They both knew that if *she* were confined to bed, a pile of books would be exactly what she'd want.

"At least you're not missing out on being outdoors in beautiful weather," Emily said. "Today's sunshine is the first we've seen all week."

"I know. Isn't it lovely? It brightens the entire bedchamber." Phoebe paused to watch a white cloud scud across the blue sky before turning away from the window to look at a vase of pink tulips sitting on the top of her bedside table. "Thank you again for sharing your flowers. They cheered up the room when it was dreary."

"I'm very glad," Emily said, grateful that Phoebe had enjoyed them so much.

The arrival of several bouquets of flowers the morning after the Tilsons' ball had caught Emily completely off guard. Mr. Poltock's daisies had arrived first. They had been quickly followed by Lord Atwood's daffodils. Lord Culham had sent two dozen tulips, while Colonel Eastberry's offering had been a more personal posy of violets.

Adam had seemed gratified by the extravagant gestures. Aunt Millward had complimented her on each spray and had asked to know the name of each sender. Emily had read each card to her, but she'd received the distinct impression that Aunt Millward had not been nearly as pleased by the deliveries as Adam had seemed to be.

In the privacy of her own bedchamber, Emily could admit to a minute portion of disappointment herself. The feeling was not so strong as to prevent her from feeling flattered by the gentlemen's gifts, but it was just enough to cause her to keep listening for another knock on the front door. It was ridiculous. She had all but abandoned Mr. Buckland on the Tilsons' patio. But she could not deny that his was the name she had most wanted to read on a card.

As it was, she could not countenance the thought of having Lord Culham's flowers in her bedchamber. Irrational or not, the mere thought of the gentleman caused her to shudder. She'd offered his flowers to Phoebe and had been pleased when she'd accepted so readily. Aunt Millward's butler had helped her find spots in the drawing room, library, and entrance hall for the other flowers. Seeing them there was a pleasant reminder that she had survived her first London ball.

Perhaps Phoebe's thoughts had also moved to the ball, because she lay back against her pillows and set one hand on the blanket where it covered her swollen abdomen.

"Forgive me, Emily. This is not how I wanted you to spend your time in London. You should be going out for afternoon tea and rides in the park and dinner engagements."

"There is nothing to forgive," Emily said. "As exciting as you may consider those things, I find them exhausting. I am more than happy to be here with you and a good book."

Phoebe looked at the volumes arranged in a small pile beside the tulips and shook her head. "It is truly remarkable that we are such good friends."

Emily laughed. "I agree." She reached out and took Phoebe's hand. "Do not fret over me. When the world has dried out a little more, I will venture forth. Perhaps Aunt Millward will take me back to Hyde Park."

"Yes. You must go again soon."

A knock sounded on the door. Emily released Phoebe's hand.

"Come in," Phoebe called.

The door opened, and Hannah, one of Aunt Millward's maid's, appeared.

"Beggin' yer pardon, m'lady." She bobbed a curtsy. "But there's a gentleman come t' visit, an' Lady Millward's askin' if Miss Norton would join 'er in t' drawin' room."

Phoebe's eyes widened even as Emily's stomach clenched.

"You have your first caller, Emily," she said, smiling delightedly.

"Who is it, Hannah?" Emily managed. "Did you catch his name?"

"Yes, miss. It's Mr. Buckland."

Emily's tightened stomach did a slow roll. She pressed her hand to her corset and took an unsteady breath. Why had he come? Was it simply a social call to see his aunt and the older lady had thought to include her in the visit? Or had he come because he'd received her letter? Her stomach lurched again. What had she been thinking? She knew better than to allow her curiosity to rule her tongue. She never should have brought up Mr. Buckland's unique eye condition with Dr. Thorndike. If she'd kept her silence, she would have been offered no reason to write to the gentleman and no temptation to overstep.

"Please tell my aunt that Miss Norton will be there momentarily," Phoebe said.

"Yes, m'lady."

Hannah bobbed another curtsy, and the next moment, she was gone.

Emily's panic swelled. She swung to face Phoebe again. "I'm not ready to go downstairs."

"Of course you are," Phoebe said. "You look perfectly lovely in that peach-colored gown."

This was probably not the time to tell Phoebe that her appearance was the least of her worries.

"Go," Phoebe urged. "I will be fine. I may even take a nap, just as Adam ordered me to do when he left to visit his banker."

Reluctantly, Emily rose to her feet. She would have to face Mr. Buckland sometime. Discussing pleasantries over a cup of tea in Aunt Millward's drawing room was surely better than almost any other alternative. "Very well. I will come back later this afternoon."

Phoebe buried her head a little lower into her pillows. "I would like that very much."

Waiting for Miss Norton to make an appearance in Aunt Millward's drawing room would have been bad enough without doing so under his aunt's watchful eye. Henry glanced at the clock on the mantel and managed to refrain from running his finger beneath his collar. Barely. It had been eight minutes since the maid had left to fetch Miss Norton. Surely it didn't take that long to deliver a message upstairs. He forced his gaze from the clock to the vase of bright-yellow flowers beside it.

"Are the daffodils from your garden, Aunt?" he asked.

"No. As a matter of fact, Lord Atwood had those delivered to Emily the morning after the Tilsons' ball."

Henry raised his eyebrows, the first inkling that he had misstepped entering his mind. "How very gallant."

"Wasn't it? Unfortunately for him, Lord Culham, Mr. Poltock, and Colonel Eastberry all had the same notion." Aunt Millward smoothed an imaginary wrinkle out of her floral gown and gave him a look that bordered on exasperation. "Thanks to all Miss Norton's admirers, we have flowers in almost every room in the house."

Henry knew full well that his aunt's home boasted far more than four rooms, but he was too busy coming to grips with the way in which his earlier unease had so quickly become burning annoyance to correct her exaggeration. Had any of those gentlemen done anything more than dance with Miss Norton? He thought it unlikely. He hadn't been that late to the ball. But she must have made her mark on them regardless.

His satchel sat on the floor beside him. He pushed it farther under the chair with his feet, his idea for an outing with Miss Norton now seeming foolish. He should have sent flowers. No matter that the weather had probably kept her housebound, she'd had five days to enjoy the daffodils, not to mention whatever blossoms the others had had delivered, and to think fondly on the senders. He gave the bright-yellow flowers an irritated look. At least some of them should have had the decency to wilt by now.

Light footsteps sounded in the passage. Aunt Millward faced the door expectantly, and Henry rose to his feet in time to watch Miss Norton cross the threshold.

"Good day, Mr. Buckland." She dropped a small curtsy. "Forgive me for keeping you waiting."

Henry inclined his head in greeting. "It is I who should apologize, Miss Norton. I came unannounced and have undoubtedly taken you from something else."

She offered him a shy smile. "I was reading to Lady Dunsbourne as she worked on her embroidery, and since her interest in the history behind the various clan tartans of Scotland is somewhat limited, I think she was rather glad of the interruption."

He chuckled. What was it about this young lady that lifted his spirits the moment he set eyes on her?

"How is her ladyship?"

"She is much improved from how she was feeling on the evening of the Tilsons' ball. For now, she is keeping to her bed, and we are hopeful that if she limits her activities over the next few weeks, all will be well with her and the baby."

"I am very glad to hear it."

She moved farther into the room and claimed a spot on the sofa beside his aunt. He sat down again, his leg inadvertently brushing against his satchel. The soft clink of the metal buckle hitting the chair leg filled the silence, and Miss Norton's gaze dropped to the bag on the floor.

"Is that the bag you use to collect your plant specimens?" she asked.

There was no hiding it now. And regardless of his second thoughts about the excursion he had planned, any excuse he could possibly contrive for having the satchel with him would surely be more awkward than the true reason.

"It is." He lifted the bag, placed it on his knee, and lifted the flap. Drawing out his trowel, he showed it to her. "I brought it because I wondered . . ." He swallowed. Lud, this was an exceptionally stupid idea. No young lady would wish to risk ruining an elegant gown to tromp through wet grass and mud in search of a weed. He cleared his throat. Forward. It was his only option. "You mentioned that you miss visiting the river near Dunsbourne Manor, and so I thought you might enjoy an outing to Clapham Common. After all the rain we've had, the foliage will be thriving, and if you are of a mind to help me search near the ponds there, the museum could use some samples of ribwort plantain or water crowfoot or lesser periwinkle. All three should be blooming at this time of year."

She stared at him, her brown eyes wide and an expression of pure delight on her face. "Truly?" she asked. "You would let me do that?"

An unfamiliar warmth filled his chest. He smiled, relief that he had somehow avoided appearing a complete dolt combining with the pleasure her enthusiastic response produced. He patted his satchel. "I have the tools we need, and my carriage is waiting outside."

She turned her brown eyes on his aunt. "May I go, Aunt Millward?"

Cocking her head slightly, Aunt Millward gave him a deliberately inquiring look. It was the same look she'd given him at the annual Millward family picnic when he'd been about eight years old. That time, he'd been so focused on choosing the biscuit with the most raisins, he'd neglected to offer the plate to her.

Henry swallowed his grin and assumed a formal tone. "Aunt Millward, would you like to accompany Miss Norton and me to Clapham Common, where we can visit the river and dig up a plant or two?"

"Well, that took you long enough," she huffed. "Did you actually think I would forfeit my role as chaperone to a maid rather than participate in so adventurous an expedition?"

"Not for a moment," Henry said. "Indeed, if you do not come with us wearing your peacock-feathered hat, I shall be sorely disappointed."

"I must say, I am twice amazed that someone who is uncommonly dense when it comes to interacting with the fairer sex would pay such close attention to their headwear." She sniffed. "But you are right, I believe my peacock-feathered hat will do very well today." She came to her feet, and Henry and Miss Norton immediately followed.

"Might I also suggest wearing your sturdiest boots?" he asked.

"Do not get ahead of yourself, Henry," Aunt Millward warned. "Just because I am choosing to wear my favorite hat does not mean that I require your direction on the remainder of my wardrobe."

Given that Henry was unable to match his own articles of clothing, it was wise counsel.

"Duly noted," he said.

She nodded gravely but was unable to fully hide the twinkle in her eyes. "Very good. I am off to fetch my hat."

Henry glanced at Miss Norton. Her lips twitched. He winked, and her smile grew.

"I'd best fetch my hat too," she said. "And since I doubtless need more direction than Aunt Millward, I will also give careful consideration to my footwear." She started after Aunt Millward, and although Henry couldn't be absolutely sure, he thought he heard the older lady chuckle as she exited the room.

CHAPTER 13

EMILY SPOTTED THE TIPS OF the trees over the rooftops and shifted a little closer to the carriage window.

"Are we getting close?" she asked.

Sitting across from her, Mr. Buckland nodded. "We'll pass the Holy Trinity Church in just a few moments. The woods and community grazing land are just beyond that." He pointed through the window. "There. You can see some of the sheep in the distance."

A gap appeared between the houses, exposing a vast grassy area dotted with white sheep. Emily's heart lightened. She'd not been gone from Berkshire long, but the pastoral sight on the outskirts of the city felt a little like a homecoming.

"I would never have imagined that I'd be so excited to see sheep," she said.

"They are a lot more pleasant to observe from the carriage than from within their field," Aunt Millward said. "I had not thought this excursion included encounters with farm animals, Henry. Will there be many of them near the pond?"

"I cannot say for certain," Mr. Buckland said. "The animals are left to roam at will."

"Hmm." For the first time since Emily had known her, Aunt Millward appeared uneasy. "If they are as prone to follow one another as I've been told, all it will take is one curious sheep and we shall have an entire flock surrounding us the moment we alight from the carriage."

"They are just as likely to ignore us," Mr. Buckland said.

Aunt Millward appeared unconvinced.

"I have no experience with these sheep, of course," Emily said, "but those that wander the fields around Dunsbourne Manor tend to amble off when any-one enters their field."

They were driving alongside the pasture. A large woodland blocked Emily's view to the left, but to the right, green grass stretched out in a large expanse.

Cattle and sheep raised their heads to watch as the carriage rolled by, and Aunt Millward's forehead creased. "The animals seem uncommonly interested in us, Henry."

"I think it more likely that the sound of the carriage's wheels has simply drawn their attention," he said.

Aunt Millward did not reply, but she maintained a watchful eye out of the window. Emily watched too, and before long, a small copse of trees appeared and she caught the shimmer of water beyond. Anticipation hummed through her, and she glanced at Mr. Buckland.

He caught her look and nodded. "This is it."

The carriage slowed and came to a stop a few yards from the trees. Mr. Buckland threaded his satchel across his shoulder and opened the carriage door. A wave of fresh air entered. Drawing her shawl more securely about her shoulders, Emily breathed deeply. It smelled of sunshine and moisture, green grass and animals.

She waited for Mr. Buckland to exit and then slid to the edge of her seat. His arm appeared in the doorway, and she took his hand. For a fleeting moment, she was swept back to the Tilsons' ball, to the wonder of the dance they had shared together. And then a goose honked, the flap of its wings sounding overhead, and instead of being in a ballroom, she was standing beside him on the damp grass with two curious sheep eyeing them from beside a nearby shrub.

He released her hand, and she stepped back, making room for him to assist Aunt Millward.

"Two rather bored-looking sheep, Aunt," he said. "That is the extent of the animal incursion at present."

The older lady joined Emily and eyed the sheep dubiously.

"I will go with you to see the pond," she said, "but if we are to be surrounded by overly bold animals, I believe it might be better for me to wait in the carriage whilst you dig."

"As you wish." He withdrew a blanket from the carriage and tucked it under one arm before offering his aunt the other. "It's an easy walk, and you might enjoy being outdoors for a little while."

They started across the grass toward the trees. Somewhere in the distance, a cow mooed. Aunt Millward stiffened, but Mr. Buckland maintained his even pace, not bothering to even glance the bovine's way. Emily walked beside them, soaking in the sights and sounds normally associated with the countryside.

It did not take long to reach the handful of scrub oaks that separated the grass from the water. Mr. Buckland guided them around the tallest tree and then paused so that both ladies might take in the view.

"Oh," Emily said. "It's lovely!"

The pond was larger than she'd imagined and was bordered by shrubs and trees. The occasional breaks between the bushes were filled by well-worn paths. No doubt the sheep and cattle knew the best routes to the water, but so, too, it seemed, did some of the locals. Not far distant, a gangly youth stood beneath the shade of an ash tree, a fishing rod in his hands and two buckets beside him.

"Very pleasant indeed," Aunt Millward agreed, her anxiety less obvious now that there were a few branches between her and the livestock.

Mr. Buckland seemed pleased. "If memory serves, there's a rather convenient log beyond this next tree. Since the ground is still so wet, I can set the blanket on it and you can sit there until you are ready to return to the carriage."

They reached the log seconds later, and in no time at all, Mr. Buckland had spread out the blanket and Aunt Millward had claimed her seat.

"This will suit me very well for the time being," she said. "Now, you'd best start looking for those worty plants or crowsfeet or whatever those all-important weeds are named."

Emily smothered her giggle with a cough, but Mr. Buckland did nothing to hide his amusement.

"If I could rename ribwort plantain to worty plant and water crowfoot to crowsfeet, I would do it in a heartbeat. I daresay the lesser periwinkle would also prefer something that makes it seem more significant." He withdrew a trowel and a notebook from his satchel. "Really, Aunt Millward, why were you not present when these poor plants were being named?"

The older lady gave him a warning look, and the peacock feathers in her hat shook with mock indignation. "I may prefer to sit on a log rather than dig in the mud, but I am not quite so old as all that, young man." She waved one hand toward the foliage at the water's edge. "Now, go and get your work done. But do not wander too far."

"Over there! Do you see?" Miss Norton pointed to half a dozen tall stems protruding from a clump of narrow leaves and topped with stubby brown heads. "Isn't that ribwort plantain?"

Henry moved closer. They'd been searching the ground between the pond and the trees for at least fifteen minutes, and he had begun to think they would have to dig up a token dandelion just so Miss Norton could wield the trowel she'd been clutching so tightly since he had given her charge of it.

"I believe you're right." He knelt beside the plant, examining the distinctive veins running parallel to each other along the length of the leaves. "You see how the leaves and stem are slightly hairy?"

"Yes." She had crouched beside him.

"That is how you differentiate between the ribwort plantain and the hoary plantain."

"How amazing." She touched the leaf gently with a gloved finger. "It grew so profusely on the grounds of Dunsbourne Manor that I've never given it the consideration it deserved."

"I'm impressed you knew it by name. If I'd not studied botany at Cambridge, I would still be calling it the pop gun plant."

Miss Norton laughed. "That's exactly what Adam called it. He was the one who taught me to pinch the long stem around the head and pull so that the head flew through the air."

Henry grinned, barely resisting the urge to pluck one of the stems and fire a flower head at her. "But you learned its proper name."

"Yes." She ducked her head, but not before he saw her cheeks pink. "We had a book about indigenous English plants in our library. I was fascinated by the illustrations."

The illustrations. Grateful for the reminder of why they were there, Henry forced his gaze away from Miss Norton's soft curls and opened his satchel. Withdrawing a piece of charcoal, he offered it to her. "Would you like to be the one to draw the plant before we dig it up?"

She shook her head. "As difficult as it is to admit, I believe my skills as an artist rank below my skills with knitting needles. If you are to have any hope of recognizing this ribwort plantain, it must be you who sketches it."

Not wanting to waste time demurring, he flipped to a clean page in his notebook and started to draw.

"How long have you known how to knit?" he asked.

"How exactly would you define 'known how to'?"

He grinned. "That bad?"

"Let's just say that Adam is the only gentleman willing to wear the scarves I've made, and I've not managed anything more complex than that."

This was probably not the time to tell her that he was quite sure that if she ever knitted him a scarf, he would immediately join Lord Dunsbourne's ranks. And in his case, the color of wool would not matter in the slightest. He cleared his throat. They were sufficiently far from Aunt Millward now to exchange a few words of a more private nature. "I've not yet thanked you for your letter or, more importantly, for discovering the name of the gentleman purportedly studying vision impairments such as mine."

Color returned to her cheeks, but this time, she did not look away. "I hope you do not consider me out of line in asking Dr. Thorndike if he had ever heard of the condition. I . . . I saw how difficult it was . . . it still is for you, and I thought that if he could suggest something that might help . . . forgive me."

"There is nothing to forgive. That you went out of your way to seek answers for me means a great deal."

"Then you are not angry?"

"How could I be? You have given me hope that I may one day come to understand my incapacity to discern colors. And even if I receive no answers, I now know that I am not facing the challenge alone. That, in and of itself, is reassuring."

"Will you write to Mr. Dalton, then?"

"I have already done so," he said.

Her smile lit up her entire face, and his heart missed a beat.

"I hope you do not have to wait long for a reply," she said.

"As do I."

He sketched another three leaves and added a stem. It was better to focus on the ribwort plantain than on Miss Norton.

She remained silent as he finished the drawing. Above his head, a bird trilled. He heard the plop of the boy's fishing hook enter the water, and a sheep bleated from somewhere closer to the carriage. He added a few tiny petal details to his drawing, closed his notebook, and glanced over his shoulder at Aunt Millward. She was facing the shrubbery, the peacock feathers on her hat gyrating wildly as her head moved from side to side.

"I think she's keeping track of the animals," Miss Norton whispered.

"It looks that way." He slid his notebook and charcoal into his satchel. "Let's dig up this 'worty plant,' and then I'll see if she's ready to relocate to the carriage."

She held up the trowel. "Tell me what to do."

Miss Norton was far better at following his instructions than she claimed to be at knitting or drawing, and in no time whatsoever, she had uprooted the plant with no obvious damage done to the roots, leaves, or flowers.

"We'll leave a little soil around the roots to prevent the plant from wilting too badly before it reaches the museum," he said, lying a piece of cheesecloth on the ground.

Without waiting for his prompt, she set the ribwort plantain in the center of the cloth. Immediately, a fat earthworm wiggled out of the damp earth clumped around the plant's roots and started squirming across the cloth. Henry's gaze shot to Miss Norton's face. If she screamed, Aunt Millward would likely fall off the log.

"Look," she said, picking up the earthworm with perfect calm. "We have an uninvited guest. Should I drop him back into the hole I dug, or do you think the young fisherman would like to use it for bait?"

Henry gaped. And then, when she set the earthworm in the palm of her hand on top of her filthy white gloves, he started to laugh.

She raised her head, a furrow creasing her brow. "Did I do something wrong?" she asked.

"No, Miss Norton." He attempted to control his laughter—for her sake and his aunt's. "You did everything right. And I am quite sure you will please that young man to no end if you offer him an earthworm."

Understanding and dismay dawned on her mud-streaked face.

"Young ladies in London do not generally handle earthworms, do they?" she asked.

"Not generally."

She sighed. "I shall have to let you in on another secret, Mr. Buckland," she said. "When I was young, I would beg Adam to allow me to go fishing with him. I wasn't tall enough or strong enough to manage the rod, but I was very good at baiting the hook, and once he was sure that I could do it without injury, it became my regular role." The earthworm on her palm contorted, and her shoulders slumped. "I'm not doing a very good job of pretending to be refined, am I?"

All at once, his amusement at her response to the earthworm felt wrong, and he knew he must say something to expel the discouragement he'd unwittingly brought upon her. "Please believe me when I say that you have no need for pretense, Miss Norton. It is my understanding that *refined* can be defined as 'pure, gracious, and educated.' If that is the case, you are the most refined young lady I know." She had yet to meet his eyes. He cleared his throat. "Might I suggest a compromise?"

"What do you mean?" Her voice was low, but her natural curiosity could not be quelled.

"I will take the earthworm to the young fisherman for you. That way, he will benefit from your kindness, but your skills as a fisherman's assistant will remain a secret."

She was silent for a moment and then gave a slight nod of her head. "I like that compromise."

"Good." It was a step in the right direction, and yet, it did not seem enough. He reached into his pocket, withdrew a handkerchief, and held it up. "You have a little mud on your face."

She groaned and raised her other hand to her face. "Oh dear. I really am no better than a waif." A second mud smear joined the first.

"Wait," he said. "Allow me."

Slowly, she lowered her hand. Leaning forward, he touched his handkerchief to her cheek. She stilled, her dark eyes meeting his. He swallowed hard and ran the cloth across the offending dirt.

"Is . . . is it gone?" she asked.

"Almost." Marveling at the softness of her skin, he gently brushed away the second smudge while working to instill some normalcy into his voice. "There." He lowered the handkerchief. "You are perfectly presentable once more."

She blinked and surveyed her soiled gloves and gown, and her muddy shoes.

"I believe your notion of presentable may be rather different from that of most people in Society."

"I have no idea why you would think so," he teased, tucking his handkerchief back into his pocket. "Don't all the most sophisticated ladies and gentlemen of the *ton* spend time digging in the dirt?"

"No." She frowned at the earthworm in her hand. "I am quite sure they do not. Indeed, this may need to be something that no one else knows about but Aunt Millward."

"We are garnering rather a lot of secrets, aren't we?"

"I'm afraid we are," she said ruefully.

He rose and extended his hand. She placed her free hand in his, and he helped her to her feet.

"Well then, since you and I now qualify as true confidants, I wonder if you would consider calling me Henry?"

Her smile was hesitant, but it was there. "Yes, so long as you call me Emily."

His heart lifted. "Gladly," he said, releasing her hand and plucking the squirming worm from her other palm. "I shall return as soon as I've gifted this to the boy, and then we will wrap up the plant and check on Aunt Millward before we look for anything more."

She nodded, and this time, her smile was more confident. "Thank you, Henry."

He smiled in return. "My pleasure, Emily."

CHAPTER 14

THE CARRIAGE WHEELS TURNED, AND with a spit of gravel and creak of leather, the vehicle rolled away from Clapham Common. Inside, Aunt Millward leaned back in her seat and gave a satisfied sigh. "Well done, Henry," she said. "That was a splendid way to spend the afternoon."

Henry. Up until half an hour ago, Emily had only ever thought of the gentleman as Mr. Buckland, but at Aunt Millward's use of his Christian name, Emily's heart warmed. He was to be Henry to her now too.

The gentleman in question eyed the mud caked on his boots and knees and gave a rueful smile. "I'm not sure that my valet will agree with you, Aunt, but I am very glad you enjoyed the excursion."

Emily made a mental note to personally apologize to Hannah for the state of her current wardrobe. Thankfully, she had taken Henry's earlier suggestion seriously and had worn her oldest gown and most serviceable boots. The fact that Aunt Millward had managed the walk from the carriage to the log by the pond and back without so much as a fleck of mud on her hem was certainly worth celebrating. Then again, the older lady's enthusiasm was more likely due to her relief that the cows and sheep had maintained their distance the whole time.

"Your valet must be used to such things by now," Aunt Millward said. "It seems to me that you make rather a habit of getting dirty."

Henry grinned. "Thankfully, he's a remarkably long-suffering chap. I'd be lost without him."

"Then, I certainly hope you are paying him well."

"He has yet to complain," Henry said.

"The good ones rarely do." Aunt Millward gave him a stern look. "You are not without means, Henry. Make sure those who are important to you recognize it in word and deed."

Henry's gaze flitted to Emily, and she felt the beginnings of another surge of warmth in her cheeks.

"That is wise counsel," he said, returning his attention to Aunt Millward.

"Yes." His aunt's stern look had yet to fade. "It is."

Emily took an unsteady breath. What was wrong with her? Digging in the mud had taken her from enjoying Henry's company above any of the other gentlemen at the Tilsons' ball to blushing whenever he so much as glanced her way. Sitting opposite him was not helping. Especially since he looked no less handsome with dirt on his clothes than he did when dressed in his finery.

Perhaps Aunt Millward's train of thought was similar to hers because with seemingly no forewarning, the older lady changed the subject to the next event on her social calendar.

"I assume you are attending Lord and Lady Southbeck's much-anticipated gathering on Saturday, Henry."

His grimace was so fleeting, Emily wondered if she'd imagined it.

"Lord Southbeck is a member of the museum's board of trustees," he said. "He holds these grand events as a means of fostering an appreciation for the arts and raising funds for the museum. Even though I oversee the natural history collection, as one of the museum's curators, I am expected to be there."

"So I imagine, but you have not told me whether you will be."

Henry leaned back against the seat, amusement sparkling in his eyes. "I defy anyone to attempt to bamboozle you, Aunt Millward. It cannot be done."

"I should certainly hope not," Aunt Millward said. "Let that be your second life lesson during this carriage ride home."

Emily bit her lip to prevent her smile from growing. Aunt Millward was a gem. A highly irregular but completely wonderful gem.

"One that I will definitely commit to memory," Henry said solemnly.

"Good. And now you can tell me if you plan to be at the Southbecks' musical event."

This time his grimace was undeniable.

"I confess, listening to an opera singer—no matter how celebrated—warble one aria after another is not my first choice of how to spend my evening."

"Yes, yes. I know you'd rather be in a library reading a book or outside hunting down plants, but one cannot spend all of one's time doing those things."

"More's the pity," Emily whispered.

The rumble of the carriage wheels prevented Aunt Millward from hearing her comment, but if his unexpectedly mischievous look was any indication, it had not escaped Henry.

"Tell me, Aunt Millward," he said, "do you intend to attend? And more to the point, do you intend to drag Emily there too?"

Aunt Millward surely noticed Henry's use of her given name, but she chose to make no mention of it.

"We shall both be there," Aunt Millward said. This was the first Emily had heard of the event, which made it seem as though Henry was not the only person whose presence was assumed. "And there will be no dragging involved. I have learned from years of experience that such events are far more enjoyable if one uses a little fabric to plug one's ears before the singing commences. I will provide Emily with ear plugs, and we shall both have a very pleasant evening."

Henry's laughter filled the carriage, and Emily could not help but join in. If Saturday's entertainment was to be as painful as Henry suggested, Aunt Millward's third life lesson may well save them all.

Henry jotted down the final entry in his ledger, set his quill aside, and reached for the blotting paper. Finally. Every piece in the Egyptian pottery collection was accounted for.

Rolling his shoulders, he rose from the chair and walked to the window. Another day of sunshine. After all the rain they'd experienced earlier in the week, everyone was glad for the warmer temperatures and drier weather. His only complaint was that for today, at least, his work demanded that he be indoors at the museum. He wished he could be outside. Preferably with Emily at his side.

A smile played across his lips as he pictured her triumphant expression when she'd handed him the perfect lesser periwinkle specimen she'd dug up after having successfully wrapped the ribwort plantain. He shook his head slightly. Was there another high-born young lady in all of England who'd be so eager to dig in the mud and handle earthworms? He did not think so. Neither did he think there was another so charming.

He moved back to the table and glanced at the calendar beside his ledger. His current commitments may prevent him from enjoying another outing with Emily right away, but at least he would see her at the Southbecks' musical evening on Saturday. His position at the museum notwithstanding, she was the only reason he had sent an acceptance to the invitation.

A knock at the door interrupted his musings.

"Enter," he called.

The door opened, and Rutherford appeared.

"My apologies for disturbing you, Mr. Buckland," he said. "I just came up to tell you that the display case you ordered some weeks back is here. The men are wondering where you'd like to have it put."

"Their timing couldn't be better," Henry said. "I have the pottery ready. Direct them to the Montagu room, would you? I shall meet them there."

"Very good, sir."

As soon as the porter left to deliver the message, Henry opened a desk drawer and withdrew a sign. Tucking it under his arm, he headed across the landing to the Montagu room. The door was open. Slowing his steps, he entered, experiencing—as he always did—a sense of wonder for lives once lived and creatures never before seen.

Cases filled with Roman artifacts and Viking relics lined one long wall. Against the other three, the skeletal remains of over thirty mammals and reptiles from around the world were displayed beneath a vast collection of animal skins. In the far corner, a space had been cleared, and if the carpenters had heeded the measurements he'd given them, it would be just the right size for the new display case.

Grateful that no one from the last tour had lingered in the room, Henry attached the sign he'd brought with him to the door. *The displays in this room are currently unavailable.* It was an unpopular sign, and whoever led the next tour group through would undoubtedly hear complaints, but it couldn't be helped. If he did his job correctly, visitors would find the new Egyptian pottery display worth the wait.

Henry heard the men before he saw them. Their grunts of exertion and called directions echoed off the high ceiling as they made their way up the wide staircase. Henry pushed the door open wide and stood back as two workmen carried a long table down the landing toward him.

"You have my thanks, gentlemen," he said. "Set it in the corner, if you would."

"Righ' you are, sir." The older of the two men tilted the table to the left to navigate the doorway. "Lift it up a bit, Tommy."

The younger fellow complied, and with a few more grunts and abbreviated commands, the older one guided the piece of furniture into its preassigned spot. Stepping back, Tommy straightened one corner and then took a moment to gaze around the room.

The other man offered Henry a slight bow. "'Ow's that, sir?"

"Excellent," Henry said. "I'm most grateful."

The older man smiled, exposing a few missing teeth. "There we are, then. Always 'appy t' do business with t' museum."

"We appreciate your service. If you'd talk to the porter on the way out, he'll see to it that you receive your payment."

"Very good, sir." He bowed again. "Come on, Tommy."

The younger fellow turned from staring at the pelt of a black bear hanging on the wall above his head. He mumbled something under his breath and tugged on the brim of his hat, then he followed his associate out of the room.

"How does it look?" Fernsby walked in, taking the workmen's place beside the display table.

"I think it will work well," Henry said, inspecting the new display case as he spoke. "It looks sturdy enough to support the weight of the pottery, and the carpenter has done a nice job on the finishing work."

A half-inch-wide and six-inch-tall strip of wood surrounded the perimeter of the rectangular table, creating a large, flat case. Three lead-framed sheets of glass were attached by hinges to the far side of the wooden frame. Henry raised the piece of glass closest to him. It lifted smoothly, allowing him easy access to the container beneath.

Fernsby whistled through his teeth. "Very nice. Did you design it?"

"Yes. I wanted something that gave the collection more protection than the open cases but gave us easier access than the cases covered by a solid sheet of glass."

"Clever," Fernsby said. "How long will it take you to have the display ready?"

"My question exactly." At the sound of another voice, both gentlemen turned to face the door.

"Lord Claridge," Henry said.

He and Fernsby inclined their heads in greeting, and the chair of the board acknowledged them with a nod.

"I would apologize for interrupting," Claridge said, "but truth be told, I'm rather glad I came when I did." He moved to stand beside the new display case and studied it with interest. "Most ingenious," he said. "And did I hear you correctly? This design is of your own making?"

"I claim credit for the design, my lord, but the carpenter and glassblower did the real work."

"Extraordinary," Claridge said. "Really. Quite extraordinary. I look forward to seeing it filled." He paused. "I believe you were about to tell Mr. Fernsby how long that will take."

"Yes, my lord. I have the cataloging complete, so it should only take a few days to have the pieces ready to display."

"Excellent. The timing couldn't be better."

"The timing?"

"Yes," Claridge said. "I've heard from Lady Grenville's solicitor again. Her donation is scheduled to arrive at the museum on Monday, and once again, she is insisting that you be the person to attend to the delivery. The board wishes you to oversee every part of the unloading and cataloging; I have given Lady Grenville's solicitor my word that you will."

"Of course," Henry said, even as misgiving tightened his stomach into a knot. The butterfly collection was well within the realm of his expertise; the literature was not.

"Glad to hear it." Claridge gave a satisfied nod. "I shall return early next week so that I might report on the progress of the Egyptian pottery display and the status of Lady Grenville's donation at our next board meeting."

Early next week. The director was giving him only a day or two to assess the vast donation of manuscripts he knew nothing about.

"Might I suggest that Mr. Townsend would be far better suited to—"

Lord Claridge raised his hand to stop Henry before he could continue. "We all know that Townsend is an expert in his field, but to be a truly effective representative of the British Museum, one must also have the social skills and business acumen to match." He offered Henry an enigmatic look. "Consider this a test of the breadth of your abilities, Buckland. A rather important one at that."

Henry had never enjoyed taking tests at university. That sentiment had yet to change. "I'm not sure I understand exactly what you are looking for, my lord."

"It's hardly complicated, Buckland. Just prove to the board that you can do what needs to be done with a multifaceted donation."

Henry had serious reservations about the assignment, but this was obviously not the time to say so. "Very well, my lord."

That, it seemed, was all Claridge needed to hear. He started toward the door. "Until next week, then."

His clipped footsteps faded along the landing, and Henry turned to Fernsby. He was staring at the open door with an odd look on his face.

"Any idea what that was all about?" Henry asked.

Fernsby's expression cleared. "Wish I could help you, old fellow."

"Almost as much as I wish you could. It's ridiculous to not bring Townsend in on this donation."

"I daresay Townsend would offer you a stronger word than *ridiculous*. Continued avoidance is likely your best strategy."

The knot in Henry's stomach tightened further. Townsend could act the role of curmudgeon, but Henry had always had a respectful working relationship with the man. He'd hoped that a new week would enable them to put their recent discord behind them. Claridge's injunction had all but ensured that it would increase. He rubbed the back of his neck. "You might be right."

"I usually am," Fernsby said. He pulled out his pocket watch. "The next tour starts in five minutes, so I'd better go. I'll bypass the Montagu room until you have the new display ready."

"I appreciate it."

Henry walked with him onto the landing and pulled the door closed behind them. The sign swung noisily back and forth, a patent reminder that Henry had no time to waste.

Chapter 15

THE SOUTHBECKS' DRAWING ROOM WAS at least twice the size of the one at Dunsbourne Manor, and it was decorated in a Grecian theme. Large urns stood on either side of the doorway, and marble busts of sightless gentlemen wearing laurel wreaths upon their heads sat on shelves in recessed archways around the room. Candles flickered from sconces on the wall and from a magnificent candelabra atop a marble stand beside a pianoforte. Chairs had been arranged in half a dozen tidy rows, facing the pianoforte, and behind the chairs, the gathering guests mingled.

Lord and Lady Southbeck greeted Aunt Millward warmly and expressed their pleasure in meeting Emily and their regret that Lord and Lady Dunsbourne were unable to join them. No one wished Adam and Phoebe were there more than Emily, but she understood Adam's decision to stay behind. Not wanting to abandon his wife was a valid excuse for opting out of an event he had never really wanted to attend anyway.

Emily allowed her gaze to traverse the room's occupants. Would Henry overcome his reluctance to sit through opera music to be here tonight? She could not deny that her hope that she would see him again had caused her to have Hannah spend a little longer on her hair and had influenced her choice of gown.

"Do you know the opera singer, Aunt Millward?" she asked.

"I have heard her sing before, but I have never been introduced," Aunt Millward said. "She is standing beside the pianoforte in a silver gown."

Emily directed her attention that way and saw the lady in question. She was a little older than Emily had imagined, but she held herself with assurance and gestured with her hands as she spoke to a lady whose gray hair was ratted to the extreme.

"Is that the Dowager Lady Pendleton with her?"

"I believe so," Aunt Millward said. "Which undoubtedly means that her granddaughter is also in attendance."

"Lady Aurelia is speaking to the gentleman from the museum," Emily said, spotting her bright-yellow gown almost immediately. "The one from the manuscript saloon."

"Mr. Townsend," Aunt Millward said. "Well, I don't suppose that will last long."

"Because he has no title?" Emily guessed.

Aunt Millward opened her fan. "Have I told you recently how uncommonly bright you are?"

Emily knew full well that whatever intelligence she could claim rarely helped her in social settings such as this. This was a situation in which the likes of Lady Aurelia shone and she sputtered. "What of the other gentleman who has just joined them?" she asked.

Mr. Townsend's somber black attire and white wig faded into obscurity when juxtaposed with the flamboyant green-and-white-striped breeches, floral waistcoat, and burgundy jacket of the gentleman who had joined him.

"That colorful peacock is Mr. Fernsby," Aunt Millward said. "He is the other curator at the museum, along with Mr. Townsend and Henry. Not only is he title-less, but I also believe the Dowager Lady Pendleton would consider his artistic background even less desirable than Mr. Townsend's devotion to literature. I fear he will be banished along with his colleague once she catches sight of him with Lady Aurelia."

The words were barely out of Aunt Millward's mouth when the sound of the Dowager Lady Pendleton's cane clicking across the polished wood floor announced her speedy passage across the room.

"Good evening, Miss Norton. How delightful to see you again."

Emily started. She'd been so consumed with Lady Aurelia's situation that she'd not noticed Lord Culham's approach.

"Lord Culham," she said, inclining her head.

He reached for her hand and pressed it to his lips. Her gloves were not barrier enough to prevent the shudder that coursed through her. She pulled her hand back.

Seemingly impervious to the snub, Lord Culham turned his oily smile on Aunt Millward. "Lady Millward." He bowed. "Always a pleasure."

"I did not know you were an opera enthusiast, Lord Culham," Aunt Millward said.

"Indeed, my lady. I enjoy all music, and of course, I am always eager to support those working so hard on behalf of the British Museum."

Given that Lord Culham's topics of conversation at the Tilsons' ball had not strayed beyond the weather, the loveliness of the ladies' gowns, and the deteriorating service at White's, it was hard to believe that he had ever given much thought to the items housed at the British Museum.

"Very good of you," Aunt Millward said. "Do you have a favorite amongst the many exhibits?"

Emily attempted to prevent a smile from growing. Aunt Millward's thoughts had obviously mirrored her own.

"Well now, that is hard to say," Lord Culham blustered. "How is one to choose when there are so many?"

"True." Aunt Millward appeared thoughtful. "I believe if I were forced to choose, however, it would have to be the collection of dishes from China. The hand-painted jugs are exquisite."

Emily did not have to think long to know that there was no such collection. Lord Culham, however, was not so fortunate.

"I could not agree more," he said. "I've never seen the like."

The last part of his statement was accurate, at least.

"Good evening, Lady Millward. Miss Norton." Colonel Eastberry stepped up from behind Lord Culham and greeted them both with a bow. "Culham," he added almost as an afterthought.

Lord Culham gave him a curt nod, but Emily was so relieved to have Lord Culham's falsehearted exchange interrupted that she greeted Colonel Eastberry with a warm smile.

"How nice to see you, Colonel."

The gentleman stood a little taller. "Thank you, Miss Norton. The feeling is mutual."

"Ladies and gentlemen, may I have your attention." Lord Southbeck's voice cut through the murmur of multiple conversations, and a hush fell upon the room. "Our special guest, Miss Sophia Ledbetter, has informed me that she is ready. If you would all be good enough to take your seats, we shall begin the concert." Lord Southbeck moved away from the pianoforte, and Miss Ledbetter stepped up to a light ripple of applause and the movement of all the guests.

"Would you do me the honor, Miss Norton?" Colonel Eastberry asked, extending his arm to her.

Emily hesitated a fraction of a second too long. She saw the confusion in his eyes and hastened to rectify it by placing her hand upon his elbow. "It would be my pleasure, sir."

Attempting to ignore Lord Culham's scowl, she allowed Colonel Eastberry to lead her toward the front of the room. It was only when she took a seat on the second row, with Aunt Millward nowhere in sight, that she realized she would be forced to sit through the entire concert without the earplugs conveniently tucked away in the older lady's reticule.

Henry slipped into the Southbecks' drawing room just as Miss Ledbetter released her first warbling notes. Two footmen stood near the door, but the other occupants were seated in six tidy rows facing the singing sensation. Henry gave the closest footman an acknowledging nod before scanning the chairs in search of Aunt Millward and Emily. He spotted Aunt Millward immediately, near the back, her dark-blue gown standing out against her bouffant white hair. The chairs at her left were filled. There was one vacant chair at her right, but there was no sign of Emily on the row. Puzzled, he scoured the remainder of the chairs. And then he saw her. On the second row, beside Eastberry.

He clenched his hands in frustration. The promise of a chance to sit beside Emily this evening had been the driving force behind his feverish efforts to finish the Egyptian pottery display today. It had taken him hours to transport the pieces, arrange them in the case, and complete the labeling. He'd been one part exhilarated by the end result and two parts exhausted by the effort it had taken, but he'd pushed aside his fatigue to hurry home to change. Even with his best efforts, however, he'd not been fast enough.

On silent feet, he crossed the distance between the door and the back row of chairs and slid into the empty chair beside Aunt Millward.

She looked at him, eyebrows raised. "Do I need to buy you a new pocket watch, or are you habitually late?"

Grateful that Miss Ledbetter's voice filled the room well enough to cover his aunt's, Henry kept his eyes forward and attempted to hide his irritation. "Neither. I had something I had to finish at the museum. Truth be told, I changed and traveled here in record time." He glanced at her. "And before you ask, I increased my valet's pay this week."

With a gratified expression, she opened her reticule. "Here," she said, handing him two tiny scraps of fabric. "We're only on the first aria. You'll be needing these before too long."

Henry accepted the makeshift earplugs with a halfhearted smile. They were poor consolation for having to stare at the back of Eastberry's head every time he bent down to exchange a word or two with Emily, but they might enable Henry to survive until the end of the concert.

"Do you understand any of the words to this song?" he whispered.

"Not one."

"And the others are likely to be in Italian too?"

"They usually are," Aunt Millward replied.

"Right, then." Henry wadded up the first piece of fabric and pressed it into his ear. "You have my sincere thanks, Aunt."

She smiled. "You are most welcome."

By Henry's pocket watch—which, contrary to Aunt Millward's belief, kept extremely good time—Miss Ledbetter sang for one hour and twenty-three minutes. As far as Henry was concerned, it was about an hour and twenty minutes too long. He may not have been the only one to feel that way, but when the audience rose to its feet and gave the singer a rousing applause, he had to concede that he appeared to be in the minority. He waited until the applause died down and then pulled out his earplugs.

His doing so was a timely reminder for Aunt Millward, who withdrew hers and tucked the fabric back into her reticule. "I rather enjoy living in a world of faded sounds for a little while," she said. "People are altogether too loud most of the time."

"I think that's one reason why Benedict enjoys being in the country so much," Henry said. "The peace and quiet certainly has its appeal."

"It does. But at this precise moment, I am glad you are here." She inclined her head toward the front of the room. "I rather think Emily might be glad to know it too."

In the short time since the concert had ended, Emily had moved from the chair where she'd been sitting toward the aisle on the far side of the room. Eastberry remained beside her, and Henry saw her turn and exchange a few words with the colonel before greeting the white-wigged gentleman dressed in black standing alone at the end of the row. Townsend? Two ladies walked by, temporarily blocking Henry's view. He leaned to the right in time to see his colleague bow and say something to Emily.

"You're quite right, Aunt Millward," Henry said. "And if you'll excuse me, I shall make my presence known to her right away."

Aunt Millward nodded her agreement, and Henry stepped out from between the chairs.

It seemed that all the Southbecks' guests were attempting to move at the same time. Civility dictated that Henry not barge through the line of people vacating their chairs nor cut through the chatting clusters of ladies and gentlemen in the aisles, but after waiting so long to speak with Emily, his patience was wearing thin, and when he caught sight of the Dowager Lady Pendleton bearing down on him, he threw courtesy to the wind.

"Excuse me," he said, stepping between Mr. and Mrs. Grisham and narrowly missing running into Mr. Dryden before darting behind the nearest Grecian urn. No matter what the Dowager Lady Pendleton thought, a grilling regarding the current location of his brother was not going to happen.

He looked to the spot where he'd last seen Emily. Townsend stood alone once more. A few feet farther away, Fernsby was talking to a couple of members of the board of trustees, but there was no sign of Emily. Releasing an exasperated breath, Henry scoured the room again. Emily's petite stature made her difficult to find, but he caught the flash of a pale-green gown behind Lord Southbeck. Notwithstanding his difficulty in discerning reds, pinks, and purples, he had little difficulty with green, and he'd been staring at the back of her gown long enough to know it when he saw it. Taking three swift steps to the left, he bypassed those gathering to express thanks to their hosts and ran directly into Emily.

"Henry!" She stumbled back a couple of paces.

Eastberry reached for her elbow. "I say, Buckland. Have a care. You all but knocked Miss Norton to the ground."

There was no logical reason why Henry should find Eastberry's comment so annoying. The man was right, after all, but the fact that he had yet to leave Emily's side or let go of her arm, even though she now appeared perfectly stable put Henry's teeth on edge. Pushing aside his frustration, he inclined his head. "I beg your pardon, Emily. I hope you are not hurt."

"Not at all." She smiled, and he was instantly reminded of why he had come. "I did not know you were here. Have you seen Aunt Millward?"

The perplexed expression that had formed on Eastberry's face at Henry's informal greeting cleared. "But of course," Eastberry said. "I had forgotten that you are cousins."

"Not at all." Henry had known Eastberry for several years and could not ever remember finding him so irksome. "We both claim a relationship to Lady Millward, but that is the extent of our familial ties."

"I see," the colonel said, even though the lines on his forehead suggested otherwise. "So you did not arrive with Miss Norton and Lady Millward?"

Given Emily's surprise at seeing him, Henry considered it an obvious assumption, but it appeared that Eastberry wanted to be sure.

"Unfortunately, no. I arrived just as the concert began."

Presumably reassured that Henry had no prior arrangement to spend the evening with Emily, Eastberry's posture relaxed. "Ah. Well, I'm glad you caught it all. Miss Ledbetter was quite marvelous, wasn't she?"

"Indeed." *Marvelous* was not the descriptor Henry would have chosen, but it would do.

"It's really quite remarkable that she could sing for so long without any loss in volume," Emily said.

"True." Henry fingered the earplug fabric in his pocket. "Although it may not have seemed so loud had you been seated on the back row."

She nodded, and he thought he caught a hint of regret. "I should like to try that next time," she said.

Eastberry gave her a surprised look. "I fear you would run the risk of not being able to see the performer, Miss Norton."

"With my short stature, not being able to see over other people's heads is so common an occurrence, I am well used to it."

Emily's admission appeared to make Eastberry all the sorrier for her, and the colonel's regretful expression deepened. Henry knew better. Although she would likely have been pleased to grow a couple more inches, Emily was not one to allow her lack of height to dim her enthusiasm for trying almost anything.

"I daresay you are always the last to be found in a game of hide-and-seek though," Henry said.

Amusement filled her eyes. "My brother has been known to complain about the length of my winning streak."

Henry chuckled. Playing hide-and-seek with Emily sounded infinitely more enjoyable than attending an operatic concert.

The colonel cleared his throat. "I can't say that I've played hide-and-seek since I was very young."

"How did you enjoy the game, Colonel?" Aunt Millward appeared at Eastberry's side, entering the conversation right away. "I would hazard a guess that you were a very diligent seeker."

He gave a gratified smile. "Yes. I rather think I was."

"An excellent quality in a military man," Aunt Millward said. She hesitated. "I don't suppose you'd be willing to help me locate Lady Southbeck, would you? With so many people in the room, I believe I may need the assistance of someone skilled in searching."

Whatever reluctance Eastberry may have owned was masked by his polite bow. "Honored to be of service, my lady," he said.

"Thank you," Aunt Millward said. "I shall express our thanks to the South-becks, Emily. With such a crush, there's no need for you to join me. If Henry would be good enough to walk you to the door, I will meet you there shortly."

"Of course," Emily said. "Thank you, Aunt Millward."

The moment Eastberry and Aunt Millward turned away, Henry offered Emily his arm. She set her hand on it, and awareness of her touch pulsed through him.

"Forgive me for not arriving sooner," he said.

She glanced at him. "I thought perhaps you'd decided to forgo coming after all."

"At the risk of having you think too highly of yourself, I weighed my options and decided that if Aunt Millward would supply me with earplugs, I would endure an hour of listening to Italian sung in an excessively high voice so that I might sit beside you and negatively influence your opinion of the concert." He grunted. "As it was, I was held up by a project at the museum, my companion was Aunt Millward, and I had to suffer through a torturous additional twenty-three minutes after the one-hour mark passed."

Emily giggled. "But at least you had earplugs."

"I did, indeed." He raised an eyebrow. "How was the second row without them?"

She shuddered, and Henry grinned. "Am I to infer that you would have preferred to be digging in the mud?"

"Yes."

They had reached the cluster of admirers surrounding Miss Ledbetter, and Emily said nothing more until they were out of earshot. To his surprise, however, when she spoke again, it was to ask about his work.

"What kept you at the museum so late?"

"An Egyptian pottery collection," he said. "A large donation is expected to arrive on Monday, and I've been charged with taking care of it. It will take a considerable amount of time to organize, and I could not leave the Montagu room locked to visitors for weeks simply because the pottery collection was not ready." He sighed. "I'd hoped to have it done in eight hours; it took nine and a half."

Her grip on his arm tightened. "You must be exhausted."

"I have tomorrow to rest before Lady Grenville's butterflies arrive."

She gasped, and her dark eyes filled with awe. "You have a butterfly collection coming?"

He smiled. "You must like butterflies."

"Do you know anyone who does not?"

"I could probably find someone if I searched long enough."

"That would be a spectacularly awful waste of your time," she said. "Especially when you could be studying the magnificent creatures themselves."

"Aren't they rather small to be considered magnificent?"

"But that's exactly it. To have so much beauty contained in such tiny wings is the very thing that makes them magnificent."

Henry's feet slowed as a new and completely irregular idea struck him. "Would you like to see them when they arrive?"

They had not quite reached the door, but she came to an abrupt halt. "May I really?"

Could she? If he were to ask Townsend or Fernsby, they'd undoubtedly say no. The public was never given access to the museum pieces until they were fully cataloged and safely displayed. But Claridge had placed him in charge. In theory, he did not need to ask permission of anyone. His offer had been rashly made, but he found that he did not regret it. "Yes," he said. "Come to the museum on Monday afternoon, and have Rutherford bring you directly upstairs."

Any doubts Henry had harbored over the wisdom of what he'd just done dissolved in the warmth of her smile.

"Thank you, Henry," she said. "I will come."

"Good." They walked the few remaining steps to the door. "I shall look forward to it."

Chapter 16

At one o'clock on Monday afternoon, Emily stepped out of Aunt Millward's carriage and approached the museum's front steps with no small amount of trepidation. She had no ticket, Henry would not be waiting in the lobby, and Aunt Millward's bolstering influence was currently being expended on Phoebe, who was lying in bed, anxiously awaiting another visit from Dr. Thorndike. Adam had offered to escort Emily to the museum, but after telling him that she'd rather him pace in Aunt Millward's drawing room than in Henry's office, he'd agreed that a maid should go in his stead. It was a suitable arrangement, even if Hannah did not instill Emily with great confidence.

"This is it, Hannah," she said, pausing to give the maid a moment to get her bearings.

"It's ever so big, miss." Hannah surveyed the stately mansion with wide eyes. "I ain't ever bin in a buildin' so big. Or so fancy."

"It is a bit overwhelming, isn't it? But never fear, we'll face it together."

Emily started up the stairs with Hannah beside her. Just as they reached the top, the doors opened, and Rutherford appeared.

"Good afternoon, Miss Norton," he said. "Welcome to the British Museum."

"Good afternoon, Rutherford. I must say, I'm impressed that you remember my name."

The porter inclined his head. "Thank you, miss. I do try to make a note of such things, especially when a visitor is a special guest of one of the curators." He lowered his voice slightly. "Of course, I was given a little extra help today seeing as Mr. Buckland told me to expect you."

Emily smiled. "I appreciate your honesty, Rutherford."

"You can always count on that, miss." He ushered Emily and Hannah inside. "If you'll follow me. Mr. Buckland is in the accessions room." He led them across the entrance hall and up the wide staircase. Their footsteps echoed off the marble flooring, and whispered words bounced off the vaulted ceiling from the small group of people following Mr. Townsend into the manuscript saloon.

"What do you think, Hannah?" Emily asked.

The maid's eyes were as round as saucers. "As I live 'n' breathe, Miss Norton, I ain't never seen the likes of this afore."

"We're approaching some of the most amazing pieces of art," Emily said. "Look over there on the right." Emily pointed to a seascape. "Have you ever seen the sea?"

"No, miss. The most water I've ever seen is in the Thames."

"Well, this is a remarkable likeness of the ocean," she said, pausing a moment before the painting.

"Is it yer favorite in 'ere, miss?" Hannah asked.

"I don't think I can pick a favorite. Not with so many to choose from. But when I came before, I was struck by an especially lifelike painting of a basket of fruit." The gallery housing that particular painting and the precious stones was just ahead. "Rutherford," Emily said. "Would you mind if I show Hannah one of the paintings in this next gallery before we join Mr. Buckland?"

"Not at all, miss." Rutherford took a position at the open doorway. "Take your time."

Emily hurried inside and led Hannah to the painting hanging on the wall. The canvas showcased a variety of grapes, figs, pears—some still clinging to their leaves—and an apple, all contained in a wicker basket. The light hit the fruit in such a way that every piece looked tempting to the taste. Except perhaps the apple. Now that she looked more closely, she noticed that the artist had included two little worm holes in that particular fruit.

"The apple reminds me of the ones growing in my family's orchard in Berkshire," Emily said.

"Worm 'oles 'an' all?" Hannah asked.

The maid had noticed the blemishes too. "I'm afraid so. Having picked many apples, I have determined that worms like apples just as much as people do." She studied the painting a moment longer. It was strange that she'd thought the apple looked like a Genet Moyle the first time she'd seen it. In today's light, the fruit appeared less red than a Genet Moyle. More like a D'Arcy Spice.

"Well, I reckon we've got t' give worms some credit fer knowin' what's good, then," Hannah said.

"You are absolutely right," Emily said. "Shall we see the butterflies now?"

Hannah nodded enthusiastically, and they followed Rutherford to the very end of the landing, where a sign proclaiming No Admittance hung on a solid wood door.

Hannah gave Emily an anxious look, but Emily raised her chin and faced the door boldly. "Is this it, Rutherford?"

"Yes, miss. Don't worry about the sign. We have to put it up while the tours are going on." He knocked, turned the brass doorknob, and stepped inside. "Miss Norton is here to see you, sir," he said.

"Thank you, Rutherford." Henry's voice reached her from behind a tall crate. "Please have her come in."

The porter nodded and moved aside to allow them entry. Natural light spilled into the room through two large windows. Shelves filled with boxes lined the walls. Crates were piled in untidy rows, and two long tables carried piles of books, sculptures, and pottery. In one corner, a tiger with glassy eyes stood on its rear legs, staring down at a shelf of stuffed tropical birds.

With a squeak of terror, Hannah backed up a few paces. "Mercy, miss. Is that a real tiger?"

"I believe so," Emily said. "But it doesn't seem to be going anywhere."

Hannah nodded numbly and inched a little farther from the fearsome creature while Emily scanned the cluttered room in search of Henry.

A third table stood a little apart from the others. An open crate sat beside it, the straw from within spilling onto the floor. Part of the table was obscured by a tall cupboard, but she could see the corner of a large display case surrounded by stacks of paper.

Chair legs scraped against the floor. Footsteps sounded, then Henry appeared around the cupboard. "Good afternoon." He smiled, and Emily discovered that not all the butterflies in the room were in the display case—a full flight were fluttering around in her stomach.

Hannah immediately bobbed a curtsy.

Pressing her hand against her corset, Emily attempted a natural smile. "Good afternoon," she said. "I hope we have not come at an inconvenient time."

"Not at all." Henry gestured toward the cluttered table. "As you can see, I have a great deal of work ahead, but the butterflies are out of the crate and ready for your perusal."

Emily stepped toward the table. "Oh!" The word escaped on a sigh.

At least a hundred butterflies, their wings outstretched, were set out in rows within the display case. Afternoon light bathed them in a warm glow, catching the iridescent quality of their wings and deepening the vast array of colors.

"They are . . . so . . . so . . ."

"Magnificent," Henry finished. "You were right. That's the perfect word."

She nodded, gazing down at the variety of shapes, sizes, and colors. "Can you see, Hannah?"

The maid moved closer. "There's so many," she gasped. "And ev'ry one is different."

"That's one of nature's greatest miracles," Emily said. She looked at Henry. "What will you do with them?"

"Lord Grenville made a valiant attempt at identifying them. I shall have to go through and verify that he has labeled them correctly. Those that are older or did not withstand the journey will be replaced, and we will house the rest in a more secure case."

Hannah stepped back, and Emily moved a little closer to Henry. She lowered her voice. "Can you identify all the colors?"

"Probably not." There was chagrin in his voice. "I shall simply have to do my best and then ask Fernsby to confirm my descriptions."

"Mr. Fernsby is the curator who wears the brightly colored clothes?"

"Yes. He seems to fancy himself as a painting." He smiled wryly. "It's probably for the best that he doesn't know I shall never fully appreciate his brightly colored wardrobe."

"I'm glad he's willing to help you," she said.

Henry eyed the piles of paper on the desk and sighed. "To be honest, ascertaining the colors of the butterflies is the least of my worries."

"What do you mean?"

"Along with the butterflies, Lady Grenville donated a substantial portion of her husband's literary collection."

"I would have thought that was a good thing," Emily said.

"Oh, it is. And the board of trustees is thrilled. But Lady Grenville has it in her head that I am the only curator sufficiently trustworthy to take care of the endowment."

"That's understandable."

Henry smiled. "Your sentiments, although generously given, are not entirely true." He pointed at the case of butterflies. "That comes firmly under the purview of the curator over natural history. That"—he shifted his arm to encompass the piles of paper—"does not. And yet, regardless of the fact that I am unqualified to classify this literature, Lord Claridge, who serves as chair of the board of trustees, has placed me in charge of the entire project. He even went so far as to say that the assignment was a test."

"What kind of test?"

"I have no idea, but I believe a pleasant test is even more rare than a person who does not like butterflies."

He had a point. The word alone conjured up anxiety.

"What kind of papers are they?" she asked.

"I've not made it past a third of the first pile," he said, "but it appears to be an assortment of things, from scientific papers to poetry to plays." He reached for a paper on the top of the nearest pile. "Have you heard of William Blake?"

"No. Should I have?"

"I have no idea." Henry waved the paper. "Some of his early work is here, but I do not know what to do with it."

"Surely Mr. Townsend would know."

"Undoubtedly, but he has not deigned to speak more than half a dozen words to me since Claridge insisted that I take charge of the Grenvilles' gift."

"Have you spoken more than half a dozen words to him?" she asked.

He considered the question. "Probably not. Townsend tends to be rather protective of his domain, and Fernsby thought it best to give him space to adjust to the idea."

"I see." Emily fiddled with the ribbons on her reticule. Who was she to offer advice? She scarcely knew the gentleman in question.

"Emily?" He was studying her too carefully. "Tell me what you're thinking."

"That I know nothing of such things."

"Actually, you know an awful lot about a great many things, and I'd be grateful for your insight."

Emily took a deep breath. "Very well. I do not claim to know Mr. Townsend well, but he strikes me as someone who is fully committed to his work—to preserving literature and making it accessible to everyone."

"He is," Henry said.

"Then it seems to me that much of his disgruntled behavior may stem from his desire to have Lord Grenville's collection taken care of correctly and from believing that he is the only one at the museum capable of that."

"He's not wrong."

"Then tell him," Emily said. "Even if Lord Claridge wounded Mr. Townsend's pride, much of it would likely be restored if he realized that you recognize his worth to the museum."

Henry rubbed the back of his neck, the creases on his brow deepening. "Even if you are right, how do I sidestep Claridge's and Lady Grenville's insistence that I be in charge of this project?"

"Being in charge does not mean that you have to do everything yourself. If that were the case, your housekeeper would be dusting, cleaning out the fireplaces, stripping beds, and a myriad other things that she currently assigns to others.

"Adam learned this the hard way in the orchard. No matter how much he wishes it were otherwise, he cannot be everywhere and do everything during the harvest. But he can hire skilled men and supervise them in such a way that the job is accomplished to the highest possible standard." She shrugged uncertainly. "Perhaps Lord Claridge wishes to test your willingness to delegate rather than your ability to do everything."

When she finished speaking, there was a terrifying moment of complete silence. She swallowed. Behind her, Hannah shifted her feet, and outside, a carriage drove by.

And then Henry released a tense breath. "Miss Emily Norton," he said, "you are the most amazing young woman."

Emily blinked. "But I—"

"Truly." The elation in his smile banished the strain that had shown on his face. "You are more magnificent than any and every butterfly. And rather than stay here to further convince you of that fact, I'm going to be inexcusably impolite and abandon you so that I might locate Townsend and beg for his help with these papers."

Happiness—warm and light—filled Emily. "Go," she said. "Hannah and I will let ourselves out and will close the door behind us."

He leaned forward and brushed his lips across her cheek. "Thank you," he whispered.

And then, before her stuttering heart could regain its beat, he was gone.

CHAPTER 17

HENRY DESCENDED THE MUSEUM'S STAIRCASE, his heart racing in time with his rapid footsteps. Heaven help him. What had he done? Hours spent struggling under the weight of his assignment must have muddled his senses. He'd been so taken with Emily's fresh perspective that brushing her cheek with his lips had felt completely natural. And right. He stifled a groan. It was time to own up to the truth. It wasn't simply Emily's fresh perspective that had captured him. It was the young lady herself. And if he were being fully honest, the presence of her maid in the room was likely the only reason he'd limited himself to kissing her cheek.

In the entrance hall below, a cluster of visitors was gathering to listen to Fernsby's introductory greeting. Grateful that it was Fernsby rather than Townsend leading this tour, Henry forced himself to slow his stride and take the last few stairs at a more sedate pace. As difficult as it was to ignore his burgeoning feelings for Emily or what had just occurred between them, he had to give all his attention to Townsend. Approaching the older curator would take every ounce of diplomacy Henry could muster.

He crossed the hall and entered the manuscript saloon. For now, it was blessedly empty, but if Fernsby chose to bring his group here first, the peace would not last long. Townsend was standing with his back to Henry, sorting through a row of books on a shelf.

Squaring his shoulders, Henry approached him. "Townsend, might I have a word?"

The older gentleman glanced his way before resuming his organizing of the books. "Why?"

"Because I believe I owe you an apology."

Townsend slid a book into place between two others and turned to fully face him. Folding his arms, he glared at Henry. "Indisputably."

At least they had found some common ground.

"Consider it wholeheartedly given," Henry said.

Townsend's eyes narrowed. "What exactly are you apologizing for?"

"For not coming to speak to you immediately after Claridge left the museum a fortnight ago. For being presumptuous enough to assume that I knew what you were thinking without actually asking you."

"Ah, but not for considering yourself an overnight authority on English literature." There was no denying the bitterness in Townsend's voice.

"For what it's worth, I have never considered myself an authority on English literature, and I never will."

"Claridge seems to think you are."

"I beg to differ. Claridge sees me as the means to acquiring Lord Grenville's collection. Why sharing three cups of tea with Lady Grenville should have had such a profound effect on the lady, I do not know, but I can tell you that not once did I assume to know the names of any of the authors her husband championed." He furrowed his brows. "Why would I need to do that when I know full well that you have a firm grasp on such things?"

Townsend's jaw tightened. "Claridge dismissed any expertise I might claim."

"You do not need Claridge's endorsement to know that you are the most qualified person to organize Lord Grenville's books and manuscripts. Lady Grenville may have insisted that I be responsible for receiving her donation, but we both know that the classification of papers will not be done properly unless it is done by you. And so, for the sake of all patrons of the museum, I ask that you please consider taking on the task."

"You do not deserve my help."

Townsend's grumpiness was as reliable as the arrival of a new day, and Henry would not allow it to deter him. "Perhaps not," he said. "But all those still-to-be-discovered authors, poets, and musicians whose work lies in the accessions room upstairs surely do."

Townsend looked away. Henry waited, instinct telling him that this was not the time to press.

Townsend sniffed. "I will not have you hovering over me."

It was not a yes, but he had refrained from giving an unqualified no, which Henry took as a good sign.

"I shall not hover over you at all. I have a rather large butterfly collection to see to. That will consume my attention for several days."

"If the compilation is as large as you claim, it will take more than a handful of days to organize," Townsend warned. "I would require you to keep your distance, no matter how long the job takes to complete."

"Agreed."

Townsend eyed him curiously. "Are you truly as desperate as you sound?"

"Completely. Tripping-over-myself desperate."

Something that sounded remarkably like a chortle rattled in Townsend's throat, but he turned back to the bookshelf before Henry could see if he actually smiled.

"I will join you in the accessions room after the next tour," Townsend said. "You can show me what you have then."

Relief, pure and lifting, flooded through Henry. "You have my thanks, Townsend."

The older gentleman grunted and pulled two books off the shelf. "Well, go on, then. Don't you have butterflies to catalog?"

Henry grinned. "I do, indeed."

The door to the manuscript saloon opened, and Fernsby walked in, leading half a dozen others. The garishly dressed gentleman's eyes instantly landed on Henry and Townsend, and he raised a questioning eyebrow.

"Good day," Henry said, acknowledging Fernsby and the guests with a nod but not stopping long enough to exchange anything further. Knowing Fernsby, he would seek out Henry at his earliest convenience to discover why Henry had been talking to Townsend. There would be time enough to explain what had happened later.

Aunt Millward's front door thudded closed, and Emily released a deep breath. She gazed at the vase full of brightly colored bluebells sitting beside the tea tray. It was the second time Colonel Eastberry had delivered flowers. This time, however, he'd brought them himself and had stayed for almost an hour. Aunt Millward had been marvelous, ordering tea and maintaining the conversation when Emily had run out of questions about India, but the entire visit had been exhausting.

"Would you mind if I go upstairs for a little while?" she asked Aunt Millward. "I promised Phoebe I'd visit her this afternoon."

"Of course not, dear. I daresay Phoebe will be anxious to hear news of your visitor and your trip to the museum."

Aunt Millward was right. Phoebe was always desperate for any news of life outside her bedchamber. A social call would rank highly compared to updates on the latest book Emily had been reading. Perhaps Emily should be glad of

Colonel Eastberry's visit after all. It would be a far safer topic to discuss with Phoebe than what she had done at the museum. Resisting the urge to touch her cheek, Emily rose from the sofa. "I won't be long."

"Not to worry." Aunt Millward picked up a book. "I have a great deal more to learn about Bengal tigers before Colonel Eastberry comes again."

"If you think he will return soon, perhaps you'd better share everything you learn with me."

Aunt Millward opened the book. "Why don't you finish the three volumes I gave you on local flora and fauna first, and then I shall tell you about India."

Emily nodded her agreement. If she was lucky, one of those books may have some illustrations of English butterflies.

Phoebe was sitting up in bed, waiting for Emily, and urged her to take a seat the moment she entered the bedchamber.

"I've been watching the clock ever since I heard the front door close," Phoebe said. "If you hadn't appeared in the next five minutes, I would have sent Hannah after you."

Emily laughed. "Forgive me. I spoke to Aunt Millward for a few minutes after Colonel Eastberry left."

"So, it was Colonel Eastberry. I thought as much." Phoebe gave her a mischievous look. "I sent Hannah down to see who had come to call. I guessed it was him from her description."

"It was very nice of him," Emily said.

Phoebe tilted her head and studied Emily carefully. "I must say, for someone who has obviously caught the eye of a very respectable gentleman, you look remarkably unaffected."

Unaffected? Was she? "Yes, I suppose I am. Unless experiencing relief that Colonel Eastberry's visit is over counts."

"Unfortunately for the colonel, I would not classify that particular emotion as a sign that you are particularly lovestruck."

"It's hard to believe anyone would be lovestruck by a discussion of the diet of monkeys, the woes of India's wet season, the difficulty in maintaining a crisp uniform while on a march, and the sorry state of the merchant ships in Calcutta."

"You might be surprised," Phoebe said. "I have discovered that when it comes to conversing with a gentleman, the subject matter has very little to do with the feelings of one's heart. One could be discussing something as banal as weeds and feel quite giddy as long as the exchange is with the right person."

Such as Henry. The words echoed through Emily's head so clearly that she wondered if Phoebe could hear them. A vision of Henry wrapping the ribwort plantain she'd uprooted in Clapham Common was quickly replaced by one of him listening to her in the museum's cluttered accessions room. She swallowed. Phoebe was right. The memories filled her with pleasure—and something that felt uncomfortably like giddiness.

"Emily?" There was a hint of concern in Phoebe's voice. "Are you quite well?"

She cleared her throat. "Forgive me. Your words simply gave me cause to think."

"About nothing too terrible, I hope."

"No." Emily summoned a smile. Was having a gentleman kiss your cheek terrible? She had a feeling Adam might think it was, but it hadn't felt the least bit terrible to her. Quite the opposite, in fact. "I suppose I must learn how to navigate this unchartered water, even if I barely know which way is downstream."

Phoebe reached out and took her hand. "I realize that while I am confined to my bed, I'm of little help to you at social functions, but I am always willing to listen if you have concerns, and I will do my best to answer any questions you might have." She lowered her voice as though imparting a secret. "I may be a little more rational about such things than Adam. He still struggles with letting you out of his sight in a ballroom."

Phoebe had been there for Emily's disastrous inaugural coming out in Berkshire and had guided her through everything from wardrobe choices to dance steps since. But the most miraculous thing Phoebe had done during that difficult time was fall in love with Emily's overly protective brother.

"Was it difficult for you to choose Adam?" she asked. "I know full well that he was not the only gentleman who pursued you."

Phoebe smiled. "No, he was not the only one. But in the end, he was the only one who mattered." She leaned back against her pillows, looking thoughtful. "If you are fortunate enough to fall in love with an honorable gentleman, Emily, you will see a change in how you view life. Any joy will be enhanced by sharing it with him; any challenge will be made easier because you face it together."

"I believe I would like that," Emily said.

Phoebe squeezed her hand and then released it. "I rather think Adam is biding his time, waiting to scare off the most persistent suitors who come to call so that he will not have to share you with another. The only hope a gentleman has of gaining your brother's consent to make you his bride is if Adam sees that kind of love between you. He would not want you to have anything less."

Emily rose from her chair and walked to the window. The sun was lowering in the sky, casting shadows along the length of Aunt Millward's small garden's walls. Had it only been a few hours ago that she'd experienced that intimate moment with Henry? She could no longer deny that she was developing feelings for him, but how was she to discern his leanings when she scarcely recognized her own? His feather-light kiss on her cheek had been impulsively given. Of that, she had no doubt. But whether he'd been motivated by gratitude or something deeper, she could not tell.

CHAPTER 18

Henry wanted to see Emily. It had been three days since she'd come to the museum and given him the advice that had turned things around for him with Townsend. But it felt like three weeks. During that time, Fernsby had repeatedly expressed his disapproval of Henry's decision to include Townsend in the project, while Henry's appreciation for the older gentleman's devotion to his field of study had continued to grow.

Townsend's passion for literature seemingly filled any void he may have felt with the absence of a wife and family, for with no one awaiting him at home, he'd repeatedly chosen to stay at the museum after it closed to work on Lord Grenville's collection. Henry could not tell exactly how well the organizing was going. The piles of paper moved occasionally, and Townsend read for long periods of time, pausing sporadically to add to the master list he was compiling. Henry did not dare interrupt, but a sense of responsibility kept him on hand regardless of the hour.

For three days, he'd arrived at the museum before anyone else and had not left until exhaustion had sent him home to bed. Today had to be different. He could not allow another twenty-four hours to pass without some sort of interaction with Emily. Rolling his shoulders, he rose from his chair in the accessions room and walked away from the catalog he was compiling. Seventeen more butterflies and he would have this portion of the recording completed.

Passing Townsend's piles of paper and tidy inventory list, he walked to the window. The sun was shining, calling him to spend time outdoors. On the museum grounds, forsythia bushes were ablaze of color. If Emily were here, she'd surely comment on the glorious sight. He could imagine the warmth in her eyes as she looked upon the blooms, and he wished he could share them with her. Unfortunately, if he were to cut off any limbs, the gardeners would come after him with their shovels. But perhaps sending flowers was a good solution. He'd failed in that area once before. He could do better.

His gaze moved from the forsythia to the daffodils and tulips swaying in the flower beds. He'd never asked Emily if she had a favorite flower. Even when she'd been deluged by bouquets after the Tilsons' ball, she'd not given any hint of her preference. He frowned. Was it prideful to want her to favor his offering over those of the other gentlemen? If so, he was currently battling an uncommonly violent surge of the vice. And he was at a loss. It was hard to imagine someone who saw beauty in the lowly red campion singling out any flower above another.

Red campion. The lines on his forehead eased, and as the first inkling of an idea developed into something larger, he smiled. He'd noticed the wild plant blooming along the hedgerow bordering the museum's property. A short walk would be good for him, and it wouldn't take long to pick enough red campion to make a small bouquet. If Rutherford would help him locate a boy willing to earn a few coins to deliver them, he could have the flowers to Emily by day's end.

Withdrawing his pocket watch, he checked the time. Townsend would be back from giving a tour in twenty minutes. Should Henry go now or wait for his colleague to return?

A knock interrupted his thoughts, and he swung to face the door as it opened to admit Claridge and Fernsby. Henry's stomach dropped. He caught Fernsby's self-assured look. It wasn't the most encouraging sign, particularly as Fernsby had stubbornly held to his opinion that bringing Townsend on to help was a mistake.

"Good day, my lord."

"Buckland." Claridge eyed the piles of paper on the long worktable, his gaze hovering over Townsend's list a fraction longer than it should. "Fernsby here tells me that you have Townsend working on the Grenville donation."

It seemed that the chair was in no mood for pleasant conversation. It also appeared that Fernsby had been as direct with Claridge as Claridge was now being with Henry. He must have seized the opportunity to bend the chair's ear the moment the gentleman had walked into the museum. Fernsby's disloyalty hurt, but Henry had no time to dwell on it. He faced Claridge without flinching. "That is correct."

Claridge's eyes flashed. "And you authorized this despite my repeated instructions to the contrary?"

Fernsby's expression had turned smug, and Henry's jaw tightened. He did not know why his colleague had suddenly turned against him, but he did know that he would not go down without a fight. "I beg your pardon, my lord, but I was under the impression that both Lady Grenville's and your instructions were that I be placed in charge of ensuring that this generous endowment be dealt with correctly."

"Exactly right."

"Then I respectfully submit that by enlisting the assistance of Mr. Townsend, I have done just that. Mr. Townsend is the only person at the museum qualified to make an accurate accounting of Lord Grenville's books and papers. Had anyone else undertaken the task, grievous errors would have been incurred that would have reflected badly on this institution."

Claridge's air of indignation was now tinged with disbelief. "Are you telling me that Townsend is a more competent curator than you?"

"No, my lord. I believe we each have our own strengths, and if we truly desire what is best for the museum, we must combine those strengths to our advantage."

"In the absence of a museum director, surely the greatest manifestation of combined strength is to follow the wishes of the board of trustees explicitly," Fernsby said.

Henry stared at him. What on earth was he about? Was he purposely trying to sabotage Henry's efforts, or was he simply being obstinate?

"Your loyalty to the board's wishes is commendable, Fernsby," Claridge said. He waved a hand toward the table. "Have you participated in this project too?"

"Not at all, my lord." Fernsby spoke as though the admission was something to be admired.

"Very well, I shall let you get back to your work while I discuss things further with Buckland," Claridge said.

Fernsby's self-assured expression cracked. "If I can be of any additional assistance—"

"Yes, yes, I know where to find you."

If Fernsby's rigid stance was anything to go by, he was not pleased by the dismissal. Henry, however, was more than happy to see him leave. Avoiding eye contact with Henry, Fernsby executed a brief bow and walked out of the room.

"Right then, Buckland," Claridge said, "I think you'd better show me exactly what you have been up to."

"With pleasure," Henry said, leading him to the display case filled with butterflies. "It has taken the best part of thirty-six hours, but I am close to—"

"I beg your pardon," Claridge interrupted. "I thought the crate arrived on Monday."

"It did, my lord. Townsend and I have been working twelve-hour days since then."

"Good heavens. Is that really necessary?"

Henry inclined his head. "Townsend is devoted to his work, my lord, and I was charged with overseeing the assignment."

The chair appeared thoughtful. "What has Townsend told you about the manuscripts?"

Almost nothing. Henry didn't think the chair would appreciate that response, even if it was the truth. Lady Grenville's take on her husband's collection might not be impartial or authoritative, but it was the best he could offer. "I believe Lord Grenville was quite discerning with regard to those authors and poets he chose to mentor. Many of the pieces are written by those likely to make a name for themselves in the future."

"Are you familiar with them?"

"No, my lord. But Townsend assuredly is." Henry hadn't actually asked him since mentioning William Blake's name, but he was counting on the fact that the gentleman who spent the majority of his day reading manuscripts was aware of more than one new author.

Claridge moved past the butterflies and stopped opposite Townsend's ledger. Henry waited in silence while the chair read the first entries. Voices sounded on the landing, a bird flew past the window, and the seconds marched on. Finally, Claridge raised his head. "I am glad to see that my confidence in your capacity to manage an important project was not unfounded, Buckland. It omens well for your future at the museum."

Relief filled him. "Thank you, my lord."

The chair walked around the table, his cane clicking in time with his footsteps. "Fernsby may have been misguided in his opinion regarding involving Townsend in the cataloging," he said, "but he was right about one thing: the museum has been without the leadership of an on-site director for far too long. To that end, you may be interested to know that a ship known to be sailing from the South Seas has been spotted in the English Channel. I am hopeful that it will contain cargo for the museum and the return of Mr. Watts."

"That is big news," Henry said, his head spinning as he thought through the ramifications of several more crates arriving at the museum within the week.

"It is indeed."

The door opened, and Townsend walked in. When he caught sight of Claridge, he came to an abrupt halt. "I beg your pardon," he said. "I did not mean to interrupt."

"Not at all," Claridge said, exhibiting no trace of his earlier reserve toward the older curator. "Buckland has been telling me what a fine job you've been doing, Townsend. I'm most grateful." He started for the door. "Far be it from me to impede your progress any longer, gentlemen. Good day to you."

Almost before Henry knew what had happened, Lord Claridge had gone, and Henry could not tell whether he or Townsend was more stunned by the gentleman's abrupt and breezy departure.

Emily and Adam completed their second circuit of the small green near Aunt Millward's home before starting back toward the house.

"Thank you for taking a walk with me, Adam," Emily said. "London has a great deal to recommend it, but I miss wandering the grounds at Dunsbourne Manor."

"I do too." Adam glanced at the misshapen beech on the corner. "And I miss the trees."

"Has your time here been productive though?" Emily asked. Adam had been gone from the house a great deal, and when he was there, he was usually in the late Lord Millward's office, poring over legal papers and catalogs.

"It has. Along with bankers and investors, I've met with several gentlemen involved in the cider production business. I'll be returning to Dunsbourne Manor with new ideas for improving the orchard's yield, and hopefully I will have learned some tips for making the apple pressing more efficient too."

"Hopefully?"

"I've been invited by Mr. Brownslow, the owner of one of the largest cider orchards in the country, to visit his facility in Wiltshire. It would be an unprecedented opportunity to see how a big operation is run."

"That's marvelous!"

"Yes," Adam said. "And no."

Emily looked at him quizzically. "Why no?"

"Because he's returning to Wiltshire tomorrow and wishes me to go with him." Adam grimaced. "I hate to leave Phoebe in her current condition, not to mention needing to be here to ward off any undesirable suitors you may acquire."

"How long would you be gone?"

"The best part of a fortnight."

Emily slipped her arm through his. "Mr. Brownslow is offering you a unique opportunity to learn from someone who has been in the cider-making business for a long time. You must go. Phoebe is doing remarkably well. She will be well taken care of in your absence. And I don't think you need worry about expelling my suitors from Aunt Millward's house. They have not exactly been beating down the door."

"I did hear that Colonel Eastberry paid you a call recently." He looked at her sternly. "And brought you flowers."

Emily tried not to squirm. "Yes. Aunt Millward offered him tea, but he did not stay long."

"And how did you feel about that?"

"Truthfully?"

Adam's expression softened. "I always want you to be truthful with me, Em. You know that."

"I was rather relieved. I was overdue to visit Phoebe, and I had run out of questions about monkeys and elephants."

Adam's laughter filled the air. "Perhaps I do not need to worry about poor Colonel Eastberry after all."

"Not as far as I'm concerned," she said. "But seeing as Aunt Millward is currently reading a book about India so as to be better prepared for their next encounter, you may yet need to be worried for the gentleman."

Adam grinned and led her up the steps to the house. "Thank goodness for Lady Millward."

The butler, Wakefield, opened the door. "Welcome back, my lord, Miss Norton," he said.

"Thank you, Wakefield." Adam handed him his hat and gloves before turning to Emily. "I think I should go and talk to Phoebe about Brownslow's offer."

Emily nodded. "I do too." She tugged at the bonnet ribbons beneath her chin. "Tell her that I will spend extra time with her while you're gone."

Giving her a grateful smile, Adam disappeared up the stairs, and Emily handed Wakefield her redingote.

"You had a delivery whilst you were out, miss," Wakefield said.

"A delivery?" Emily's stomach knotted. If it was from Colonel Eastberry, she truly might need to enlist Aunt Millward's assistance to discourage the gentleman.

"Yes, miss. Flowers and a note. A young lad brought them, and Lady Millward had Hannah take them to your bedchamber."

Startled, Emily glanced up the stairs. Aunt Millward had never had any of the flowers she'd received sent directly to her room. She'd always had them set in the drawing room until Emily had read the accompanying notes and determined where she would like them placed. "Where is Lady Millward now?" she asked.

"I believe she is catching up on her correspondence in her chambers, miss."

Not readily available for questioning, then. She'd best go upstairs and see the mystery delivery for herself.

"Thank you, Wakefield."

By the time Emily reached the door of her bedchamber, her curiosity was bubbling. She turned the knob and entered.

At first glance, nothing in the room appeared any different from the way it had looked when she'd left about an hour before. The bed, covered in a pale-yellow eiderdown quilt, was tidily made. The two chairs with light-blue upholstery and yellow cushions sat empty on either side of the fireplace. The door of the large wooden wardrobe at her left was closed, as were the drawers beneath the dressing table. A quill and a few sheets of paper were the only things lying on the writing desk beneath the window, and the mantel bore the same two candlesticks and china figurines that had been there since the day Emily had arrived.

She stepped farther into the room, dropping her bonnet and gloves onto the bed and turning a slow circle. She had almost completed a full rotation when she saw the vase of tiny pink blossoms standing on the bedside table. Crossing the distance between the end of the bed and the table, she reached out to touch the delicate flowers.

"Red campion," she whispered over the pounding of her heart. There was only one person who would choose to pick these wildflowers for her rather than purchase a more traditional bouquet from a flower vendor.

A small white envelope lay propped against the vase. Reaching for it with trembling fingers, Emily broke the seal and withdrew a single sheet of paper. A quick glance at the bottom of the page confirmed what she had already known. It was from Henry.

Taking a seat on the bed, Emily read the short note.

Dear Emily,

You were right. Asking Mr. Townsend for his assistance with Lady Grenville's donation was the correct thing to do. He has been invaluable, and we have already put in many long hours of work together.

Unfortunately, with another much larger delivery expected within days, it is unlikely that I will be granted the opportunity to visit you at Aunt Millward's home anytime soon, so I am sending these still-poorly-named red campions as a token of my gratitude for your friendship and wise counsel.

Yours sincerely,
Henry
PS Lest you worry about the number of plants I picked to create this bouquet, I would have you know that I did leave a few for others to enjoy in the hedgerow.

When Emily reached the postscript, she smiled. She read the note again and then set it on the bedside table. Lifting the flowers to her face, she closed her eyes and breathed in their faint scent. Henry had gifted her a hint of the English countryside. She opened her eyes, and as she touched one of the delicate petals, she came to a disquieting realization. Colonel Eastberry may know a great deal about India, but Henry was coming to understand her.

CHAPTER 19

EXACTLY A WEEK AFTER HENRY sent Emily the red campion flowers, two horse-drawn carts pulled up outside the museum, each bearing multiple large crates recently unloaded from the merchant ship *Roselle*. Word of the *Roselle's* arrival at the Thames dock had reached the museum two days before, and the curators had used that time to clear space in the accessions room for whatever Mr. Watts had decided to send their way.

Lord Grenvilles' butterflies had been put on display in the same room as Sir Hans Sloan's collection; his books and papers had been cataloged and relocated to the manuscript saloon. Henry had cleared the tables in the accessions room, and given that no one knew exactly what to expect, he considered them to be as prepared as they could be.

"Looks like seven crates," Fernsby said.

He'd arrived in the entrance hall ahead of Henry and was standing at the window, watching the dock workers untie the rope strapping the large boxes to the carts. With the gentleman's natural curiosity, Henry shouldn't have been surprised that he was there, but neither he nor Townsend had seen much of Fernsby since Claridge had approved Townsend's involvement with categorizing Lord Grenville's manuscripts. Fernsby had come and gone from the museum at his normal times, but when he wasn't taking his assigned tours, he was in his office with the door firmly closed.

If Henry hadn't been so desperately preoccupied, he probably would have made a greater effort to talk to his colleague. To clear the air between them, at least. As it was, he assumed Fernsby was as busy as he was and had left him to get on with his work. With this shipment, they would be forced to coordinate their efforts again, which was just as well. Watts would want to see them working as a team.

Henry joined him at the window. "Any sign of Watts?"

They'd heard nothing from the returning museum director since the ship docked in London.

"Not that I can see," Fernsby said. He eyed Henry warily. "Has Claridge been here since the *Roselle* arrived?"

"No." Now that he thought on it, the absence of both the chair and the director was rather odd. He would have assumed they would want to be here to see the crates safely deposited at the museum.

Fernsby, it seemed, disagreed. "Sounds about right."

Puzzled by Fernsby's take on the situation, Henry turned his attention to Rutherford, who was opening the museum doors wide to admit the first two dock workers carrying a crate.

"Up the stairs, if you please," Rutherford said.

The shorter of the dock workers scowled. "'Ow many steps 'ave ya got in this massive place?"

"Altogether too many when you're hauling crates," Henry said. "You have my apologies."

His companion, taller, thinner, but with an equally weatherworn complexion, grunted. "Which way when we're at t' top, then?"

"Follow me," Henry said.

Fernsby and Rutherford could monitor things on this level. His time would be better served if he supervised the depositing of the crates in the accessions room.

Two hours later, the large room was unrecognizable. The seven crates took up almost all the floor space. The wooden lids that Fernsby and Rutherford had pried off lay in disarray around the room. Straw that had been used to pack the items within had spilled out, covering everything in sight, and the tables were laden with the most eclectic assortment of items ever to arrive in one shipment.

Running his fingers through his hair, Henry surveyed the chaos. He couldn't think about how long it would take to organize everything. At present, it was impossible for him to reach the door without vaulting at least two boxes.

"What do you think these are, Buckland?" Fernsby stood behind the nearest table, studying two wooden statues that stood about three feet high. The creatures—whatever they were—had large eyes and mouths with grotesquely long tongues.

"Idols, perhaps," Henry said.

Fernsby nodded thoughtfully. "These are similar, but they have stones in the foreheads." He picked up one of five miniature versions of a similar creature.

Henry climbed over one of the crates and studied the intricately carved pieces. Most of the weapons, headdresses, woven baskets, feathered capes, and handcrafted bowls littering the table were larger. They drew the eye because of their size and unfamiliar style. Polished to a shine, these smaller pieces spoke of the creator's meticulous care.

"They look to be a set," Henry said.

Fernsby lifted another. "Each one bears a stone of a different color."

Henry studied them more carefully. One stone was opaque white. If he had to guess, he'd say it was an opal. Another stone was green. Jade, perhaps. The other three were so similar in color to the wood, it was hard to make them out.

"What do you think the stones are?" Henry fished.

"That's your area, not mine," Fernsby said. "If I had to guess, opal, jade, ruby, carnelian, and garnet. Given where they've come from, one of them could be an agate."

"True."

"Which do you think would be the most valuable?"

Henry picked up the closest one. Why were there so many red gemstones? They were almost as prevalent as red flowers.

"It's hard to tell without a thorough examination," he said, "but generally, rubies are considered one of the rarest stones."

Rapid footsteps sounded on the landing. Henry set the figurine back on the table and turned to see Townsend burst through the door.

"It's missing!" he said.

Given the current state of the room, Henry could have said the same of his sanity and all sense of order. But he didn't think that was what Townsend was referring to.

"What's missing?" he asked.

"A print from an etching by William Blake."

Henry tensed. "From Lord Grenville's collection?"

"Of course," Townsend barked. "Where else would it be from? I had it sitting atop the fellow's poetry."

"In here or in the manuscript saloon?" Henry asked.

"Here. Both." Townsend mopped his brow with a large white handkerchief. "I thought I had it on the table downstairs, but now I cannot be sure."

Henry surveyed the accessions room, his heart sinking. If the print was here, it could take days to uncover it. If it wasn't . . . He would not consider that possibility. Townsend's distress was a sufficient clue that the paper was too valuable to lose.

"We won't find anything here until we've returned the room to some semblance of order," Henry said. "I'll come with you to the manuscript saloon, and we'll check there one more time."

"You won't find it." Townsend mopped his brow again, his agitation mounting. "I've searched countless times."

Henry clambered over the nearest crate, but before he could go any farther, another set of footsteps reached them. There was a firm rap on the half-open door, and Claridge walked in.

"Good day, gentlemen." Scarcely sparing the chaos a second glance, the chair did not wait for a response. "Rutherford told me that I might find you here. I apologize for not arriving sooner. The last couple of days have been somewhat hectic."

If Claridge was hoping to escape commotion, he had come to the wrong place.

"The arrival of the *Roselle* was bound to do that," Fernsby said.

"Indeed." Claridge shifted his feet, and the straw rustled. "As the contents of these crates attest, Mr. Watts is dedicated to seeking out artifacts for the museum, so it should not come as a complete surprise to any of us that he has chosen to continue his quest rather than return to England."

Henry stared at Claridge. Had he heard the gentleman aright? Watts had not sailed with the crates? Henry glanced at his companions. Townsend's brows were drawn together in a deep frown. Fernsby looked neither shocked nor perturbed. In fact, if Henry had to use one word to describe the man's expression, it would be calculating.

"So what happens now?" Fernsby asked.

"Mr. Watts sent a lengthy letter with the shipment," Claridge said. "He outlined his reasons for staying in the Pacific, including the countries he hopes to visit. He will continue to ship items to the museum but has asked that we replace him as its director. To that end, I have called for an emergency board meeting to appoint his successor." He cleared his throat. "Mr. Watts has recommended that we choose his replacement from amongst our current curators, and I am inclined to agree with him. I am come to ask if each of you would present yourselves before the board at Lord Southbeck's house at one o'clock on Friday afternoon."

Friday? That was tomorrow. Henry ran an unsteady hand across the back of his neck, the condition of the accessions room suddenly fading in significance.

"Might I have a word, my lord?" Townsend spoke for the first time, his tone grave.

"Of course." Claridge gestured toward the open door. "Why don't we walk downstairs together."

Townsend inclined his head in thanks and followed the chair out of the room.

"What do you think that was about?" Fernsby asked. "Townsend rarely wants to talk to anyone."

Henry was still trying to wrap his mind around Claridge's explosive news and had given no thought whatsoever to Townsend's request. "I could not tell you."

Fernsby navigated his way around a crate and stood at the doorway, watching the disappearing men with narrowed eyes. "I'd give a lot to know."

Memory of Townsend's distress over the missing William Blake etching flooded back.

"You don't suppose he's admitting to losing that document, do you?"

Fernsby shook his head. "Townsend is a curmudgeon, but he's not idiotic. He'll scour the entire museum before he admits to mislaying it."

"You think it's about the director position?"

Fernsby raised an eyebrow. "It stands to reason, doesn't it?"

It struck Henry, then. Fernsby wasn't nearly as taken aback by the news as he or Townsend were. When they'd been downstairs, he'd shown no surprise over Watts's lack of appearance.

"Did you know about Watts before this?" Henry asked.

Fernsby tugged on the lace protruding from beneath the sleeve of his pin-striped green jacket. "I keep my ear to the ground, Buckland. It's a skill you'd be wise to acquire. Nobody knew for certain, but there were members of the board at Southbeck's musicale who weren't averse to speculating over Watts's long absence or what it would mean for the directorship."

Henry remembered the evening well—primarily because his long hours at work had made him too late to sit beside Emily. Fernsby must have been working the room before and after the concert. But had he simply been gathering information from among the influential attendees at the fundraising event, or had he been actively ingratiating himself? "I see," Henry said.

Fernsby snorted. "I seriously doubt it. You rarely raise your head long enough from studying butterflies, rocks, and plants to see anything else." He stepped out of the room. "Good day, Buckland. And if I do not see you again before tomorrow's meeting, may the best man win."

As Fernsby's footsteps faded, an unfamiliar weight settled in Henry's chest. Fernsby wanted the director's position more than he wanted a friendship with Henry. The recent change in his colleague's attitude toward him made sense now, but understanding the reason did little to lessen the loss.

His thoughts spinning, Henry scooped up an armful of straw from the floor and stuffed it into the nearest crate. Then he reached for more. Ten minutes later, he'd cleared a wide path between the tables and the door, but the physical exertion was not enough to silence the echoes of Fernsby's taunts. Leaving the room, he shut the door behind him, locked it, and walked the short distance to his office. Another door clicked closed. It was probably Fernsby's office. Perhaps it was just as well that the man had kept to himself for the last couple of weeks. Henry had become used to seeing his door firmly shut.

The afternoon sun was reflecting off the windows, painting his office with bright squares. Henry crossed the room and stood, staring at the grounds below and feeling unaccountably lonely. The emptiness was reminiscent of the way he'd felt during his first few weeks at boarding school. He managed a wry smile. Given that he was craving being with Emily rather than a basket of feather-light scones from home, perhaps he'd matured a little since those early school days.

He wished Emily were here. She would brighten the room and lighten his mood with a single smile. But more than that, he knew he could talk to her and she would listen. He sighed and turned away from the window, only then noticing that Rutherford had placed today's post on the corner of his desk. He reached for the small pile and flipped through the letters one by one. When he reached the last envelope, he hesitated. He did not recognize the script or the seal. Curious, he opened it and withdrew a single sheet of paper before dropping his gaze to the signature at the bottom. John Dalton. His breath caught. The scientist known to Dr. Thorndike had written back.

Not bothering to take a seat, Henry started to read.

> *Moulton House,*
> *Manchester*
> *7 April 1790*
>
> *Dear Mr. Buckland,*
>
> *I was grateful to receive your recent letter and to know that Dr. Thorndike is aware of my work. My research into the reality of differences in color perception is still in its infancy, but early findings are both fascinating and promising.*
>
> *Although the primary focus of my scientific studies thus far has been the chemical composition of matter, I am drawn to discover*

more about what I have named "color blindness" because it is a condition claimed by both my brother and me. I am convinced that there is a medical reason for this disorder, and I am determined to uncover it.

I believe it might be advantageous to schedule a meeting. It would grant me an opportunity to learn more about your experiences and, if you are willing, allow me to examine your eyes. For my part, I would be happy to answer any questions you may have regarding my research thus far.

I will watch for your letter informing me of a convenient date.

Yours sincerely,
John Dalton

Henry lowered the paper and stared unseeingly at his office door. Nothing about his situation with Fernsby or the directorship had altered since he'd opened Dalton's letter, but something else—something significant and deep—had changed. Just as Emily had thought might happen, a few penned words had lifted the feeling of isolation he'd known since first realizing that he could not differentiate colors the same way everyone else did. He now knew for a surety that he was not alone. There were others, including this renowned scientist, who saw the world as he did.

His earlier desire to see Emily was now a need. She was the one who had done this for him; she was the one he must tell.

Picking up his satchel, he slung it over his shoulder and exited his office. Locking his door behind him, he started down the stairs. Thankfully, the arrival of the crates had prompted Claridge to cancel today's museum tours. Henry could depart early without leaving his colleagues in the lurch. Except, perhaps, for Townsend. His feet slowed as he reached the bottom of the stairs. He'd promised Townsend he would help him search for the missing document.

Suppressing his mounting impatience to be gone, Henry crossed to the manuscript saloon and opened the door. Townsend was alone, sifting through an enormous pile of papers.

"Any luck, Townsend?" Henry asked.

Townsend looked up with a start. When he saw Henry, he set the manuscripts in his hand on the table and released a tense breath. "No." He pointed to a second pile. "That is where it should be—where it was."

Henry knew better than to question the man. If he'd learned anything from working beside him in the accessions room, it was that Townsend was meticulous at record keeping.

"I offered to help you search . . ." Henry began.

"There's no need," Townsend said. "I shall go through the piles once more, but I am quite certain it's not here."

"We'll search the accessions room tomorrow," Henry promised.

Townsend's grim expression became grimmer. "Very well, although it's as likely to be in the butterfly display as on one of those tables. We cleared that room before the crates arrived."

He was right, but saying so would not help.

"Did you mention the loss to Claridge?"

"I'm not quite ready to declare my neglect yet, Buckland," he said gruffly.

Henry's lips twitched. "Good. Neither am I."

Townsend gave a noncommittal grunt and picked up the manuscripts again. "I shall not be at the meeting tomorrow," he said, keeping his eyes on the papers in his hand. "I told Claridge that I have no interest in becoming museum director. I am too old for the job and have no desire to expand my responsibilities beyond literature. I also told him that if the board of trustees knows what's good for them, they'll vote to put you in Watts's place." He set down a few pages. "Fernsby's far more interested in forwarding himself than in furthering the growth of the museum."

Henry opened his mouth and then closed it again. How did one respond to such a comment?

Townsend eyed him wryly. "As much as I welcome your silence, I would advise you to remove yourself quickly. It won't take me long to come up with a list of criticisms that will keep you firmly in your place."

This time, Henry allowed himself to smile. "Duly noted, Townsend. Thank you."

Townsend grunted again, and when he didn't bother looking up, Henry beat a hasty retreat.

Chapter 20

Emily wound the wool around her knitting needle and pulled it through to cast off the last stitch in the row.

"There," she said, setting aside her needles and raising her arms so that her ten-inch-wide knitted creation started above her head and flowed into a heap at her feet. "What do you think?"

From her throne of pillows on the bed, Phoebe grinned. "It's marvelous. But unless the recipient is eight feet tall or intends to wind it around his head half a dozen times, it's a good thing that you have brought this scarf's creation to an end."

Emily eyed the enormous dark-green ribbon ruefully. "It is a bit long, isn't it? I wasn't really thinking about how fast it was growing; I just kept knitting."

"Comments like that make me realize how far I am from your skill level. If I were to attempt it, I would be counting every painful stitch and row."

"This is not an example of skill," Emily said. "This is a manifestation of my unsettled state. And if the awfully wobbly edges are any indication, there is significant reason for concern."

Phoebe laughed. "We are quite a pair. I have embroidered half a dozen baby gowns since Adam left."

"And I have made a muffler fit for a giant even though I may never see Henry again."

"He will come. He said he would."

"Did he though?" Emily had read Henry's note so many times she had it memorized. She'd also read it to Phoebe.

It had taken less than a day after Adam left for Phoebe to coax Emily into confessing what was distracting her from her reading and causing her to alternately pace the bedchamber and blindly gaze off into the distance. And since

Emily had never been this upended over anyone or anything before, it had been a relief to share her fledgling feelings with her sister-in-law.

"He said that his work would prevent him from visiting, not that he *would* visit," Emily said.

"Calm yourself. A gentleman does not send flowers and a note to declare his disinterest."

Emily pressed her palm to her forehead. Phoebe was right. But this waiting, not knowing, was more torturous than she could have imagined.

"What shall I do with myself now that the scarf is complete?"

"You could try making matching mittens," Phoebe suggested.

"I fear they would be so misshapen and of such differing sizes that they would be completely unrecognizable," Emily said.

"Perhaps you could offer them to the museum for the stuffed animals to wear. The larger one could go to the bear, and the smaller one could go to a squirrel."

Emily gave her an indignant scowl, and Phoebe broke into peals of laughter.

"Can you imagine stuffy Mr. Townsend trying to explain your mittens to the visitors on his tour?" Phoebe said, gasping for air.

The image was so ludicrous it was impossible for Emily to remain straight-faced. "Stop, Phoebe," she laughed.

But Phoebe's mirth was uncontainable. "You could even take orders for pets," she said, and then they both collapsed in a fit of giggles.

Emily barely heard the knock on the door, but when Hannah peeked around the narrow opening with wide eyes, she and Phoebe attempted to regain some semblance of control.

"Forgive us, Hannah," Phoebe said. "I blame being cooped up in bed for too long."

Hannah offered her a sympathetic smile and stepped farther into the room. "A caller's come fer you, Miss Norton. 'E's in the drawing room with Lady Millward."

Emily's breath caught. After all these days, had Henry finally come? "Who . . . who is it, Hannah?"

"I believe Wakefield announced 'im as Lord Culham, miss."

Lord Culham? Emily's stomach dropped. It was bad enough that the visitor was not Henry, but to have it be the one gentleman she'd most like to avoid made the disappointment one hundred times worse. She turned to Phoebe, not bothering to hide her panic. "What do I do?" she whispered.

"You must go down," Phoebe said. "He has already been admitted, and Aunt Millward is expecting you."

"But Lord Culham is . . ." She grimaced.

"I know," Phoebe said. "I'm so sorry, Emily. I wish Adam were here."

So did Emily, but bemoaning his absence would not help. Setting her needles, wool, and completed scarf in the basket beside the chair, she rose to her feet.

"Aunt Millward and I will survive. She knows what kind of man he is."

"Yes, she does," Phoebe said. "And she's rather good at navigating difficult social situations."

A vision of Aunt Millward's coming out victor after having gone head-to-head with the Dowager Lady Pendleton at the Farwells' home filled her mind. Aunt Millward had discouraged the viscountess's overbearing matchmaking by dwelling on Lord Benning's involvement with farm animals. Perhaps, if Emily were to follow her example and paint herself in a less than favorable light, she might dissuade Lord Culham from pursuing her further. She squared her small shoulders. Together she and Aunt Millward could surely manage the odious gentleman.

"I fancy Aunt Millward's intelligence over Lord Culham's, don't you?" Emily said.

"Absolutely," Phoebe agreed. "Yours too. In fact, I believe I shall spend the entire time you are gone feeling terribly sorry for Lord Culham."

Raising her eyes to the ceiling, Emily picked up her knitting basket and handed it to the maid. "Would you take this to my bedchamber, Hannah? It seems that I am off to engage in a battle of wits."

Aunt Millward's voice rang out as Emily reached the bottom of the stairs. "Do you plan to attend the Morrises' ball, my lord?"

"Oh, most assuredly. The Morrises' ball really should not be missed." He paused. "You and your family members will be there, I assume. I confess, I shall be quite crushed if Miss Norton is not present."

Emily made a mental note to discover the date of the Morrises' ball so that she might be unwell that day.

"I cannot say for certain," Aunt Millward said. "Miss Norton's social calendar is of her own making, you understand, and she tends to prefer less popular activities."

The large potted plant in the corner of the entrance hall caught Emily's attention, and an idea settled upon her. If Lord Culham's fixation on the clothing worn by those attending the Tilsons' ball was any indication, he was a gentleman for whom a young lady's appearance mattered a great deal. It might be for the best if he were to learn that she was not always so well turned out or refined as he believed.

She could not be sure whether Aunt Millward had heard her descent on the stairs, but the older lady was doing a marvelous job of setting up her entrance. Hurrying over to the plant, Emily slid her hands beneath the leaves and reached for the soil below. She burrowed her fingers in the moist dirt and then quickly withdrew them. Content that enough soil clung to her fingers and nails to make her ruse plausible, she walked directly into the drawing room.

Lord Culham was sitting on the sofa opposite the chair Aunt Millward was currently occupying. His fair hair was pulled back in a ribbon of the same light-blue hue as his jacket and breeches. The lace at his neck and sleeves was crisp white, and his shoe buckles were polished to a shine. His smug expression and the arrogant angle of his weak jaw spoke of the gentleman's overconfidence, and Emily's resolve to avoid any form of encouragement deepened.

At Emily's entrance, he rose to his feet and bowed.

"Good day, Lord Culham." Making sure to keep her dirty hands clearly displayed and away from her gown, Emily curtsied. "I apologize for keeping you waiting." She glanced at her fingers. "As you can see, I was otherwise engaged, but perhaps I should have taken the time to clean up a little before joining you."

"Good gracious, my dear, have you been digging up plants again?" Aunt Millward's suitably shocked expression was perfect. "You really can leave such things to the gardener."

"So you have said." Emily took the chair beside Aunt Millward, studiously avoiding the sofa. "But you have no need to fear. This time there were no worms involved."

Aunt Millward placed one hand on her heart. "I am very glad to hear it." She leaned a little closer to Lord Culham. "Miss Norton is totally fearless when it comes to such creatures, my lord. She's really quite remarkable."

Lord Culham shifted uncomfortably. "Worms, you say? Well now, that is quite something."

"Caterpillars and ladybirds tend to remain in the plant's leaves if I remove it by the roots, but worms appear to take exception to the disruption," Emily said. "I find myself feeling quite sorry for them. After all, we would feel equally put out if a giant shook the very foundations of our homes."

Aunt Millward took in Lord Culham's glazed expression and smiled. "You will join us for tea, won't you, my lord?" Without waiting for a response, she pulled the bell and turned to Emily. "Lord Culham was wondering if you plan to attend the Morrises' ball."

"I've heard wonderful things about it," she said.

"You must go, Miss Norton." Lord Culham reentered familiar territory with an ingratiating smile. "Everyone of importance will be there, and I have great hopes of securing the first dance with you before I leave today."

Those two things alone were enough to keep Emily at home, but she mustered a smile. "That is very kind of you, my lord, but I would not have you miss a dance on my account."

"Miss a dance?" He was clearly confused.

Emily clasped her soiled hands on her knee and sighed. "Unfortunately, my attendance at the ball is fully dependent upon the weather. And as England's weather is notoriously fickle, I can make you no promise."

He blinked. "The weather, Miss Norton?"

Vaguely aware of a knock on the front door, Emily pinned a regretful expression to her face. "Why, yes, my lord. I'm sure you are aware that when we have rain, worms vacate their holes in the ground."

"Can you imagine how many worms meet an untimely demise on the wet roads of London when every member of the *ton* is out in their carriage?" Aunt Millward asked.

Something that looked remarkably like panic flashed in Lord Culham's eyes. "I cannot say that I have ever considered—" he began, but he was interrupted by the arrival of the butler.

"I beg your pardon, my lord, my lady, Miss Norton," he said. "Mr. Buckland is come."

Wakefield stepped aside, and Henry walked into the room wearing a dark-blue jacket and brown breeches, with his satchel across his shoulder.

Henry's annoyance at seeing Lord Culham seated in Aunt Millward's drawing room was immediately followed by an intense—and uncomfortably telling—stab of jealousy.

At Wakefield's announcement, the dandy rose. "Good day, Buckland."

"Culham."

Henry barely acknowledged the man before turning his gaze on Emily's sweet face. She smiled, and his heart responded. He'd been a fool to stay away so long. How many other gentlemen had come to call on her while he'd been immersed in identifying artifacts?

"Henry, how lovely to see you."

Aunt Millward's voice was a timely reminder that Emily was not the only lady in the room. He turned and bowed. "Thank you, Aunt."

"I hope you will join us for tea." She gave him a pointed look. "Lord Culham, Emily, and I were just talking about worms."

Worms? He must have misheard her. "I beg your pardon?"

"Worms," his aunt repeated firmly. "Such as the ones Emily is wont to dig up occasionally."

His head swiveled back to face Emily, and for the first time, he noticed her hands. They were clasped tightly, the dirt caked on her fingers clearly visible against her cream-colored gown. He lifted his gaze and caught her subtle nod.

"Forgive me," he said. "I did not realize that Lord Culham shared Emily's interest in invertebrates."

Culham, Henry was gratified to note, was looking distinctly uneasy and had yet to resume his seat.

"Fascinating creatures," Culham blustered. "Although, I can't say that I have ever studied them extensively."

"Then you are come to the right place, my lord. Miss Norton can tell you anything you wish to know on the subject," Aunt Millward said.

A lady who dug up worms. A titled gentleman who delivered sheep. Henry recognized the pattern and the motive. Aunt Millward was up to her old tricks, and she had his wholehearted support.

"Most certainly," Henry said. "Indeed, if you are a fishing enthusiast, Culham, Miss Norton can also advise you on the most effective bait."

Culham's narrow-set eyes widened, and his Adam's apple bobbed, but he was saved from responding by the arrival of a footman.

"Ah, here is the tea," Aunt Millward said, exhibiting no qualms whatsoever about partaking of a hot drink and a piece of cake after speaking of worms and fish bait. "Please, sit down, gentlemen."

"As loath as I am to leave, I fear I must decline your offer of refreshment, my lady." Culham had found his voice, and if his stiffened stance was any indication, he had no intention of reclaiming his seat. "I thank you and Miss Norton for your hospitality and enlightening conversation, but I have a matter of business that I must attend to before day's end."

"What a shame." Aunt Millward's expression was so sorrowful, Henry half expected her to invite the gentleman back another time. Instead, she and Emily stood. "Thank you for coming, my lord."

Culham bowed. "Of course." He turned to Emily, his jaw tightening as his gaze landed on her soiled fingers. "Miss Norton, I bid you farewell."

Emily bobbed a curtsy. "Farewell, my lord."

With a cursory nod directed at Henry, Culham walked out of the room. No one else moved. Silence descended on the drawing room until the front door thudded closed, and then Aunt Millward dropped into her chair with an unladylike whoosh.

"Praise the heavens," she said.

Henry grinned. "Is that what you say every time I leave too?"

"I almost said it when you walked in." His aunt gave him a stern look. "You gave me quite a scare when you questioned our choice of subject matter, but thankfully, you rallied in the end."

With a chuckle, Henry waited for Emily to take her seat and then slid his satchel off his shoulder and placed it on the floor before claiming Culham's spot on the sofa. "Emily's dirty hands were a nice touch. I shall have to suggest to Benedict that he acquire some props."

Emily gasped. "I must go and wash them before we have tea."

"You do that, dear," Aunt Millward said. "I shall entertain this dilatory gentleman until you return."

CHAPTER 21

Accepting a cup of tea from Aunt Millward with her newly cleaned hands, Emily listened to Henry and his aunt banter back and forth and smiled. It seemed ridiculous that her happiness over Henry's arrival was even greater than her relief that Lord Culham was gone, but she rather thought that Aunt Millward felt similarly.

"You are wearing yourself out, putting in such long hours at the museum, Henry," Aunt Millward said. "It really must stop."

"I am touched that you care so deeply for my wellbeing, Aunt."

"Nonsense. I am simply concerned for those guests who have waited weeks to visit the museum only to walk through the rooms with a curator who is too tired to remember his own name let alone the names of anything on display."

"My name is Horacio Blackguard." He raised an amused eyebrow. "Are you content now?"

Aunt Millward shook her head. "You are impossible."

"True. But I am glad you feed me tea and cake regardless."

Emily smiled behind her teacup. The tension that had filled the room when Lord Culham had been here was gone. Henry made her heart feel lighter. "Did the large delivery you expected at the museum arrive?" she asked.

"It did." He put down his teacup, suddenly serious. "Seven crates from the museum's director in the South Seas."

"Good gracious." Aunt Millward was suitably startled.

Henry pulled a face. "The accessions room may never recover."

He paused, and Emily received the distinct impression that there was something else—something significant—that was weighing on him. Would he share it? She waited, sensing his indecision.

"I don't suppose tidying up was ever your strong suit," Aunt Millward said.

"Unfortunately, you are correct."

It was a trivial comment, but it had the power to shift his attention. His moment of vacillation was gone, and Emily desperately wanted it back. Whatever was bothering Henry had nothing to do with sorting clutter. Of that, she was sure.

She glanced at the french doors. Twilight was falling, but the evening chill had yet to arrive. "Aunt Millward," she said, "if Henry and I promise not to dig anything up, would you allow me to show him the lily of the valley that bloomed this week?"

Aunt Millward appeared surprisingly pleased by her request. Emily did not dare look at Henry. She hoped he would be happy to go outside with her. Or, at the very least, be willing to do so.

"With pleasure," Aunt Millward said. "Although, for the sake of my gardener's nerves, I think his satchel and its contents should remain indoors."

Emily hazarded a quick look at Henry. He was already on his feet.

"A walk in the garden sans trowel would be welcome," he said.

Emily smiled and rose to stand beside him. He offered her his arm, and she took it, distractingly aware of how strong it felt beneath her fingers.

"Shall we?" he asked, pointing to the french doors.

She nodded, and he led her outside.

A robin was singing on a nearby branch and took off in a flurry of feathers as they stepped onto the stone path that circled the small lawn. Higher up the tree, a crow issued a mocking caw at the fleeing robin and remained firmly on its perch, watching them as they walked past.

The distant rumble of carriage wheels and horses' hooves reached them from beyond the terraced houses and garden wall, but the enclosed area of greenery contained a welcome tranquility.

"Henry?"

He slowed his footsteps and looked at her questioningly. "Yes?"

Emily wavered. Had she imagined the anxiety in his expression earlier? Out here, with the late afternoon sun behind him and the steady drone of bees circling the pear tree blossoms above their heads, her concern seemed fanciful.

He was still waiting for her to speak.

She met his gaze, the kindness in his eyes giving her courage. "Is there something weighing on you? In the house, I sensed . . ." She shook her head. This was harder than she'd thought it would be. "You . . . you seemed troubled."

Surprise lit his hazel eyes. "You took the Dowager Lady Pendleton's measure within minutes of meeting her, saw through Lord Culham's facade without prompting, and now this. Such discernment is a rare thing."

"I would never claim that gift," Emily said, "but I have always been more comfortable observing others than being the center of attention."

"And you observed something in me today."

"I thought so." She wrinkled her nose. "Was I wrong?"

He looked away and sighed. "No, you were not wrong."

The heaviness in his voice caused her heart to ache. "Would it help to talk about it? You can count on my discretion."

"True." His smile was strained. "We are the holders of each other's secrets, after all."

"Yes, we are."

They walked a little farther in silence. Up ahead, the robin that had been so recently displaced from the tree swooped down to land on the edge of a stone birdbath. He bent his head to take a drink, noticed Henry and Emily's approach, and took to the sky again.

Raising his head, Henry watched it go until it disappeared over the garden wall. "I had thought I enjoyed a good friendship with Mr. Fernsby, my colleague at the museum," he said. "Today, I came to realize that I may not know him at all."

Emily tightened her grip on his arm. The loss of a friendship, no matter how it occurred, was a painful thing. "Tell me," she encouraged.

He took a deep breath. "This afternoon, I learned that the museum director, Mr. Watts, did not return to England with the items he collected in the South Seas, and the board of trustees have decided to appoint a new director from amongst the curators."

Emily bit her lip to prevent an exclamation. For Henry to have avoided mentioning something so monumental—something that might place him in so prestigious a position—gave reason to believe that the situation was more complicated than it initially appeared.

"The museum has three curators," he continued. "Townsend, Fernsby, and me. Soon before I arrived here, I learned that Townsend has taken himself out of contention. He does not want the position. Fernsby, on the other hand, seems to want it above all else." He tightened his jaw. "I noticed a change in his behavior about a fortnight ago, but I did not know what to attribute it to. I learned today that he caught wind of the director stepping down and has been attempting to position himself as Watts's replacement by actively undermining the chair's confidence in me and Townsend."

"He shall not succeed," Emily said. "How could he? Your work and character speak for themselves."

Henry smiled. "As much as I appreciate your sentiments, the members of the board are unlikely to perceive Fernsby's maneuvering for what it is. Flattery goes a long way amongst members of Society."

"That is ridiculous! Can they not see that you are clearly the best person for the job?"

Henry's smile widened. "A gentleman could not ask for a more valiant champion."

"I am useless," she countered. "I can do nothing more than express my frustration."

"On the contrary." He stopped walking and met her eyes. "Your listening ear and support make a huge difference to me."

"But, Henry—"

"I mean it, Emily. Up until a few hours ago, I had never even considered becoming director of the British Museum. Even now, I am not sure that it is what I want. I recognize the honor and prestige that come with the position, but I am fully aware that such things often come at the cost of one's freedom. Mr. Watts's decision to step down and remain in the South Seas is proof of that." He set his hand over hers on his other arm. "Regardless of what happens, I am truly touched that you believe me so capable."

Emily could not fully identify the emotion in Henry's eyes, but surely, discussing his position at the museum should not make the simple act of breathing so difficult. She needed a distraction. Something safer than Henry's eyes. "We have almost reached the lily of the valley." With her free hand, she pointed to the end of the garden. "It's beneath the wall over there. Do you see it?"

"I do." He smiled, but she did not miss the resignation in his tone. "It helps that they're white."

She winced at the reminder of his difficulty with colors. "How did you manage with the butterflies?"

"Townsend helped," he said. "He was in the accessions room with me most of the time, so it was easy enough to casually ask for his opinion when I needed it."

"I'm glad." Her concern suddenly felt foolish. Of course he would know how to overcome the obstacle. He'd been doing it all his life.

"You are kind to ask. And I'm doubly grateful for this chance to speak with you alone." He slipped his free hand into his pocket, withdrew a piece of paper, and offered it to her. "Along with the crates and their attendant issues, this letter arrived today."

"You wish me to read it?" she asked, surprised.

"Yes."

Puzzled, she lowered her hand from his arm and took the proffered letter. Raising questioning eyes to his, she hesitated.

"Go ahead," he encouraged.

Unfolding the piece of paper, she began to read. By the time she finished the second paragraph, a lump had formed in her throat. "Mr. Dalton wants to meet with you," she said. "Will you agree to it?"

"Yes." There was no vacillating. "I will do everything in my power to aid him in his research."

"And now you know for certain that you are not alone in suffering from this ailment."

He nodded. "Dalton confirmed it, but it was you who offered me the first glimmer of hope that I might find some answers. You are the one to whom I owe my deepest gratitude." He reached out and brushed a stray hair from her face, his fingers skimming her skin. Her breath caught, and his gaze darted from her eyes to her lips. His fingers stilled.

"Henry?" she whispered.

"Forgive me, Emily." His low voice sent a tremor through her. "I did not tell you the whole truth. My feelings for you, they are . . . they are so much more than gratitude."

She met his eyes and saw a reflection of her own vulnerability there. "What makes you think so?" she whispered.

"They're urging me to do very ungrateful-like things."

A thousand butterflies danced in her stomach. "What do you mean?"

"I have an overwhelming compulsion to personally escort Culham off Aunt Millward's property if he ever comes to call upon you again."

"*I* would be very grateful for that," she said.

"What about my strong desire to hold your hand in mine whenever the opportunity arises?"

She felt her cheeks color but did not look away. "I like that one just as much as the first."

"So do I." He threaded his fingers between hers. "And it leads directly into my desperate wish to officially court you."

Joy filled her heart. "I believe that is your very best ungrateful-like feeling of all."

"Does that mean you are willing to allow this red-campion digging gentleman to claim that role in your life?"

"Yes." She laughed. "A hundred times yes." And then a thought struck her. "Do you need to ask Adam? He is gone for several more days."

"I will speak with him upon his return, but in his absence, I will tell Aunt Millward that she is to turn away any other gentleman who comes to the door."

"I rather think she will be pleased with that assignment."

"Good," he said, releasing her hand so that he might wrap his arms around her and draw her close. "Because I've just been hit with another very ungrateful-like inclination."

She did not ask what it was. There was no need. The air around them seemed to still, and all she could hear was the pounding of her heart in her chest. Slowly, he lowered his head until he was so close she could see the flecks of gold in his hazel eyes. He whispered her name, and a wave of longing coursed through her. She leaned into him, and his lips met hers.

CHAPTER 22

HENRY WAS LOST. COMPLETELY AND utterly. He'd not meant for his kiss to be anything more than a fleeting manifestation of his growing affection for Emily, but now that she was in his arms and her lips were on his, he didn't want to be found. Ever.

Somewhere high above him, a bird sang. A light breeze teased his hair, bringing with it the faint scent of lily of the valley and a renewed awareness of where he was. Emily shifted slightly, and he released his hold on her, reluctantly drawing back. She blinked as though struggling to bring her eyes into focus, and then she saw him watching her and smiled. A sweet, shy smile that made his heart ache to gather her into his arms once more. She was as pure as she was kind, as intelligent as she was beautiful, and if his current feelings were anything to go by, he had fallen headlong in love with her.

"Perhaps it's a good thing Adam is not here at the moment," she said.

It was a mindful reminder, and Henry took another step back. "It's a very good thing," he agreed, reaching for her hand as the reality of their situation sank in. If the baron had witnessed that kiss, Henry would have been fortunate to escape the house with his life. Even now, he may have to face an all-too-knowing Aunt Millward. He glanced at the white flowers nearby. "What can you tell me about the lily of the valley if Aunt Millward asks?"

"They are thriving, and she has every reason to be very proud of them."

"Perfect." He started back toward the house, gently pulling her close to him. "We should probably return to the drawing room before she comes looking for us."

Emily tilted her head and eyed him mischievously. "Mr. Henry Buckland, are you afraid of your aunt?"

"Absolutely and completely," he said. "Culham was lucky to escape with only the likelihood of nightmares about worms tonight."

Her laughter brought a smile to his face and resolve to his heart. He would do whatever he must do to be worthy of this incredible young woman.

They reached the pear tree, and her fingers tightened around his.

"I . . . I have something for you," she said. "Would you wait in the drawing room while I fetch it?"

"Of course," he said, halting outside the french door. "May I ask what it is?"

In the dimming light, he sensed her self-consciousness. "It's nothing important, but I made it, and I would like you to have it."

"Gladly," he said.

She withdrew her hand from his. "It will not take me long to retrieve it, but if Aunt Millward questions you regarding more than the lily of the valley, the foxgloves will be coming on soon, and the forsythia blooms on the other side of the garden are spectacular."

He smiled. "Thank you, Emily. I could not ask for a better confidant."

Emily floated up the stairs. Henry had kissed her. He wished to court her. She touched her fingers to her lips, the memory of that earth-shattering moment still lingering. Somehow, over the last month, friendship had become affection, and affection had blossomed into love. She was in love with Henry. It was the only reason she could give for having spent the last week yearning to be with him, for caring so deeply about what he was going through, and for having her knees all but buckle beneath her at his kiss.

She was not sure what had prompted her to offer him the scarf she'd made. Thinking of Henry while she'd been furiously knitting was one thing; giving him the wobbly-edged, overly long final creation was something else entirely. Racked with sudden gnawing doubt, she slowed her footsteps. What had she been thinking? She released a tense breath. That was just it. She hadn't been thinking; she'd been feeling. And now her elation was being choked by misgiving.

Reaching her bedchamber, she opened the door and stepped inside. She spotted her knitting basket immediately, on the hearth beside the fireplace, where Hannah had set it. Hurrying over to it, Emily took out the scarf. The edges really were terribly uneven. And she should have kept better track of how quickly it had grown. But she could not change either of those things now, and Henry was downstairs waiting for her. Waiting for it. Swallowing her pride, she folded the scarf into a fat square and carried it out of the bedchamber.

She heard Henry's voice as she approached the drawing room. He was praising Aunt Millward for her forsythia bush.

"It remains spectacular, even though it is past its prime." He paused. "I daresay your roses will be in bloom soon."

"So the gardener tells me," Aunt Millward replied. "But I will not have you doing anything to those either. Even if you have a sudden yen to give a rose or two to Emily."

Emily entered the room and the conversation. "I do love roses," she said. "My mother planted some bushes at Dunsbourne Manor that produce glorious flowers, but recently, I've been quite taken with red campion."

She did not dare look at Henry, but Aunt Millward eyed her with a knowing mien.

"I grant you, the plant has quite pretty flowers," she said. "Albeit, usually regarded as a weed."

"Weeds are simply flowers planted by a heavenly gardener," Henry said. "And they're altogether underrated."

"Perhaps I should request a bouquet of dandelions for my next birthday," Aunt Millward said dryly.

"A splendid idea," Henry said. "I shall see to it myself. They will be just as bright and cheerful as your forsythia blooms."

Aunt Millward shook her head helplessly, and Emily tried not to laugh.

"He is incorrigible, Emily. Do not encourage him."

"She's not encouraging me," Henry said, "but I believe she has brought me a gift."

Aunt Millward's attention shifted to the square of green wool in Emily's hands. "Did you really, my dear? I did not realize you were fetching something for Henry. How very kind of you."

Desperately wishing that this gift giving had not mushroomed into a somewhat public, overblown affair, Emily offered the lopsided neckwear to Henry. "It's a scarf," she said, thinking it probably needed an explanation. "Not a very well made one, I'm afraid. But Adam tells me that the one I made for him keeps his neck quite warm."

"You knitted this for me?" There was no humor in Henry's voice now. He'd unrolled it, and it hung all the way to the floor. "It must have taken you weeks."

"One week," Emily said, battling discomfiture. "I have become quite fast, even if the quality of my work has not improved significantly."

"It's marvelous." Henry draped it over his shoulders, the wonder in his eyes attesting to the sincerity of his words. "Truly."

"It's lovely, my dear," Aunt Millward said.

"Thank you. I'm glad you like it."

Henry wound the scarf around his neck three times and stood with his arms extended. "What do you think?"

"I think you are a very fortunate gentleman," Aunt Millward said. "And that you will be far too hot if you wear it in a hackney cab all the way home."

"You are right on both counts." Henry began unwinding the scarf. "I shall put it in my satchel for safe-keeping and will wear it when I walk to the museum first thing in the morning."

With the scarf in one hand, he reached for the satchel he'd set beside the sofa with his other. Lifting the flap, he went to put the scarf inside and froze.

"Emily," he said, "would you hold this for me?"

Puzzled, she stepped closer and took the proffered scarf. Henry reached into his satchel and withdrew something small. Opening his hand, he stared at the wooden object lying on his palm with shock.

"Devil take him!" he said.

Aunt Millward rose from her chair. "What is it, Henry?"

He swung around, extending his hand so that Emily and Aunt Millward could see the polished piece for themselves.

"It's one of the artifacts that arrived in the shipment from the South Seas today," he said. "I assume it's a likeness of one of the indigenous peoples' gods. This one is part of a set of five."

"Where are the others?" Emily asked.

"The last time I saw them, they were all in the accessions room at the museum."

His grim face expressed far more than his words, and Emily's throat went dry. Henry had not known the piece was in his bag, and she did not need to be a museum employee to know that valuable artifacts did not belong there. "Was it Fernsby?" she asked.

"It must have been. He was the only one in the room after Claridge left."

"What does that gentleman masquerading as a peacock have to do with this?" Aunt Millward asked.

Henry clenched his jaw. "Everything."

Aunt Millward's gaze flitted from Henry's pale face to Emily's. "Sit," she said. "Both of you. I believe an explanation is in order."

Emily lowered herself onto the sofa, grateful when Henry chose to sit beside her. Aunt Millward reclaimed the chair she'd been using earlier, her posture rigid, obviously waiting for Henry to begin. Henry's attention remained on the carved object in his hand.

"Look at the stone in the creature's forehead," he said, moving it closer to Emily. "Describe it to me."

"It's red and lustrous," Emily said.

He nodded. "Do you see any marbling? Any other colors?"

"No."

He released a hissing breath. "It's the ruby. It has to be."

"Enough enigmatic muttering, Henry." Aunt Millward's patience was at an end. "Tell me exactly what is going on."

"I was informed today that Mr. Watts, the director of the British Museum, did not return to England with the shipment from the South Seas and has decided to step down from his post. An emergency meeting of the board of trustees has been called for tomorrow afternoon at one o'clock at Lord Southbeck's residence. The chair of the board, Lord Claridge, wishes to choose Watts's successor from amongst the current curators. Townsend has already refused the position, leaving Fernsby and me as the only contenders." He tightened his grip on the carving. "It seems that Fernsby wants the job badly enough to place a stolen artifact in my bag, presumably so that he might accuse me of the crime before the board."

"That is preposterous!"

"Preposterous, scandalous, underhanded," Henry said. "Call it what you will, for a reason known only to Fernsby, he considers the directorship position to be of greater value than our friendship or his integrity."

"Why did you ask about the embedded stone?" Emily said.

"Each of the pieces in the set sports a different jewel. Fernsby asked me which I thought was the most valuable. Having not examined them thoroughly, I could only guess."

"But you suggested the ruby," Emily finished for him.

"Yes." Henry appeared contemplative. "Fernsby left the accessions room soon after that discussion. I stayed behind to clear a path through the crates to the tables. It did not take me long, but it must have been enough time for him to transfer this from his pocket to my satchel."

"He cannot be allowed to get away with this," Aunt Millward said.

"He won't." Henry was adamant. He wrapped the artifact in Emily's scarf, placed the bundle in his bag, and stood. "I must return this to the museum tonight and make sure the other pieces of the set are where they should be. In the morning, I will confront Fernsby, and the board of trustees will hear the truth."

A prickle of fear skittered down Emily's spine. She did not know Mr. Fernsby like Henry did, but she'd witnessed Adam challenge a criminal and had firsthand knowledge of the terror such a person could unleash when he was cornered. "You must not face him alone." She rose to stand beside him, her hands clasped tightly. "Please, Henry."

His expression softened. "Do not concern yourself over me. Fernsby is always the last to arrive in the morning; Townsend and Rutherford will be there."

"Emily is right, Henry." Aunt Millward was firm. "Whatever is motivating Mr. Fernsby's despicable actions is not likely to disappear when he learns he's been found out. Quite the opposite, in fact. He is more than likely to act rashly."

"If it will allay your fears, I will send word to you after I have spoken to him."

"You must do that much, at least," Aunt Millward said.

"Very well."

Aunt Millward appeared satisfied.

Emily, on the other hand, could not rid herself of her disquiet. "Promise me that you will be careful," she said.

He leaned forward and brushed her cheek with his lips. "Do not fret," he whispered. "I shall see you again soon."

"Henry Buckland! What are you thinking?"

At Aunt Millward's exclamation, Henry's lips curved upward. "Forgive me, Aunt Millward, I should have mentioned it earlier." He slipped the strap of his satchel over his shoulder. "As of this evening, Emily and I are officially courting."

It was not exactly how Emily had envisioned him sharing the news with the older lady, but given the gratified expression on Aunt Millward's face, it seemed that he had done enough. Henry must have thought so too, because his smile widened.

"Good evening, ladies," he said. And then he hurried out of the room.

CHAPTER 23

THE HACKNEY CAB ROLLED UP the drive and stopped at the base of the stairs leading to the British Museum's front doors. Cutting a large black block out of the star-filled sky, the imposing building loomed over the darkened grounds. Devoid of light or the usual sound of voices, it had a mausoleum-like air, which, given the building's contents, was not far from the truth.

Henry exited the hackney. His feet crunched on the gravel, and the driver looked down from his perch.

"Want me t' wait fer a bit?" he asked, his face illuminated by the moonlight.

"Thank you, but no." Henry reached up to pay the man. "I'm not sure how long I will be."

"Righto." The driver tugged on the brim of his hat. "Good evenin' to ya, sir."

The wheels started rolling, and as the carriage disappeared into the gloom, Henry mounted the steps. When he reached the top, he opened his satchel and dug out his keys.

The bolt on the large front door slid back with a solid thud, but the door opened without a squeak. Rutherford obviously kept the hinges well oiled. Keeping the door ajar to allow a small portion of moonlight into the entrance hall, Henry approached the porter's desk. There had been many times during the winter when Henry had left work after dusk. Rutherford had always lit the candle he placed on the corner of the table with a flint stored in the drawer beneath. Fortunately, both items were still there.

It took only a moment for the wick to catch. Holding the candle high, Henry relocked the front door and walked across the entrance hall. Glassy eyes watched him from the stuffed giraffe and bear standing guard on either side of the staircase. Purposely ignoring them, he started upward. The candle flickered, sending dancing shadows up the walls and onto the ceiling high above. He cupped his hand around the flame and continued ascending until he arrived on the landing.

Upon reaching his office, he unlocked the door and walked inside. Setting the candle on his desk, he slid his satchel off his shoulder and opened it. He withdrew the scarf and carefully unrolled the fabric until the wooden idol appeared. Moving closer to the candle, he held the figure within the circle of light. The stone in the creature's forehead winked at him, igniting Henry's ire. If Fernsby's attempt to implicate him in the theft of something so rare had been successful, the repercussions for Henry and the museum would have been disastrous. Henry could only hope that restoring this item to the accessions room would complete the set once more.

Leaving his bag on the floor and his scarf across the back of his chair, he picked up the candle and left his office. From somewhere outside, a dog howled, the eerie sound filtering through the windows and into the empty landing. There was a muffled bump. Henry stopped, raising the candle and moving it in a slow circle to better see the doorways of the nearby rooms. All the doors were closed. Shaking off his unease, he continued along the landing until he reached the accessions room. A twist of the doorknob confirmed that it was locked.

He turned the key in the keyhole. The bolt slid back with a click that filled the empty space around him. He held perfectly still. Hearing no other sounds, he opened the door and walked inside.

The room looked just as it had when he'd left it. His attempt at clearing some of the straw from the floor was clearly visible, as was the rudimentary path leading from the door to the nearest table. Keeping the candle low enough to watch for anything on the ground that might trip him, he made his way across the room. Shadows of every shape and form surrounded him, but he kept his focus on the items gathered atop the table, scouring the area for the matching idols.

A wooden mask, three rustic bowls, an assortment of spears, and then he spotted them. Four polished wood idols lined up behind a rolled-up rattan mat. Releasing a tense breath, Henry set the idol that had been in his satchel beside its mates and raised the candle above them. The stones embedded in each one gleamed back at him. He had no way of knowing if anything else had been stolen from the room, but this set, at least, was complete once more.

Retracing his footsteps, he exited the room and closed the door. He had just turned the key in the lock when he heard another click, this one coming from farther down the landing. Swinging around, he saw the faint light of an approaching candle coming around the corner. His pulse racing, he blew out his own flame and pressed himself into the shadows of the accessions room doorway right before someone came into view.

Height and wardrobe identified the person as a male. He was moving purposefully, his footsteps brisk and sure. In the darkness, it was impossible to spot any identifying features on his face or the color of his clothing, but a long shadow followed his movement along the tiled floor and accentuated a rectangular object in his arms. Henry strained to see better. Who was it? And what was he doing?

The footsteps slowed near the door to the Montagu room, and Henry heard the jingle of keys. Unless they'd been stolen, being in possession of keys narrowed down the number of suspects considerably. The lock clicked, and the man pushed open the door. Before entering the room, he raised the candle, and for that split second, Henry saw his face, his ostentatious cravat, and the white pinstripes on his jacket.

Leaning his head against the accessions room door, Henry took a couple of deep breaths, attempting to control the anger roiling within him. He did not know what Fernsby was about, but given the current circumstances and the man's recent activities, he was convinced it was nothing honorable.

Waiting only until Fernsby disappeared inside the room, Henry stepped away from the accessions room doorway. The faint glow coming from Fernsby's candle guided Henry the short distance to the open door. Pressing himself against the wall, he peered around the doorframe. Fernsby had set the candle on one of the display cases, and by its light, he was removing a canvas from the wall. A glimpse of green and its location in the room was enough to remind Henry of the painting's details. It was a pastoral scene—one that reminded him of the rolling hills near his property in Shropshire—created by Jacob Hackert.

Fernsby set the painting on the display case next to the candle and picked up the rectangular object beside it. This must have been what he had been carrying earlier. The candlelight picked up the gilded frame of another painting. Fernsby held it aloft, studying it. As far as Henry could tell, the green and brown tones were the same. Exactly the same, in fact.

A gaping pit formed in Henry's stomach as he watched Fernsby hang the new canvas where the other one had been. Fernsby stepped back to ensure that it was straight, and Henry entered the room.

"Which one is the original, Fernsby?" he asked.

Fernsby pivoted. "Buckland! What are you doing here?"

"I could ask you the same thing," Henry said, balling his fists. "Although, perhaps creeping through the museum at night is a routine occurrence for you."

Fernsby flinched. He was not completely without feeling, then.

"You know nothing about what I do," he said.

"So I have recently learned," Henry said. "Why don't you enlighten me."

"Spare me the attitude of moral superiority, Buckland. Taking the higher ground is all too easy when there are no obstacles in your way."

"Do you happen to know anyone whose life is completely without hindrance?"

"Yes," Fernsby spat. "You."

Henry's lifelong struggle with color vision flashed through his mind, but he dismissed it. This conversation was not about him; it was about Fernsby. "If you truly believe that, then your knowledge of my life is as limited as mine is of yours."

Fernsby snorted. "Have you ever had to wonder how to pay your bills? Of course not. You have an inheritance, an income wholly separate from this curator hobby of yours. What of the crushing burden of knowing that you and your passions are nothing more than a disappointment to your family? No. That one is equally foreign to you, isn't it?

"I am an artist, Buckland. A blasted good one, at that. I spent three years in Paris honing my craft, and do you know who cares? No one. No one but me. I could barely sell one of my paintings for enough money to keep bread on the table. My father was so ashamed of my chosen profession that he cut me off—told me that I must put aside my ridiculous penchant for painting and actually make something of myself. And so here I am." He waved his arm to encompass the Montagu room. "A curator at the British Museum. Is it enough for my father? No. He will not be happy until I am the director. And is it enough for me? No." His eyes flashed wildly. "I was born to paint."

"And so you use your talent to make forgeries," Henry guessed.

Fernsby smirked contemptuously. "You would be amazed at how many members of the *ton* have dismissed my original artwork as not worth their time only to unwittingly purchase one for an obscene amount simply because I put another artist's signature on it."

If Henry allowed himself to consider the full ramifications of what Fernsby was doing—what he had already done—to the original artists, to those who bought the paintings, and to the museum, he would be unable to contain his fury. Somehow, he must set aside his abhorrence of Fernsby's actions long enough to think through a means of preventing him from following through with his present and future nefarious activities. "So who is to receive your version of Hackert's painting?" he asked.

Fernsby laughed. It was a mirthless sound that set Henry's teeth on edge. "My broker takes care of such details, but even if I knew, I would not tell you. I am not so foolhardy as all that." He tucked the painting under his arm. "And now, as pleasant as this discussion has been, I think it is time to end it."

Henry stepped in front of him. "Leave the painting behind."

"Move out of my way, Buckland."

"Only after you've set down the painting."

Fernsby glared at him with narrowed eyes. "You'll have to do better than that."

Henry did not need a second invitation. He pulled back his arm and swung. His fist connected with Fernsby's jaw. The man's head jerked back, and with a curse, he stumbled sideways.

"Put the painting down," Henry repeated.

"As you wish." In one swift movement, Fernsby set the frame on top of the display and spun around, his fist plowing into Henry's abdomen.

Henry doubled over, and Fernsby let his fist fly again. This time, Henry anticipated the punch, stumbling to the left before Fernsby's hand could connect with his face. Still winded, he shifted right, stepping just outside the circle of candlelight as Fernsby darted forward.

Henry moved again, this time to the left. Fernsby was cloaked in darkness, moving on silent feet. Only the occasional rasp of breath hinted that someone else was in the room. With arms extended, Henry inched forward, knowing the fossil display was close. Behind him, a thud was followed by a smothered curse. If Fernsby had run into the ancient coins case, he was fewer than three yards away.

Switching directions so that he was moving toward the wall, Henry mentally reviewed the items in this room. He could hardly use a painting or valuable museum piece as a weapon. The risk of doing irrevocable damage to the objects was too great. Beyond those articles, his only option was a wooden chair that sat near the door. He turned to work his way toward the exit.

A flicker of movement on the fringes of the candlelight caught his attention. He backed right and clipped the corner of another display case. His grunt was barely audible, but Fernsby must have been listening. The man rushed forward, his head low, and barreled into Henry. Henry swung right and then left, connecting with Fernsby's stomach twice before going down with Fernsby on top of him.

Like a hammer against an anvil, Henry's head hit the floor with a resounding crack. Pain consumed him, stealing his breath, slowing his motion, and clouding his thoughts. And then there was nothing.

CHAPTER 24

EMILY LOOKED AT THE CLOCK on the drawing room mantel for about the tenth time in the last eight minutes. Quarter past eleven in the morning. Surely Henry had had the opportunity to speak with Mr. Fernsby by now. They both should have arrived at the museum hours ago. But if that was the case, where was the messenger he'd promised to send?

Closing her book, she set it on the nearby end table. She'd reread the same lines at least half a dozen times but could not repeat a single word. All she could think of was what Henry might be facing. Terrifying memories of Adam's run-in with a criminal a year and a half ago had haunted her night, and though it was extremely unlikely that Fernsby was nearly so vicious as Adam's nemesis, she could not countenance the thought that a man she loved was once again facing someone who wished him ill.

Attempting to quell her rising anxiety, she thought through what little she knew. Henry had said the meeting with the board of trustees was scheduled for one o'clock at Lord Southbeck's house. According to Aunt Millward, it would take a carriage fifteen minutes to travel there from the museum. Henry would not want to be late. Neither would Mr. Fernsby. They would likely leave for the meeting soon after half past twelve.

She took an unsteady breath. Another fifteen minutes. If a messenger did not arrive from Henry by then, she would order Aunt Millward's carriage and discover what had happened for herself.

"Ah, there you are, Emily."

Emily turned to see Aunt Millward walk into the room, a shawl over her shoulders and her peacock feather hat upon her head.

Emily rose to greet her. "Good day, Aunt Millward."

"Yes, well, that remains to be seen, doesn't it?" The older lady pressed her fingers into her gloves. "I believe the time has come to discover what has happened to Henry and the message he was supposed to send us. I am off to visit the Farwells' home, and if he is not there, I shall continue on to the museum. Would you like to accompany me?"

"Yes!" The single word doubled as a cry of relief, and Emily was across the room in an instant. "I will join you in the hall as soon as I have my hat and gloves."

Half an hour later, Emily descended from the carriage in front of Lord and Lady Farwell's house and took her place at Aunt Millward's side. Together, they mounted the steps to the front door. Aunt Millward raised the knocker. The rat-a-tat-tat reverberated through the door, jarring Emily's frayed nerves. She understood Aunt Millward's desire to check the house first. It was closer than the museum, and if Henry was not here, surely someone within—either Henry's parents or a servant—would know where he was.

The door opened, and the butler who had welcomed Emily when she'd come to the dinner party bowed in greeting. "Good day, Lady Millward," he said. "Miss Norton."

"Good day, Akers," Aunt Millward said. "We are come to talk to Mr. Buckland."

"I'm afraid Mr. Buckland is unavailable, my lady."

Emily's heart sank, but Aunt Millward appeared undeterred.

"Very well. I will speak to Lady Farwell."

Maintaining an unruffled expression, Akers delivered further bad news. "Lord and Lady Farwell have gone to the country, my lady. They left a few days ago and won't be back for a fortnight or more."

"Good heavens." Aunt Millward's peacock feathers bobbed up and down in indignation. "How inconvenient."

"I am sorry that I cannot be of greater assistance, my lady."

"Oh, but you can." Aunt Millward smiled. "We simply need to know what time Mr. Buckland left for the museum this morning."

"I cannot say, my lady."

"Akers," Aunt Millward huffed. "As much as I appreciate your discretion, this is not the time for it. We have known each other for over thirty years. You know full well that I have Mr. Buckland's best interests at heart. I need you to tell me how long he has been gone."

For the first time since their arrival at the door, Akers appeared mildly uncomfortable. "To the best of my knowledge, Mr. Buckland did not return home last night, my lady. I have not seen him since yesterday morning at about nine o'clock, and neither has Felix."

Emily's heart faltered. Henry had not come home after going back to the museum. She did not know what that meant exactly, but she was positive that it was nothing good.

"You are sure of this?" Aunt Millward's tone suddenly became more urgent.

"Yes, my lady."

"Thank you, Akers."

She turned to go, and Emily followed. They said nothing until they reached the carriage.

"To the British Museum, Robert," Aunt Millward called to her driver. "As fast as you can."

"Yes, my lady."

Aunt Millward climbed into the carriage and took her seat.

"I fear this does not omen well, Emily," she said, her expression uncharacteristically grim. "Either Henry did something that has caused him to come afoul of Mr. Fernsby, or he slept the night at the museum and will come afoul of me for causing us such anxiety."

"If we have a choice," Emily said, "I would prefer the second option."

"As would I. Although, Henry might not."

Emily attempted a half smile. They would find him at the museum. They had to.

The ride to the museum was agonizingly long. Occasionally, their carriage would slow to allow another carriage to pass by. Pedestrians filled the pavement, each intent on their own destinations. Vendors stood on the corners, hawking their wares with stray dogs looking on. Not one of them knew of Emily's inner turmoil or her need for haste.

At last, the crunch of the gravel drive beneath the carriage wheels announced their arrival at the museum. Emily slid to the edge of her seat, exiting as soon as Aunt Millward was clear of the door.

"Calmly now," Aunt Millward said, straightening her shoulders and facing the door. "We must appear to be making a casual visit."

"Will we be allowed in without tickets?"

"Yes."

Emily slipped her arm through the older lady's. She had no idea how Aunt Millward planned to circumvent the usual requirement for entry, but whatever method she used, Emily would be right beside her.

When they reached the top step, the porter was there to greet them with the door open. "Good day, Lady Millward," he said, bowing. "Miss Norton."

"Good day, Rutherford," Aunt Millward said. "We are here to see Mr. Buckland."

Rutherford frowned. "I can't say that I've seen Mr. Buckland this morning, my lady."

"How very odd." Aunt Millward looked suitably perplexed. "He specifically told us to come today, did he not, Emily?"

"Yes," Emily said. "He was quite clear. We were to come before one o'clock."

"I believe some of the curators have a meeting to attend at Lord Southbeck's house at that time," Rutherford said. "Is it possible he's gone ahead?"

"Most unlikely," Aunt Millward said. She appeared to ponder the idea a moment. "Has Mr. Fernsby left already?"

"No, my lady. He offered to take Mr. Buckland's tour since the gentleman hadn't arrived." He glanced at his pocket watch. "It should be finishing anytime now."

"How very noble of him."

If Rutherford caught the bite in Aunt Millward's compliment, he did not show it.

"Mr. Townsend will take the rest of the tours this afternoon," he said.

"Well, Miss Norton and I don't want to keep you from your duties or get in the way of your other guests," Aunt Millward said. "We will just slip upstairs to check Mr. Buckland's office. We won't be long."

"Allow me to go for you, my lady."

Rutherford had obviously practiced polite ways of telling guests that they could not roam freely around the museum.

"No, no." Aunt Millward dismissed the idea with a wave of her hand and the peacock feathers. "We both know exactly where it is."

Voices sounded outside. Rutherford opened his mouth, glanced at the door, and then appeared to change his mind. "If you wouldn't mind restricting yourself to visiting Mr. Buckland's office only, I'd be much obliged," he said. "The tours—"

"I understand completely," Aunt Millward said, already moving across the entrance hall. "We shall be back downstairs before you know it."

A knock sounded, and Rutherford stepped forward to admit the latest visitors.

"Straight up the stairs, Emily," Aunt Millward said softly. "We have no time to waste."

A murmur of voices met them when they reached the landing. It seemed that the current visitors had reached the gallery of antiquity. It would be only a matter of minutes before Mr. Fernsby completed the tour and led them downstairs again.

Turning away from the gallery, they hurried along the landing to Henry's office. Emily reached it first and gave a light knock on the door before trying the handle.

"It's unlocked," she said, pushing it open.

Aunt Millward followed her in, and Emily closed the door behind them. Sunlight was streaming in through the large windows, illuminating dust particles hanging in the air and reflecting off the shiny inkwell on Henry's desk.

"It doesn't look like he's been here for some time," Aunt Millward said, eyeing the open book lying beside the inkwell. "His quill is dry, and the most recent entry in the ledger is dated yesterday."

Emily walked around the desk, coming to a halt when she reached the chair.

"He may not have been here today, but he was here last night," she said, lifting Henry's satchel off the ground and setting it on the desk. "Henry doesn't go anywhere without this."

Aunt Millward joined her and reached for the green scarf draped across the back of the chair. "And he wouldn't willingly leave this behind either."

Swallowing the lump in her throat, Emily lifted the satchel's flap and riffled through the contents.

"The wood carving is gone," she said. "Henry either put it back with the others, or Fernsby took it."

"Are Henry's keys in there?"

"No."

Were they with Henry, or had they been stolen with the artifact?

"Rutherford will have another set," Aunt Millward said. "We need access to every room in this building."

On the other side of the closed door, footsteps and muted voices passed by.

"The tour is leaving," Emily whispered.

Aunt Millward nodded. "As soon as they're gone, we'll go downstairs and talk to Rutherford again."

Setting down the satchel and scarf where they'd found them, they waited. When it had been at least two minutes since they'd last heard a voice, Emily opened the door a crack. The landing was clear. Pulling the door fully open, she stepped out, waiting for Aunt Millward to follow before she softly closed the door behind her.

"Good day, Lady Millward."

Emily's heart leaped to her throat as Mr. Fernsby appeared at the top of the stairs. Dressed in a yellow brocade jacket with blue breeches, he eyed them guardedly.

"Mr. Fernsby!" Aunt Millward placed her hand to her chest. "You gave me quite a fright."

"My apologies." He bowed. "Visitors are not generally permitted in this portion of the museum unless they are part of a tour, so I confess, I was equally startled to see you." He paused. "May I be of assistance?"

"Not unless you can tell us where Mr. Buckland might be," she said.

Emily watched his face. A twitch in his jaw was the only indication that anything might be amiss, but the slight movement drew her attention to an area of purple discoloration on his chin. Was it a bruise?

"I'm afraid not." There was a polite hint of regret in Mr. Fernsby's response to Aunt Millward. "He hasn't been seen at the museum all day."

Aunt Millward frowned. "How very odd. Try the door one more time, my dear."

Mentally applauding the older lady's quick thinking, Emily knocked on the empty office door. As expected, they were met with silence.

"He appears to be gone," Emily said. "We shall have to try visiting him another day."

"Well, I daresay artifacts that have remained hidden for centuries will not change much in a week," Aunt Millward said. She took Emily's arm. "Come. We shall console ourselves by going to the milliner's shop. No young lady should be without a hat decorated by peacock feathers, do you not think, Mr. Fernsby?"

"Peacock feathers have much to recommend them, my lady."

He smiled, and Emily sensed more than a little relief in the expression. She had yet to be formally introduced to the man, and for that, she was glad. As much as she never wished to wear a hat sporting bouncing feathers of any kind, she itched to be out of his presence.

"A new bonnet is a wonderful idea," she said.

Aunt Millward gave a pleased nod. "It seems that we are embarking on an alternate activity for the afternoon, Mr. Fernsby. Good day to you."

"Allow me to walk you out," he said.

"Thank you, but there is no need for you to trouble yourself."

"It is no trouble at all." He raised one arm and gestured toward the stairs. "I was planning on leaving for a meeting myself."

To demure further would have raised his suspicions, so with an acquiescent nod, Aunt Millward and Emily started across the landing. Mr. Fernsby followed close behind. His footsteps echoed theirs down the marble stairs, the steady rhythm marking their removal from the museum like the beat of an ominous drum.

Emily felt his eyes upon her and suppressed her instinctive shudder. The man may have perfected an impressive facade, but he could not replicate the light that shone from a person's eyes when they went about doing good. Like the light that shone in Henry's eyes. She tightened her grip on Aunt Millward's arm. If that light had been snuffed out by this awful pretender, she did not know what she would do.

"Take heart, my dear." They had reached the entrance hall, and Aunt Millward had picked up her pace. "I believe we shall find exactly what you are looking for today."

Pushing past the despair threatening to creep into her heart, Emily managed a weak smile. "I have that same hope."

"I am glad to hear it. Over the years, I have learned that hope wields a great deal of power."

Grateful for the reminder, Emily raised her chin a fraction. Hope would get her through until she had something more tangible to hold on to. They would find Henry because they would not give up until they did.

"No luck, my lady?" Rutherford stepped out from behind his table. The visitors he'd admitted earlier must already be in the manuscript saloon with Mr. Townsend.

"I'm afraid not, Rutherford," Aunt Millward said. "We shall return again before long."

"Very good, my lady." He moved to open the door for them.

"You may resume your other responsibilities, Rutherford." Mr. Fernsby spoke from directly behind Emily. "I shall walk the ladies out."

"As you wish, sir."

They exited the building. Aunt Millward's carriage was parked not far from where they'd disembarked. Two more carriages were parked a little farther up the driveway, presumably awaiting the return of the museum's visitors, and as they started down the shallow steps, a hackney cab rolled up the drive toward them.

Aunt Millward's driver saw them coming and left his perch to open the carriage door for them.

"Thank you, Robert," Aunt Millward said.

"Of course, my lady." He bowed and offered her his hand to assist her into the vehicle. It did not escape Emily's notice that Aunt Millward had failed to acknowledge Mr. Fernsby again after their removal from the upper floor of the museum. He stood nearby, but Emily considered Aunt Millward's example worthy of emulation, and so without so much as a glance his direction, she accepted the driver's assistance into carriage.

Robert closed the door and climbed onto his perch again. Mr. Fernsby took one step back from the carriage, and it rolled forward.

"Are we really leaving?" Emily asked.

"Yes."

Panic welled. "But Henry . . ."

Aunt Millward raised her hand to stop her. "I refuse to turn around to give that odious man my attention, but you are faced the right way. Tell me, can you see what he is about now that we are on our way?"

Emily leaned slightly to her left. "He's entering the hackney cab."

"Excellent." Aunt Millward leaned back in her seat. "If—as I suspect—he is headed to Lord Southbeck's house, he will instruct the hackney driver to turn left at the gate. We shall turn right."

It was true. To return to Aunt Millward's house would require a right turn, but Emily did not wish to return to Aunt Millward's house. Or to go to the milliner's shop. Or anywhere else, for that matter.

"But what of Henry?"

"Did Mr. Fernsby turn left?" Aunt Millward asked.

Tamping down her frustration, Emily checked the window. "Yes."

"Perfect."

Emily could see nothing whatsoever that was perfect about their current situation, but without further explanation, Aunt Millward reached for a cane lying below her seat, raised it, and tapped the side of the carriage three times. The vehicle slowed, coming to a stop a few yards farther down the street.

"Drop the window, Emily," Aunt Millward said.

Emily did as she asked, and moments later, Robert appeared at the door.

"You signaled, my lady?"

"I did." Aunt Millward spoke through the open window. "Miss Norton and I have some unfinished business at the museum. Drive around the building and then take us back to the front door. The faster, the better."

"Right away, my lady."

Robert disappeared, and Emily barely had time to process what Aunt Millward had said before the carriage wheels began rolling at a far greater speed than before.

CHAPTER 25

HENRY NEEDED WATER. HE TRIED swallowing, but his swollen tongue was blocked by the fabric tied around mouth. Closing his eyes against the pain pulsating through his head, he pulled against the rope at his wrists once more. He could not see his hands—they were tied behind his back—but if the discomfort he was experiencing was anything to go by, his skin was raw and bleeding.

He had to hand it to Fernsby. The man had done a thorough job. Henry had no idea how he'd managed to get him into one of the recently emptied crates on his own, but if the throbbing in his right shoulder and hip was any indication, he'd been dragged and then dropped—more than once. His body barely fit in the confined space. His knees were bent and his shoulders hunched. Turning his head slightly, he groaned at the searing pain the slight movement produced, even as the gag in his mouth muffled the sound.

The angle of the light coming in through the chinks between the slats had changed since he'd first awoken to find himself trussed hand and foot in the confined space. If he had to guess, he would say the crate was still in the accessions room and that it was now nearing noon—which was dangerously close to the time of the board of trustees meeting. He tugged at the ropes around his wrists in futile frustration. It was highly unlikely that Townsend or Rutherford would have reason to enter the accessions room today, and the locked door would prevent any visitors from inadvertently stumbling in. The likelihood of his being discovered soon was bleak, at best; his chances of escaping on his own were almost none.

His thoughts turned to Emily, and his heart ached. He'd failed her. She'd begged him to be careful, to not approach Fernsby alone. He should have listened. She was probably at Aunt Millward's house now, patiently reading a book while waiting for a messenger who would never come. Closing his eyes to the agony that vision produced, he offered a silent prayer. At this point, prayer was all he had left.

If Rutherford was surprised by Lady Millward and Emily's hasty return to the museum, he was sufficiently well-trained to hide it. He opened the door, admitting them into the empty entrance hall with a bow. "May I be of assistance, Lady Millward?"

"You may," Aunt Millward said briskly. "I require your keys."

He stared at her. "I beg your pardon, my lady?"

"Your keys, Rutherford. Mr. Buckland is missing, and Miss Norton and I intend to search every room in the museum to find him."

"I grant that it is highly irregular for Mr. Buckland to be absent without sending word ahead of time, my lady, but I am honor bound to uphold the rules of the museum, and they clearly state that guests cannot roam freely within the building."

Aunt Millward stiffened, but before she could retort, Emily stepped forward. "Perhaps you could accompany us," she said. "That way you could ensure that we do nothing untoward, and we would benefit from your knowledge of the building's floor plan."

Rutherford shifted his feet uneasily. "It is not my place to give tours, miss."

"I realize that, but we do not need a tour in the normal sense of the word. We simply need to have a quick look inside every room."

"Is there a reason why you believe Mr. Buckland to be here?" he asked.

"He left Lady Millward's house last evening, intent on returning to the museum," Emily said. "He has not been seen since."

Rutherford's furrowed brow showed his concern. "Could he have been involved in an accident?"

"We believe it likely," Aunt Millward said. "But if it occurred on a public road, word would have reached Benning House by now. As it is, no one there has seen or heard from Mr. Buckland since yesterday."

"So you believe he met with a serious injury here?"

It sounded far-fetched even to Emily's ears, but Rutherford did not know of Mr. Fernsby's duplicity. "It is a possibility we wish to confirm or rule out by checking every room," she said.

Rutherford glanced at the manuscript saloon. A faint hum of voices came from beyond the closed door. Emily did not know how much longer the museum's visitors would be there, but they had to act before the tour group started upstairs.

"Time is of the essence, Rutherford." Aunt Millward's patience was wearing thin; Emily's was in shreds.

"Please, Rutherford," Emily begged. "If we go now, we would not interfere with Mr. Townsend's tour."

The porter hesitated for a few seconds more, and then he gave a slight nod. "Very well. I'll take you around. But only because it's Mr. Buckland who's missing."

"Thank you, Rutherford." Emily's voice caught. It was only the first step, but it was a significant one.

He opened a drawer in the desk beside the front door and withdrew a large ring of keys.

"Where do you want to start?" he asked.

"Mr. Fernsby's office," Aunt Millward said firmly.

Rutherford straightened, apprehension in his eyes. "Going into the locked storage and collection rooms is one thing; going into the curators' private offices seems like something else entirely."

"We've already been in Mr. Buckland's office, and I'm more than happy to speak to Mr. Townsend before entering his. Mr. Fernsby's is the only remaining one, and it cannot be missed." Aunt Millward began marching toward the stairs. "Come. We've wasted enough time already."

Emily hurried after Aunt Millward, and with another quick look at the manuscript saloon door, Rutherford followed after them.

Aunt Millward maintained her rapid momentum all the way up the stairs. By the time she reached the landing, she was breathing heavily, but she pointed down the hall. "Mr. Fernsby's office, if you please."

Squaring his shoulders, Rutherford led the way. They passed Henry's office and three display rooms before the porter stopped and sorted through the keys on the ring in his hand. Singling out one, he slid it into the lock and turned it. Emily's heart pounded uncomfortably in her chest. Rutherford opened the door and then stepped back so that Aunt Millward and Emily could enter.

The small room was surprisingly spartan. A large table and two chairs took up the bulk of the space. The only objects on the table were an inkwell, quill, and small pile of clean paper. Three large easels stood holding canvases, and a pile of empty frames lay on the floor beside them. A box containing paint and brushes sat on the end of a shelf, and the remainder of the space was taken by books.

It was obvious that the usual occupant of the room enjoyed painting, but that appeared to be the only clue to his identity. The personal touches common in most gentlemen's studies were missing. There was no hat or scarf. No handwritten notes. No plants on the shelf and no art on the wall. It appeared that Mr. Fernsby hung paintings everywhere in the museum except within his own office.

Aunt Millward circled the table before returning to join Emily and Rutherford at the door. Nothing needed to be said. There was no sign of Henry or any hint of a physical struggle.

"What is the next locked door, Rutherford?" she asked.

"That would be the art storage room, my lady."

"Very well. We shall go there now."

Rutherford waited for them to exit Mr. Fernsby's room before closing the door and locking it behind him. He then moved to the next door and unlocked it. Once again, he stood aside to allow the ladies to enter. This room was long and narrow. The walls were covered in deep shelves that housed stacks of framed art. Emily walked the length of the room, glancing at the artwork as she searched for anything that might be out of place. It did not take long.

"Next," Aunt Millward said.

Rutherford locked the door behind them and continued across the landing, leading them past four display rooms before stopping at another door. Emily stared at it, tears pricking the back of her eyes. She'd been here before on a happier day. This was the room that had housed the butterfly collection when it had first arrived. And it was where Henry had first kissed her. The light brush of his lips against her cheek hadn't been anything like the earth-shattering kiss they'd shared in the garden so recently, but the tenderness behind it had opened Emily's eyes to what her heart had already known.

"This is the accessions room," Rutherford said, inserting the key in the lock.

Emily took an unsteady breath and blinked away the moisture in her eyes.

Aunt Millward reached for her hand and squeezed it. "We shall find him, Emily. I am sure of it."

The room was almost unrecognizable. Large crates filled what had previously been an open area. Wisps of straw clung to the crates' wooden slats and lay littered across the floor. Most of the crates' lids leaned haphazardly against the open boxes. Two of them—the largest and the smallest—lay on top of their respective crates. The tables that had once housed the butterfly collection and piles of literature were now covered in wooden statues, primitive masks, feather capes, headdresses, earthenware bowls, and spears.

Emily navigated the narrow path between the boxes to the table. She spotted the row of carved idols immediately. Five of them, each bearing a different jewel. Picking up the one containing the ruby, she held it out so that Aunt Millward could see. "Henry was here," she said.

Aunt Millward eyed the piece grimly. "So the all-important question is, Where did he go afterward?"

The sound of voices roused Henry from his stupor. Emily. He'd been thinking of her when he'd lost consciousness again, and now he was hearing her. He forced his eyes open. In his cramped quarters, his eyes were almost the only things he could move without incurring more pain. The narrow beams of light filtering in through the chinks had moved only a little since the last time he'd checked. Perhaps he hadn't been insensible so long this time.

"Check that side of the room, Emily. Rutherford and I will look over here."

Henry's breath caught. Aunt Millward. Surely the words had been too clear to be caused by delirium. Footsteps sounded, coming nearer. Hope fortified by desperation gave his aching limbs strength. He tried calling out but managed nothing more than a soft moan. He swung his knees to the left. They hit the side of the crate. Ignoring the pain, he drew them back and swung again. The thud was muffled by the fabric of his breeches, but he did it a third time.

"Did you hear that?"

It was Emily's voice.

"Emily!" Henry's attempt at calling her name had the same pathetic results as crying out had done. His dry tongue could barely formulate the word, and all sound was stolen by the fabric in his mouth.

"It sounds like the visitors in Mr. Townsend's tour have arrived on this floor."

That was Rutherford, and he sounded anxious.

"No," Emily said. "It wasn't that."

Light footsteps drew closer. Henry thumped the side of the crate with his knees again and again.

"It's coming from over here!" Emily cried. "From the big crate."

More hurried footsteps, this time solid and firm.

"Stand back, Miss Norton. Let me see to the lid."

Above his head, the wood creaked, and then there was an ear-splitting crack. One of the strips of wood flew clear, letting in a stream of light. Henry blinked, instinctively turning away from the bright sunlight only to moan in pain as the tender spot on the back of his head rubbed against the side of the crate.

"Mr. Buckland!" Rutherford's shock was mingled with horror, and it appeared to give the porter additional strength. The remainder of the lid flew off in one giant piece and clattered to the ground. "Don't you worry, sir. We'll have you out of there in no time."

"Dear heaven, what did that terrible man do to you, Henry?" Aunt Millward said.

Henry attempted to focus on the faces swimming above him. Peacock feathers swayed in and out of his vision. He turned his head slightly, ignoring the pain in his desperate search for Emily. And then he saw her. Her dark eyes were filled with tears. She leaned over the edge of the box and reached for his face. He closed his eyes, drawing strength from her soft touch.

"Rutherford, see if you can remove the cravat from his mouth without injuring him further," Aunt Millward said.

Emily disappeared, replaced by Rutherford, who started tugging at the cloth. Henry groaned.

"Gently," Aunt Millward warned.

The force of Rutherford's tugging lessened slightly, but he did not give up. "It's almost there, sir."

One more pull and Henry felt the fabric loosen. He held perfectly still as Rutherford drew it out of his mouth and away from his face. Carefully, Henry moved his jaw up and down. It did not appear to be broken.

"Here!" Emily said, handing Rutherford a lethal-looking knife. "This dagger was on the table. See if you can use it to cut his bindings."

"Spare my legs and arms, if you would," Henry croaked. The words were almost incomprehensible.

"Water," Aunt Millward said. "Where can we find water?"

"Henry has some in his office," Emily said. "I noticed the bowl and pitcher earlier."

Henry attempted to nod but quickly changed his mind. Emily didn't need the painful confirmation. She was observant enough to know exactly where to find it.

"Would you like me to fetch the water, my lady?" Rutherford asked.

"I'll go," Emily said before Aunt Millward replied. "Rutherford is needed here to help Henry out of the crate."

"Thank you, my dear. I think you will manage it faster than I would."

Emily didn't reply; she'd already left.

Chapter 26

Throwing all decorum to the wind, Emily ran the entire distance between the accessions room and Henry's office. Vaguely aware that Mr. Townsend's tour was in the Montagu room, she gave no thought to the heads that turned to watch as she raced by. Her sole focus was on getting the water Henry so desperately needed. Bursting through the door to his office, she came to a stumbling halt beside the workbench.

The pitcher standing on the corner was almost completely full. Henry would not need that much water right away, and it would be far easier for her to carry it quickly if the pitcher were not so heavy. Pouring half the water into the bowl that Henry likely used to wash his hands after working with plants and animals, she carried the pitcher out of the office.

She made the return trip to the accessions room at a hasty shuffle rather than a full sprint. Keeping her eyes on the sloshing water, she attempted to keep the pitcher level as she hurried across the marble floor. The door to the accessions room remained open, and she slipped in.

"That's it, sir. Slow and steady."

Emily stopped, her ragged breathing catching at the sight before her. Rutherford stood behind Henry, his arms around Henry's chest, supporting him as he helped pull him to his feet in the crate. Henry swayed, and Rutherford shifted one leg, anchoring himself more firmly.

"Take your time, sir. I'll help you out as soon as you're ready," Rutherford said.

"Now," Henry croaked. Slowly, he raised one leg, gingerly lifting it over the side of the crate and lowering it to the floor. He paused, his chest heaving as he stood straddling the edge. Rutherford continued to hold him. "Again," Henry panted. This time, he placed his weight on the foot outside the crate and lifted his other leg over. He stumbled. Rutherford staggered back a pace, and Aunt

Millward gasped. Henry reached for the side of the crate, grasping it with one hand as Rutherford steadied himself.

"All right, sir?" Rutherford asked.

Henry's lowered head nodded slightly, but his arm was trembling, and the lace at his cuffs was stained with blood.

"Chair," Henry rasped.

Maintaining his hold on Henry with one arm, Rutherford leaned for the chair beside him and dragged it into position beside Henry. "The chair is at your right, sir," Rutherford said. "On the count of three, I'll help you onto it."

Henry grunted his agreement, and Rutherford began to count. When he reached three, Henry lowered himself onto the seat, and Rutherford released him.

"Nicely done, sir," Rutherford said.

"Let him have some water before he attempts anything more," Aunt Millward said. "Emily is here."

Emily glanced at the pitcher in her hands, suddenly wondering what to do with it. "Can he manage without a cup?"

"Absolutely," Aunt Millward said. "As long as some of it gets down his throat, it doesn't matter if his shirt and vest become wet in the process."

Henry raised his head, his eyes softening at Emily's approach.

"I'm sorry, Henry," she whispered brokenly. "I hate to see you so badly hurt."

He reached out and touched her face and hair. "You are come," he rasped. "That's all that matters."

"And that you are safe," she said, raising the jug. "You must drink. I will do my best not to spill."

Without waiting for a response, Emily pressed the pitcher to his lips. Cautiously, she tipped it, watching for the first sign of water. A dribble ran down his chin. She held the pitcher steady, letting him drink before tipping it a little more. After several thirsty gulps, he leaned back, and she lowered the jug.

"Thank you," he said.

The words were a little slurred, but far more recognizable.

"Would you like more?"

He shook his head and then winced. "Not yet."

She set the pitcher on the floor. "Are you well enough to tell us what happened?"

"When I returned to the museum last night, Fernsby was here, exchanging priceless artwork for forged paintings."

Rutherford muttered a curse. "Mr. Fernsby did this to you?"

"He's obviously a lot stronger than I gave him credit for." Henry winced as he swallowed, and Emily lifted the pitcher to his mouth again.

"I have seen the kind of desperation that leads men to do terrible things manifest in a burst of extraordinary strength," Aunt Millward said.

Emily waited for Henry to take a few more sips of water before lowering the pitcher.

"I don't know what Mr. Fernsby's end goal is," she said, "but leaving you for dead in a crate suggests that he'd rather you not be part of it."

"He wants to be the director of the British Museum," Henry said.

"That would make it far easier to maintain a clandestine forgery business," Aunt Millward said. "You became expendable the moment you stumbled upon that."

Henry grimaced. "I daresay he intended to leave me here for dead. Why else would he nail the crate lid closed? It would be easy enough to have the dock workers come back to carry away that crate with the others needing to be burned. We've been known to fill crates with damaged goods and refuse before. They wouldn't question the extra weight."

The pitcher in Emily's hands trembled as she visualized the dreadful scenario Henry described.

"Mr. Fernsby must be stopped," Aunt Millward said.

"What time is it?" Henry asked.

Rutherford reached into his waistcoat pocket and withdrew a pocket watch. "Quarter past one."

"The board of trustees meeting." Henry pushed himself onto unsteady feet. "I must go. They must hear what Fernsby is about."

He teetered, and Rutherford grabbed his arm. "Are you certain that is wise, sir? You're coming off a serious injury."

"I have no time or energy to argue, Rutherford." He looked to Aunt Millward. "Is your carriage outside?"

"It is, and if Rutherford will help you into it, Emily and I will take you to the meeting at Lord Southbeck's house."

Aunt Millward started for the door, but she had scarcely circumvented the crate when Mr. Townsend appeared in the doorway, a menacing scowl on his face. "What the blazes is going on?" he said. "A young lady running wild through the museum. No porter assisting guests in the entrance hall. Unticketed visitors in the accessions room. A missing curator . . ." His voice trailed off as he focused on Henry. "Buckland? You look as though you've recently escaped a brawl in the Rookeries."

"You're not far off," Henry said, reaching for Emily's hand and taking his first shaky steps toward the door with Rutherford at his other side. "If you want the details, you'll have to ride with us to Southbeck's house."

"You're going there in that condition?"

"I'm going there to prevent the man who put me in this condition from being made director," Henry said.

Mr. Townsend's jaw tightened. "I'll come," he said, stepping aside so they could all exit the room.

Somehow, Henry made it down the grand staircase, across the entrance hall, down the steps, and into Aunt Millward's carriage without collapsing. Rutherford's physical support was invaluable, but having Emily at his side helped him block out the pain associated with every movement. He was alive, and she was with him. For now, that was all that mattered.

"You have my deepest thanks, Rutherford," he said as the porter hurriedly backed away from the carriage to allow Townsend entry.

"I dismissed my tour early, Rutherford," the curator said, climbing in as quickly as his aging joints allowed. "There are two more scheduled. Offer those who come later today the museum's regrets, and have them reschedule, would you?"

"Yes, Mr. Townsend."

"One more thing," Aunt Millward called through the carriage's open door. "Send a message to Bow Street and ask that they send a runner—Mr. Toole, preferably—to Lord Southbeck's house immediately."

"I'll see to it right away, my lady," Rutherford said, closing the carriage door with a thud and raising his hand to signal the driver.

The vehicle pitched forward, and Henry stifled a moan.

"Does it hurt terribly?" Emily asked.

"Like the dickens," he muttered, tightening his grip on her hand. He had no desire to release it anytime soon. "My head's the worst. There's a decent-sized goose egg where it hit the tile."

"About that," Townsend said. "A full explanation—or, at least, as full as you can make it, given your current state—would be helpful before we reach Southbeck's place."

Townsend was right. Everyone in the carriage deserved to be alerted to the tempest Henry would be unleashing if he arrived in time to speak to the board of trustees.

"What time is it?" he asked again.

Townsend glanced at his pocket watch. "Half past one."

Henry grimaced. He had never descended the museum stairs so slowly. It had taken them a quarter of an hour to reach the carriage from the accessions room, and it would take at least that to reach Southbeck's house.

"Locating and apprehending Fernsby must be our first priority when we arrive," he said. "There's no accounting for what he may do if he sees that I am free and can testify against him."

"It will be your word against his," Townsend warned. "Fernsby is a social creature and is well versed in flattery and charm."

"Henry's obvious wounds will add to his credibility," Aunt Millward said. "Quite apart from the fact that Emily and I witnessed him bound, gagged, and confined in that awful crate."

"If they want further proof of Fernsby's crimes, they need go no further than the paintings hanging on the walls in the museum," Henry said.

Townsend's face paled. "I sincerely hope you are not suggesting that they are forgeries."

Henry rubbed his aching jaw. No matter his fatigue, it was time to start his account at its beginning.

Chapter 27

THE CARRIAGE TURNED THE CORNER, and Henry leaned forward to better see through the window. Southbeck's house, a grand mansion built of red-brick, with multipaned, white-framed windows, appeared up ahead. A narrow lawn lined by a hedge and low wall separated the house from the row of black carriages parked along the length of the road.

Henry released a tense breath. The meeting must not yet have adjourned. "The members of the board are still here," he said. "I recognize Lord Bradbury's crest on the nearest barouche."

"Good." Aunt Millward's carriage came to a stop behind one of the others, and she slid to the edge of her seat. "They shall not leave until they have heard what you have to say." She turned to Townsend. "Are you ready, sir?"

"I am." Townsend pressed his hat more firmly to his head, as though the action secured his courage as well as his wig. "Will you need assistance alighting the carriage, Buckland?"

Although the pain caused by his many injuries had yet to subside, Henry's movement and speech had improved greatly since he was first helped out of the crate. He was not ready to run a footrace, but he could likely manage a few shallow stairs.

"I believe I can cope."

"If that is the case, Mr. Townsend and I shall go ahead and apprise the butler of your need to gain entry into the meeting," Aunt Millward said.

Townsend nodded his agreement. Always a man of few words, he had listened to Henry's report of Fernsby's activities in grim silence. Henry's observations of Fernsby's recent change in behavior had likely come as no surprise, but when he'd recounted his experience with the man last evening, Townsend's expression had hardened. The older gentleman may not be an artist, but he was an authority on literary works. Stealing another man's words was not so very different from stealing another artist's painting, and Henry could tell that Fernsby's criminality did not sit well with Townsend at all.

The driver opened the carriage door, and Townsend climbed out of the vehicle immediately. "Come, Lady Millward," he said, extending his arm to her.

Aunt Millward exited and started up the steps leading to the house with Townsend at her side. Emily hurried out, too, but stood beside the open door, waiting for Henry. Henry reached for the carriage's door frame, and using it as an anchor, he pulled himself off the seat. The bloodied lace at his wrists chafed the raw skin, but he kept his hold on the piece of wood, using it to steady himself as he clumsily disembarked. A wave of dizziness hit him. He closed his eyes and breathed through his nose.

Emily's small arm slipped through his. "Lean on me if you must," she said.

He managed a wan smile. "That does not sound very gallant."

"Rescuing me from an afternoon with Lord Culham amassed you an excess of gallantry. You may lose some on these steps and still be ahead."

Gratitude overwhelmed him. Even when he was in extremis, Emily lifted his spirits and made anything seem possible.

"I shall remember that if I lose what little decorum is left to me and punch Fernsby in the jaw again," he said.

She raised an eyebrow. "Again?"

"Again," he repeated, starting up the stairs. "And I sincerely hope the bruise is visible."

Emily gave a gratified smile. "It is."

The front door was open, and Aunt Millward's voice was rising.

"I am fully aware that Lord Southbeck is in a private meeting," she said. "That is exactly why we are here."

"If you wish to make an appointment to see Lord Southbeck at a later date, I am happy to make arrangements for you." The butler had positioned himself in the center of the doorway and showed no sign of moving.

Aunt Millward glared at the man. "Do you know who I am?"

"Yes, my lady."

The question was a testament to Aunt Millward's level of anxiety. Henry had never heard her pull rank on anyone before. And unfortunately, it did not seem to be having its desired effect. He and Emily joined his aunt and Townsend on the top step.

"My name is Buckland," Henry said. "I am one of the British Museum's curators. Lord Claridge personally invited me and my colleague, Mr. Townsend, to attend this meeting of the board of trustees. I grant that we are late, but it is imperative that we join the other gentlemen before they dismiss."

"Mr. Buckland, you say."

"That is correct. And Mr. Townsend."

The butler eyed Henry's disheveled appearance, then he withdrew a slip of paper from his waistcoat pocket and consulted it. "I beg your pardon, sir."

Henry might not have a title or a cravat, but it seemed that he had the right connection.

The butler replaced the slip of paper and stepped aside to admit them into the hall.

"This way, if you please."

He led them through the entry hall and into a long passage lined on one side with windows and on the other with paintings. Three doors punctuated the long row of paintings, and beside each door was an elegant chair upholstered in gold brocade.

"Please take a seat, Lady Millward," the butler said, stopping beside the first door and its accompanying chair. "And you, miss," he added, gesturing toward the chair a little farther down the passage.

"I shall attend the meeting," Aunt Millward said.

The butler tucked his hands behind his back and inclined his head. "With all due respect, my lady, only those whose names are on the paper Lord Southbeck gave me are allowed entry."

"Good heavens!"

Aunt Millward's indignation was reaching new, unchartered levels, but before Henry could intervene, Emily stepped forward and laid her hand on the older lady's arm. "Henry is not entering the lion's den alone, Aunt Millward. Mr. Townsend will be with him."

With a frown, Aunt Millward dropped onto the chair. "I am not happy about this arrangement."

"Neither am I," Emily whispered, "but seeing as Lord Southbeck's butler is so diligent, someone will need to listen for Mr. Toole's arrival, because the poor man will not be allowed in otherwise."

Henry had never met Mr. Toole, but he thought it highly unlikely that a Bow Street runner would need the assistance of either Aunt Millward or Emily.

His aunt did not seem to be of the same mind, however, for with a surreptitious glance at the butler, who was now standing guard over the nearby door, she clasped her hands upon her knee and leaned back in the chair.

"You'd best go and say your piece, Henry," she said. "Emily and I shall be here if you need us."

Henry did not hesitate. Assuming that Townsend was at his heels, he approached the butler. The conscientious servant offered Henry a small bow, knocked, and then opened the door. Someone was speaking. Henry did not recognize the voice, but at the butler's sudden interruption, whoever it was stopped talking midsentence.

"Mr. Buckland and Mr. Townsend," the butler announced.

Henry walked in. Eight men were seated on either side of a large rectangular table. At one end sat Lord Claridge; at the other end sat Fernsby.

"My lords, gentlemen." Henry bowed and then immediately wished he hadn't. The room tipped, and the faces swam. He sensed Townsend stepping up beside him.

"Steady, Buckland," he muttered, placing a hand on his elbow.

It was the grounding he needed. Clearing his throat, Henry gave his vision a moment to clear and began again. "Please forgive my late arrival. I was detained by a rather violent encounter with my colleague Mr. Fernsby."

He turned slowly so that he was facing his erstwhile friend. Fernsby's fingers were splayed on the table, his palms pressed against its surface as if he were preparing to propel himself out of the chair. His pale face accentuated the dark bruise running along the right side of his jaw, but he was as impeccably and brightly dressed as always.

"You are come too late, Buckland." Fernsby was the first to speak, his eyes flashing a toxic combination of fear and derision. "The board has just voted to put me in as the new museum director."

"I daresay they will reconsider their vote when they hear what I have to say."

Claridge rose to his feet, his cheeks flushed. "I had not thought you a gentleman of such inferior comportment, Buckland. You have considerable gall showing up an hour after the appointed time in such a shoddy state and throwing threats at your colleague."

"If those of you in the *haut ton* are truly so fixated with the inappropriateness of a gentleman's soiled clothing and lack of punctuality that you would not even think to ask what prompted those things, you are as narrow-minded as so many poets and essayists claim. Indeed, you deserve to have a gaudy, amoral criminal as the museum director, and I formally submit my resignation."

It was the longest speech Henry had ever heard Townsend give outside a lecture on a piece of literature, and it left the remaining occupants of the room staring at him in stunned silence.

Fernsby was the first to recover. "It appears that your insular existence has finally caused you to crack, Townsend. You have my deepest sympathies."

Claridge glared at Fernsby, but Southbeck rose to his feet.

"If I may take the floor, Claridge?" Southbeck said.

"Granted," the chair said.

"Before any more accusations or resignations are made, I should like to ask Mr. Buckland to explain himself further."

"With pleasure, my lord." It was exactly the opening Henry needed, and he seized it. "For the sake of brevity, I shall limit myself to the events of the last twenty-four hours, for they are the ones of most import to you.

"Last evening, I discovered a valuable artifact in the bottom of my satchel. Although I had not placed it there, I recognized it immediately as part of a set I had unloaded a few hours earlier from one of the crates sent to the museum by Mr. Watts. My alarm at finding the piece in my possession and outside the accessions room was quickly followed by determination to replace it immediately. Regardless of the lateness of the hour, I returned to the museum only to find Mr. Fernsby there, making use of the darkness to exchange a prized painting on the wall for one of his own. I accused him of creating and selling forgeries, and we came to blows.

"A hit to the head against the marble flooring rendered me unconscious. I awoke this morning, gagged, tied hand and foot, and trapped within one of the crates so recently come from the South Seas. I was discovered not long ago and came directly here."

"That is preposterous!" Fernsby was on his feet.

"I agree," Henry said. "Preposterous, deceiving, and unlawful."

"Where's the proof of all this?" Mr. Hibbard, the gentleman seated beside Southbeck, yelled.

"Hear, hear." The gentleman across from him called out, and suddenly, everyone was shouting at once.

"Silence!" Lord Claridge bellowed.

The ruckus calmed, but Fernsby did not resume his seat. His muscles tense, he watched the chair warily.

"One at a time, we shall each ask a question of Mr. Buckland, Mr. Townsend, or Mr. Fernsby," Claridge said. "Southbeck, you may start us off."

Emily reached the end of the passage, pivoted, and started back the way she had come. She had walked the length of the long, narrow room twice already.

The first time, she had studied the intricate pattern on the exotic rug and attempted to block out the sound of rising voices in the room Henry and Mr. Townsend had entered. The second time, she had paused to admire the view from each window, secretly hoping to also catch a glimpse of a hackney cab dropping off at least one Bow Street runner. Not one carriage had passed by, so this time, she turned her attention to the opposite wall and concentrated on the paintings.

The first two were pastoral scenes. The third portrayed a foxhunt.

"What can possibly be taking so long?" Aunt Millward had chosen to remain seated by the door and was straining to hear what was occurring in the other room now that the men's voices had lowered. "Mr. Fernsby should have been escorted out by now."

"The longer the wait, the greater the chance that Mr. Toole will arrive," Emily said. It was the only consoling thought she could muster, and she clung to it.

Another glance through the nearest window showed no traffic on the other side of the stone wall, so she returned to her forced study of the paintings. The next canvas showed a flock of doves in flight. Emily counted the birds. It was only marginally better than counting minutes. She continued a few more steps. This painting showed a bowl of fruit. She stared at the masterfully recreated apple—the one she'd once thought was a Genet Moyle and later had thought appeared more like a D'Arcy Spice—and a gaping pit formed in her stomach. She did not know if this was a replica or if Lord Southbeck had purchased the original, but she was quite sure that Lord Southbeck was unaware that either he or the museum was displaying a forgery.

Clenching her fists, she tried to gather her scattered thoughts. She must tell someone. Lord Southbeck needed to know, and if she acted now, it could be the proof Henry needed to convict Mr. Fernsby of the crime he alone had witnessed. She eyed the door to the meeting room. The butler was gone, but he'd sent a footman to watch over Aunt Millward and her. The young man was unlikely to be quite as attentive as his superior, but he had yet to leave his post at the other end of the passage.

Forcing herself to keep her pace even, she retraced her steps until she reached Aunt Millward. Turning her back to the footman, she lowered her head slightly. "I need a distraction," she whispered.

"Yes, dear. We both do."

"No, I mean I need you to create a distraction."

Aunt Millward's head jerked up. "Why?"

"I've just discovered something that will enable Henry to prove that Mr. Fernsby has been copying the paintings in the museum."

The older lady's eyes widened, and the peacock feathers bounced. "On Lord Southbeck's wall?"

Emily nodded.

"Dear heaven." Aunt Millward placed her hand on her heart. "The gentleman takes great pride in his art collection. He will be devastated."

"Yes, but he will be more devastated if Mr. Fernsby gets away with what he has done." The rumble of voices continued from behind the closed door. "I must tell him immediately."

"Indeed, you must." Now that she had something useful to do, Aunt Millward had perked up considerably. "You shall have your distraction. I am uncommonly good at those." Rising to her feet, she started toward the footman. "Excuse me, young man."

The startled footman bowed. "Yes, my lady."

"I find that I am in desperate need of some air." She swayed a little dramatically and reached for the footman's arm. "Would you be so good as to guide me to the nearest exit?"

"Of course, my lady." His concern was obvious, and Emily might have felt truly sorry for him had she not known that Aunt Millward would treat him kindly. Besides which, Emily was desperate.

She waited only until Aunt Millward and the footman were facing the other way, then she took ahold of the door handle. Turning it, she eased open the door, stepped inside, and closed it softly behind her.

Chapter 28

Henry tugged his sleeves back into place and glanced at Fernsby. The mood in the room had changed after Lord Brooks had asked to see Henry's wrists. Fernsby now had tiny beads of perspiration running across his brow, and his eyes kept darting between the door to the passage and the french doors leading to the garden.

"So let me be clear," Lord Southbeck said. "You claim that what you witnessed last night was not the first time Fernsby has replaced a painting in the museum? That he has been producing counterfeit paintings for some time?"

"Yes, my lord." Henry said.

"Can you prove that?"

"Yes, he can."

At the sound of Emily's voice, the eyes of every gentleman in the room turned on her.

"Who are you, and what the blazes are you doing in here?" Lord Claridge bellowed.

Henry instinctively stepped closer to her, but she did not waver.

"My name is Miss Norton, and I am here with Mr. Buckland, Mr. Townsend, and Lady Millward. Lord Southbeck's butler insisted that Lady Millward and I wait outside while you gentlemen discuss Mr. Fernsby's recent activities."

"Which is exactly where you should be now," Hibbard growled.

Henry stiffened, attempting to control his mounting anger. "I believe an apology is in order, sir. I don't care what you think of me or my claims, but to speak to Miss Norton like that was completely out of line. The same goes for you, Claridge."

"He's absolutely right," Southbeck said firmly. "It's not done. Especially whilst you're guests in my house."

Claridge flushed at the reproof. "You have my apologies, Miss Norton."

"And mine," Hibbard mumbled, looking far less contrite.

"Thank you, my lord. Sir." She raised her chin slightly, and Henry had the irrational urge to kiss her for her courage and comportment. "I believe that if you are willing to hear me out, you will find it worth your time."

"Go ahead, Miss Norton." Given Claridge's faux pas, Southbeck had obviously decided to take charge of Emily's interruption.

"It is information that you, in particular, must hear, my lord." She caught her lower lip in her first show of anxiety. "There is a painting in the passage outside this room of a bowl overflowing with fruit."

"I know the one to which you refer. It is one of my wife's favorites."

"It is lovely," Emily agreed. "And you undoubtedly purchased it believing that it was one of a kind. Unfortunately, you are mistaken. I do not know which was created by Mr. Caravaggio and which is Mr. Fernsby's work, but an identical painting hangs in the Montagu room of the British Museum."

The chair behind Fernsby toppled to the floor as he bolted for the french doors.

"Catch him!" Southbeck shouted.

Half a dozen men rose from their seats and were already in pursuit when Fernsby threw open the doors and disappeared outside.

Henry started after them, but Townsend caught his arm. "Not this time, Buckland. You don't have the strength. Let the others go."

Henry attempted to brush him off, but the older man was tougher than he appeared. And he was right. In his present condition, he could not catch Fernsby in a footrace. But he might be able to trap him.

Older and less agile than some of the other board members, Southbeck had not quite reached the open glass door.

"Where do the french doors lead?" Henry called.

"Into a walled garden." Southbeck anticipated his next question. "An eight-feet-tall wall all the way around."

"Any other way out?"

"There's another set of doors leading into the library, but they would be locked. And a gate." Southbeck froze. "There's a gate! We don't use it much, but it leads to the front of the house."

That was it. There was no way of knowing if the fiend would notice the access, but given his desperate state, he would most certainly be searching for one. If Fernsby were given an option that did not risk ruining his precious clothing on a gritty brick wall, he would take it.

Henry hurried to the door leading to the passage. The floor tilted sightly, and nausea assailed him, but he reached for the handle and yanked it open. "What's the fastest way out there?" he yelled.

"The front door." Southbeck had reversed course and joined him in the passage. "This way!"

Vaguely aware of footsteps behind him, Henry kept his eyes on Southbeck and attempted to keep his balance. They ran through the passage and into the entry hall.

"Open the door!" Southbeck ordered.

Southbeck's butler hastened to do his master's bidding, pulling the door wide and standing aside as the men rushed through.

Three people stood on the narrow strip of grass in front of the house: Aunt Millward, a footman, and a gentleman Henry did not recognize. What they were doing there, Henry could not fathom, but he needed Aunt Millward somewhere else entirely.

"Move away!" Henry cried. "Fernsby's on the run."

Instantly, the stranger moved. "Which way is he coming?"

Southbeck pointed to the left as the creak of a little-used metal hinge filled the air and a man dressed in a bright-yellow jacket bolted out from between two bushes.

"Stop him, James!" Southbeck shouted, and the footman, who was the closest person to the fleeing man, darted across the lawn to intercept him.

Fernsby saw him coming and dodged right. James countered. Fernsby pivoted and rushed past him, heading directly for the front gate, with Henry right behind him. The stranger stepped into his path and pulled a pistol from his pocket. Fernsby veered toward Aunt Millward. A few more yards and he'd be close enough to use her as a shield or hostage. Henry changed his trajectory. A flurry of skirts appeared in his peripheral vision.

Emily appeared out of nowhere and lunged for Aunt Millward's arm. "This way," she cried, pulling her back toward the house.

Fernsby thrust his arm out, sweeping the air as his hand grasped for the excessive fabric of Aunt Millward's gown. Emily yanked her out of reach, and Fernsby missed. He stumbled, enabling Henry to take the three extra steps he needed. Launching himself into the air, he seized Fernsby around the waist, and they both went down. Fernsby's curse was cut short by the thud of his head hitting the ground. He moaned, and Henry pushed himself to a kneeling position beside Fernsby's prostrate form.

"Fair's fair, Fernsby," Henry said through gritted teeth. "Good luck with that headache."

Emily delivered a shaken Aunt Millward into Mr. Townsend's care and raced back across the short lawn to where Lord Southbeck was aiding Henry to his feet. The Bow Street runner, Mr. Toole, was standing over Mr. Fernsby, his pistol in hand.

"This is the art copyist, I assume?" Mr. Toole said.

"Amongst other things." Henry steadied himself, and upon his giving Lord Southbeck a subtle nod, the gentleman released his arm. "His list of crimes has grown significantly over the last twenty-four hours."

Mr. Toole slid his weapon back into his pocket and exchanged it for a piece of rope. Dropping to his knees beside Mr. Fernsby, he rolled him onto his side and drew his wrists together behind his back. With well-practiced expertise, he wrapped the rope around them and cinched it tight before rising to his feet again.

"Grateful though I am for your assistance," Lord Southbeck said, "I do not believe we have met."

"I wouldn't wish the need of a Bow Street runner on anyone, my lord, so it's just as well for you that we're as yet unacquainted." He bowed. "Hugh Toole at your service. I received a message from someone at the British Museum and arrived whilst Lady Millward was taking the air. She told me a little about what this fellow's been up to right before he came barreling out from between the bushes."

Emily stepped forward to stand beside Henry. "Thank you for coming so promptly, Mr. Toole. As usual, your timing is impeccable."

Mr. Toole hid any surprise he may have harbored at her unexpected presence with his usual calm. "Miss Norton." He bowed a second time. "Nice to see you again, although I wish it were under slightly better circumstances."

"As do I."

At their feet, Mr. Fernsby groaned and shifted slightly.

"He's coming around," Lord Southbeck warned.

"Well, that'll make moving him easier," Mr. Toole said. He raised a questioning eyebrow at Lord Southbeck. "Where do you want him, my lord?"

"Off my property."

Mr. Toole inclined his head. "Easy enough. I daresay the warden at Newgate can find room for him while we get things sorted."

Emily shuddered. Newgate was one place in London that she never wished to see.

"You have my thanks, Toole." Henry slipped his hand around hers. It was strong and warm and a poignant reminder of how close she had come to losing him. "You know where to find me if you need me."

"I do, sir." He paused. "Lady Millward recounted a portion of what you recently endured. I'll give you a day or two to recover before I come calling."

"I appreciate it."

Lord Claridge arrived on the scene, breathing heavily. Behind him, half a dozen more members of the board were crossing the lawn from the side gate.

"What happened, Southbeck?" Lord Claridge asked.

"Buckland brought him down," Lord Southbeck said.

"Good heavens." Lord Claridge looked from Henry to the man lying on the ground with his hands bound.

Fernsby's eyes flickered open. For a moment, he simply stared at the men standing above him, and then awareness of his situation dawned. Fear shone in his eyes, and he tugged at his bindings. "I can explain!" he shouted. "Let me loose. I can explain!"

Henry turned away from him. "Come, Emily," he said, leading her away. "We're not needed here any longer."

Aunt Millward hurried across the grass to meet them. "Henry! I've been so worried. Are you all right?"

He gave her a tired smile. "I daresay I will be after about twenty-four hours of solid sleep."

"Home," she said firmly. "I do not care what Mr. Toole, Lord Southbeck, or any of these other gentlemen say. I am taking you home right away."

"If you'd be good enough to drop me off at the townhouse, I'd be most grateful."

"Nonsense. Neither of your parents is home. I know your housekeeper and valet are fully capable and reliable employees, but they are not family. I could never face your mother again if I simply dropped you off in this state." She started across the lawn toward the waiting carriage. "Besides," she added, seemingly as an afterthought, "if you come home with me, you will not have to travel any distance at all to see Emily."

CHAPTER 29

"Look!" Emily bent down beside a rosebush and pointed to a dark caterpillar with yellow markings wiggling its way across a leaf. "Isn't it incredible? Not much longer and it will be a painted lady butterfly."

Henry loved that Emily found such joy in discovering a caterpillar on a leaf, loved that she could identify it by name. He crouched beside her, the delight on her beautiful face causing his heart to swell. Aunt Millward had been correct. As usual. Spending the last three days in her home with Emily had been better than any medicine Dr. Thorndike could have prescribed.

"Do you know its scientific name?" he asked.

She turned her expressive brown eyes on him. "Tell me."

"*Vanessa cardui.*"

"*Vanessa cardui,*" she repeated. "That's pretty. It's a good fit for such a beautiful butterfly."

Smiling, he rose to his full height again, grateful that the movement no longer caused the loss of equilibrium he'd endured for the first couple of days after his run-in with Fernsby. Aunt Millward had insisted upon calling in Dr. Thorndike as soon as they had returned from Southbeck's house, and the physician had given Henry a thorough examination, recommending that he apply the housekeeper's salve to the broken skin at his wrists and ankles, which had been far easier to fulfil than the doctor's admonition to rest.

Henry was not used to lying around the house, but Emily had made it bearable. Whenever dizziness had threatened to cause him to lose the contents of his stomach, she'd read out loud to him from one of the books in the late Lord Millward's library until the discomfort had passed. When his bruised shoulder and sore wrists had made the easiest of movements difficult, she'd discretely passed him a second roll at dinner and moved his chess pieces for him. He smiled at the memory of her excitement at trouncing him at chess the night before.

She'd blamed it on his recuperation, but Henry knew better. When it came to strategic thinking and intelligence, Emily was brighter than most of his peers at Cambridge. It was one more thing he loved about her.

Thankfully, he'd seen improvement in his balance every day, and the short walk they'd taken together around Aunt Millward's garden on the first day had become longer and longer rambles every day since.

"Do you think the foxgloves have fully bloomed yet?" she asked, leaving the caterpillar to continue its journey up the rosebush unmonitored. "They were so close yesterday."

"We can walk there next." He took her hand, and she threaded her fingers through his. It was a natural response now, but it thrilled him every time.

"Yes." She smiled at him. "Your unsteadiness is all but gone."

He nodded. As grateful as he was for his recovery, he knew what it meant. Sometime very soon, he was going to have to return to his own home and determine what his future might be at the museum. He tightened his grip on Emily's hand, already dreading having this time with her end.

"I beg your pardon, Mr. Buckland."

Startled out of his contemplations, Henry turned to see one of Aunt Millward's footmen approaching.

"Yes, Frederick."

"Lord Claridge is here to see you, sir. Lady Millward thought it best to inform you rather than tell him you are unavailable, but she wished you to know that she is willing to offer the gentleman that response should you desire it."

There could be no doubt about it, Aunt Millward was his greatest ally, but he could not put off the inevitable forever. "Thank you, Frederick. Please tell my aunt that I shall join Lord Claridge momentarily."

"Very good, sir." The footman bowed and started back the way he had come.

"I wonder what news Lord Claridge brings," Emily said, watching Frederick go.

"We shall find out soon enough." He raised her hand to his lips and kissed it. "Forgive me for cutting our walk short."

"Of course." She smiled, and his desire to kiss her lips all but upended his decision to go. "You must meet with him."

She was right, but he didn't have to like it. "I will seek you out as soon as he is gone," he promised.

She nodded, and he released her hand. Frederick was gone, and Claridge would be waiting.

Henry and Lord Claridge had chosen to meet in the library, which made Emily's return to the house much easier. Entering the drawing room from the garden, she loosened her bonnet ribbons and crossed the empty room to the passage. Aunt Millward was probably meeting with her housekeeper to go over the menu for next week, which saved Emily from feeling torn over what to do. She had neglected Aunt Millward and Phoebe since Henry's arrival. But whereas Aunt Millward had often joined them in the drawing room, poor Phoebe was still limited to life in her bedchamber. She was long overdue for a visit.

After depositing her hat in her own bedchamber, Emily knocked on Phoebe's door.

"Come in!" Phoebe called.

Emily entered, took a couple of steps inside, and stopped short. Phoebe was sitting at the dressing table, wearing one of her favorite gowns, and Hannah was putting the last few pins in her hair.

"Phoebe," Emily gasped. "You're out of bed!"

"Isn't it marvelous?" Phoebe beamed. "Never again will I take dressing for dinner for granted."

"But are you . . . I mean to say, is it safe?"

Phoebe reached out her arm, and Emily walked closer to take her hand.

"I pray that it is," Phoebe said. "Dr. Thorndike stopped to see me after he checked on Mr. Buckland's injuries. He told me that since I had gone over a fortnight without any pains, I could go down for dinner as long as I promised not to be on my feet any longer than it took me to go downstairs and back. An hour or two a day is not much, but after having been confined to my bed for so long, it feels like complete freedom."

"I am so happy for you! Adam will be thrilled."

Phoebe laughed. "He will fuss over me like a mother hen; we both know that."

"Yes, he will. But to see you so much improved will do much to alleviate his concern."

"That is why I waited until today," Phoebe said. She reached for a letter on the dressing table. "I received this from Adam right after Dr. Thorndike's visit. He plans to be back this evening. And I want to be downstairs when he comes."

Adam was returning. Emily's initial excitement was muted by a sudden wave of nervousness. Henry would ask to speak with him, and she had no idea how Adam would respond. "How did I not know all this before now?"

As though she had read her thoughts, Phoebe smiled. "You have been somewhat preoccupied with another of Aunt Millward's guests."

Emily felt her cheeks color. "Forgive me, I should not have waited so long to visit you again after I came to tell you all that happened at the museum and Lord Southbeck's house."

Mindful that they were not alone, Phoebe smiled at Hannah. "Thank you, Hannah. You've dressed my hair beautifully."

"Welcome, m'lady." The young maid looked pleased. "Will you be needin' anythin' else?"

"No, thank you."

"Very good, m'lady." She bobbed a curtsy and exited the room.

Phoebe waited only until the door closed behind her before tugging on Emily's hand. "Tell me," she said. "I have been dying to know. How are things progressing with Mr. Buckland?"

There was no point in hiding her feelings from Phoebe. Not only did Phoebe know her too well for Emily to successfully dissemble, but it was also quite possible Emily would need her assistance with Adam. "I have fallen in love with him," she admitted. "I am at my happiest when I am with him, and I miss him terribly when we are apart."

"What of his feelings?"

The warmth in her face increased. "He intends to speak with Adam when Adam returns."

"Oh, Emily!" She squeezed Emily's hand. "I so badly wanted for you to have the kind of marriage Adam and I enjoy. If Aunt Millward approves of Mr. Buckland, I have no doubt he is an honorable gentleman. This is the best possible news."

Happiness bubbled within Emily's chest. "I hope Adam will feel similarly."

"He will." Phoebe cocked her head to one side and appeared thoughtful. "Perhaps if he learns it after he's had a large helping of bread pudding."

Emily giggled. There were some days when her gratitude for Phoebe's friendship knew no bounds. She had a feeling that today would be one of them.

Henry considered twelve minutes of responding to polite questions regarding his health and welfare to be more than enough. He was ready to start asking Claridge some questions of his own. "Have you ascertained how many of the paintings at the museum are forgeries?"

The lines in Claridge's forehead deepened. "Thus far, Mr. Woolley has identified three from amongst those currently hanging on the walls, but he tells me that he has yet to go through the canvases in the storage room." He paused. "It appears likely that Fernsby also stole and sold a valuable print from the Grenville donation."

The manuscript Townsend had found missing. Henry's heart sank. He had held out a slim measure of hope that Fernsby's crimes had begun very recently, but if there were three forgeries in addition to the one at Southbeck's house and the one Henry had seen him switching out, the man had been at it for some time.

"What happens now?"

"Fernsby has refused to divulge the name of his broker. Southbeck, on the other hand, has been invaluable, assisting Toole by giving him details of his own unfortunate purchase. Toole claims to have already made good headway with the case. Ultimately, we hope to discover the names of all those who purchased paintings from Fernsby and will restore as many as possible to the museum."

"And Fernsby?"

"He will have his comeuppance in court," Claridge said severely. "Mr. Woolley is unwilling to leave his position at the Royal Academy of Art but has offered to assist at the museum until we hire a permanent replacement for Fernsby. He has given us the names of several Academy members whom he considers qualified for the job, and Southbeck is following up with each of them."

"What of Townsend?" Henry asked. The last time he'd been with the older gentleman, Townsend had declared his intention to resign.

"I have reassured Townsend that he is needed at the British Museum and that the entire board wishes him to remain." Claridge shifted uncomfortably in his seat. "To say that I have begged him to stay might be closer to the truth."

Henry fought to contain his grin. It was time that Townsend was given the recognition he deserved. "His knowledge and dedication to British literature are second to none."

"Indeed, and the board has unanimously agreed to increase his salary."

"I am very glad to hear it. Am I to assume, therefore, that he has agreed to stay on?"

"Provisionally," Claridge said. "He will not fully commit until he learns who is to be made museum director."

"I see." Henry had had three long nights to consider the question of the directorship since Fernsby had been taken out of the running. He'd not known if the board would consider him for the position again, but he'd wanted to be prepared for the possibility.

Claridge leaned forward in his seat. "The board owes you an apology for not responding to your accusations of Fernsby's misdeeds in a more appropriate manner. We are all heartily sorry for what you endured, are grateful for your unparalleled commitment to the museum's success, and are unanimous in our desire to offer you the position of museum director."

Henry took a moment to absorb Claridge's words. Hours of pondering had left him uncertain of the path he should take, but less than a minute after Claridge voiced the offer, Henry knew his answer with surety.

"I thank you and the board for your sentiments and am honored by your vote of confidence. It should not come as a surprise, however, to learn that my passion lies with the natural sciences, and if the board is willing to extend my tenure, I would prefer to stay on as curator over that area of the museum."

Claridge stared at him in stunned disbelief. "Do I understand you correctly? You are turning the directorship down?"

"Yes, my lord. And if my opinion is of any worth to you, I would submit that Lord Southbeck would be an excellent choice for the position. He has exhibited consistent support of the museum through fundraising efforts and his work on the board. His strengths for acting in an administrative capacity would far outweigh mine." He allowed himself a small smile. "And I believe that if I am held on as curator, I might be able to persuade Townsend to consider doing the same under Southbeck's leadership."

"Well, I never." Claridge appeared completely bemused. "I confess, this is not the outcome I had imagined, but I see the wisdom in your suggestion. And if you were to stay on in your current capacity, the board would be spared the necessity of finding another expert in the field of natural sciences to take your place."

He may have been unprepared for Henry's answer, but the chair was warming up to the change of direction quite quickly.

"That is correct," Henry said. "Although I went to Cambridge with several fellows who enjoy digging up fossils and plants, we are rather a unique breed. I imagine replacing Southbeck on the board might be an easier opening to fill."

"By Jove, I believe you're right." Claridge's expression cleared. "You have my thanks, Buckland. And I think I may speak for the board when I say that Townsend is not the only curator who will be receiving a raise in salary."

Henry inclined his head. "That is very good of you, my lord."

"Nonsense." Claridge rose to his feet, and Henry followed suit. "The museum, its board, and its guests shall be forever indebted to you, Buckland."

"I look forward to returning to my work," Henry said. He'd been too long without his satchel and trowel. "You can expect me at the museum tomorrow morning."

"Good man," Claridge said. "I shall tell Rutherford, Townsend, and Woolley to expect you."

Chapter 30

Emily had barely helped settle Phoebe into a chair beside the drawing room fireplace and across from an extremely pleased Aunt Millward when the sound of men's voices reached them from the entry hall. She looked to the door. If Lord Claridge was not staying for tea, his visit must have been purely business related.

"Is that Lord Claridge leaving?" Aunt Millward asked.

"I believe so."

She'd heard the front door open and close, but it seemed there was still more than one male voice in the passage. Perhaps Henry was talking to Wakefield. The voices drew nearer.

"It's Adam," Phoebe gasped. "He's arrived back early."

One moment later, Adam and Henry walked into the drawing room together.

Henry's eyes instantly found Emily's, and his thoughtful expression softened into a smile meant just for her. Her heartbeat quickened, and she smiled in return. How quickly she had come to recognize his moods and gestures. How thankful she was for their intimate, unseen connection—that at a time when the ramifications of Lord Claridge's and Adam's arrivals were surely filling his mind and social protocols kept them standing apart, his eyes sought hers.

"Phoebe!" Adam crossed the room in a few rapid strides. Dropping to his knees beside Phoebe's chair, he reached out and cupped her face in his hand. "What are you doing out of your bedchamber?"

"I have been without pains for over a fortnight, and Dr. Thorndike told me I might come downstairs for a few hours each day as long as I remained seated." Her smile was radiant. "Today is my first day, but he says that if I can manage it for another fortnight without regressing, I can make the drive home."

"That is the best possible news." He brushed her cheek with a soft kiss. "I have missed you desperately, my love."

She lowered her eyes. "I have missed you too."

Adam seemed to suddenly recall that they were not alone. Coming to his feet, he ran his hand across the back of his neck. "Forgive me," he said. "I did not mean to be impolite."

"Nothing of the sort," Aunt Millward said. "It's a pleasure to see your love for each other, and we all rejoice in Phoebe's improvement along with you."

"To see such a positive change in her is more than I had dared hope," he said.

"There have been some other significant changes since you've been gone," Phoebe said.

Adam raised an eyebrow. "It has not been that long."

Phoebe glanced at Emily, and Emily's stomach dropped. No, she wouldn't. Adam had not even partaken of a cup of tea, let alone a large helping of bread pudding. Phoebe's eyes twinkled. It was the same mischievous look she'd worn when she'd tricked Adam into leaving Emily with Aunt Millward at the Tilsons' ball. "What has always been your greatest wish for Emily?" Phoebe asked.

Adam looked at Emily. "That she never grow up."

It was true. He had told Emily that many times.

Phoebe sighed and tried again. "What was your hope for her when you brought her to London?"

Adam frowned, clearly uncomfortable with this line of questioning. "That she would find a gentleman worthy of her, who would love her as deeply as I love you."

"Yes." With a gentle smile, she set her hands atop her swollen abdomen. "Your first hope was always destined to fail, my love, and your second hope seemed almost inconceivable. And yet, I believe we all have reason to celebrate that the latter was not, after all, a complete impossibility."

Adam's frown deepened. Emily did not dare look at Henry, so she kept her eyes on Phoebe, silently willing her to say no more.

Henry, however, seemed to have decided that there was no time like the present. He cleared his throat. "Might I have a word with you in private, my lord?"

Adam's jaw tightened, shock temporarily stealing his tongue.

"The answer is yes," Phoebe prompted.

Straightening his shoulders, Adam turned to face Henry. "You may."

"Use the library," Aunt Millward said, reaching for the bell. "I shall order tea."

Henry followed Dunsbourne out of the drawing room. This was not how he had imagined orchestrating the conversation he must have with the gentleman. Allowing him a day or two to recover from his journey or, at the very least, waiting until he'd eaten a solid meal had seemed a wiser course. But the longer he'd stood in the drawing room separated from Emily by protocol, the less inclined he'd been to wait for either of those things.

Lady Dunsbourne's prompting had, in fact, been an unforeseen gift. Especially after witnessing the obvious affection she and her husband shared. Henry wanted the same thing. He wanted to walk into a room knowing that he could rightfully sit beside Emily, hold her hand, or even place a gentle kiss on her cheek. And he could only pray that her brother would grant him the permission he so desperately desired.

Dunsbourne entered the library and walked to the fireplace. The gentleman's rigid posture spoke volumes. There was to be no sitting and discussing niceties, it appeared. So much the better. Henry had endured a sufficiently long preamble during Claridge's visit to be more than happy to cut to the chase this time.

"What are your intentions toward my sister, Buckland?"

No preamble whatsoever.

Henry met the baron's steely eyes without flinching. "I wish to marry her."

"Why?"

Why? Lud, how was he to verbalize the way he felt about Emily? His overwhelming desire to always be with her, to support her in her every endeavor, to protect her, to work together to create a home filled with happiness?

"I love her, my lord. Her goodness and intelligence are all the more remarkable because she does not recognize them in herself. She is the most genuine, lovely young lady I have ever had the good fortune to meet."

"No one deserves her."

Henry suspected Dunsbourne's gruffness masked how difficult this was for him. "I agree," he said. "That Emily has singled me out to be the recipient of her particular affection is almost beyond my comprehension, but I can promise you this: I will strive to be worthy of her love every single day of my life."

"Exactly how would you do that?"

Henry took a deep breath. He could not fault the man, but Dunsbourne was not making this easy. He took a moment to think of Emily's sweet face, of her enthusiasm for everything they had done together, whether great or small. "I will escort her out of a crowded ballroom if ever she's in need of time away from the crowd, I will stand by her side to watch a caterpillar turn into a butterfly, I will dig up flowers with her whenever she wishes, and I will proudly wear any eight-foot-long scarf she makes."

Dunsbourne's lips twitched, and his stance relaxed a fraction. "You have come to know Emily well in a relatively short period of time."

"I look forward to getting to know her even better."

"Can you financially support her in such a way that she will never want for any essentials?"

"I can." There was something in the way Dunsbourne phrased the question that led Henry to wonder if the baron had a markedly different view of affluence than the one held by most members of the *ton*. "I own property in Shropshire: a rather lovely house once owned by my maternal grandfather that sits on almost one thousand acres of forested and arable land. My inherited income is sufficient to keep a family comfortably, but I choose to work at the museum because of my passion for the natural sciences."

"I enjoy a similar passion, but mine is for my apple orchard and cider production." Dunsbourne inclined his head as though conceding a point. "I daresay you shall see both before long."

Hope rose in his chest. "I should like that very much, my lord."

"Giving Emily away in marriage will be difficult for me, Buckland. I am entrusting you with someone who is very precious to me."

"I understand, my lord. And although I have not spent nearly as much time with her as you have, she is also extremely precious to me."

Dunsbourne gave a resigned nod. "I shall speak with Emily. If, as you claim, she reciprocates your feelings for her, I will grant my permission for you to marry."

Relief, gratitude, and joy washed over Henry in quick succession.

"You have my heartfelt thanks, my lord."

"I am happy for you, Buckland. And for Emily." He eyed Henry curiously. "Before we return to the drawing room, however, I do have one more question."

Henry braced himself. "Yes, my lord."

"What color is your scarf?"

He fought back a smile. "Green."

Dunsbourne chuckled. "If it's any consolation, she is getting better at them."

Henry completed his fifth circuit of Aunt Millward's garden, fighting the urge to check his pocket watch again. Emily had been talking to her brother for over twenty-five agonizing minutes already. What could possibly be taking them this long? More to the point, how could Aunt Millward and Lady Dunsbourne contentedly sip tea in the drawing room all this time? Did neither of them entertain the slightest concern about Dunsbourne's and Emily's ongoing absence?

He rolled his shoulders and began his sixth lap. A bird flapped overhead, a cat slunk along the top of the garden wall, and a man's shout reached him from the distant road. He focused on each one, drawing calm from the commonplace occurrences.

The click of the french door's latch sent the cat leaping off the wall. Henry swung around. It was Emily.

She ran to him in a rustle of silk skirts. He wrapped her in his arms and drew her close. She pressed the palms of her hands to his chest, raised her beautiful dark eyes to his, and smiled. His breath caught in his throat.

"Adam has given us his blessing," she said.

It was all he had longed to hear. But there was one more thing he must tell her.

"Claridge offered me the position of museum director," he said, "but I turned it down."

She tilted her head back a little farther so she could see him better. "You chose happiness over social standing," she said.

"Yes."

She smiled. "I'm glad."

He had refused a prestigious position, and she was glad. Heaven help him. Dunsbourne was right. He did not deserve her. But, oh, how he needed her.

"As a second son and a museum curator, I cannot offer you a title or an elevated position in Society, my darling, but I can offer you my whole heart, a secure home, and ready access to all the collections at the British Museum."

Her radiant smile was almost his undoing. "May I occasionally join you when you go hunting for plants? And perhaps even wield your trowel every once in a while?"

"Whenever you wish."

"Yes," she said. "To everything. But most especially to being your wife."

With love for this remarkable young woman filling him to overflowing, he cupped her cheek in his hand and ran his thumb gently across her lips. They were soft and warm, and he ached for more. He lowered his head. "I love you, Emily."

"I love you too." Emily's whispered words barely escaped before his lips met hers.

Her arms encircled his neck, her fingers finding his hair. A tremor coursed through him, and he deepened the kiss, surrendering himself to the pure joy of being with her and sharing this moment together.

A blackbird sang, its persistent call gradually penetrating Henry's consciousness. Slowly, he raised his head. Aunt Millward's garden came into focus, and with it, the realization that no matter their new status, they must not be gone from the house too long. Emily shifted in his arms, and reluctantly, he loosened his hold on her.

"Perhaps we could take a turn around the garden before we go back in," he said.

She slipped her arm through his. "I would like that."

They started walking, passing the blooming lily of the valley and foxgloves and the tightly budded roses.

"Look, Henry." Emily pointed to a small plant growing in the shadow of one of the rosebushes. "Is that red campion?"

Releasing her arm, Henry crouched down to examine the delicate flowers. "It is indeed, and I shall never begrudge it for its misnomer again."

"Nor shall I," Emily said. "Coming across a gentleman digging red campion out of the hedgerow remains one of the most intriguing things I have ever seen."

Rising to his full height, he lifted an amused eyebrow. "More intriguing than Indian elephants?"

"Most assuredly."

"Or hats bedecked with rare ostrich feathers?"

"Definitely."

He chuckled. "It seems to me that a regular delivery of red campion bouquets may be in order so that you might continue to remember the event with such fondness."

With a smile that warmed his heart, she tucked her arm securely through his again. "That would be most welcome," she said. "But if red campion is unavailable, a bunch of ribwort plantain would do almost as well."

Author's Note

Over the course of his lifetime, Sir Hans Sloane gathered over 80,000 objects from around the world, amassed a library of over 40,000 books and manuscripts (including hundreds of volumes of dried plants), and collected 32,000 coins and medals. Upon his death in 1753, he bequeathed them all to the British public, and his collection became the founding exhibit of the British Museum. The museum's board of trustees purchased Montagu House in 1759, and the building functioned as the home of the museum until the 1840s when it was demolished to make way for a new structure.

The British Museum was the first of a new kind of museum—one not owned by the church or the crown but that was open to the community. Visitors had to apply for a limited supply of tickets and were given tours of the exhibits by the curators. The number of exhibits continued to increase as well-connected families donated collections and as items were acquired from regions within the British Commonwealth.

Over the years, the British Museum's wide-ranging collections have grown to about eight million objects and cover over two million years of human history. Tickets are no longer necessary to enter the museum, and it now welcomes approximately six million visitors annually.

Although it has always housed priceless works of art, the British Museum has never displayed the oil painting *Basket of Fruit* by Michelangelo Merisi da Caravaggio. That particular masterpiece, created in approximately 1599, is housed in the Biblioteca Ambrosiana in Milan.

John Dalton was born on September 6, 1766, in Cumberland, England. He was a chemist, physicist, and meteorologist and is best known for introducing atomic theory to the scientific world. Remarkably, he is also the first person to study color blindness. Both he and his brother suffered from color vision deficiency, and he conducted many rudimentary tests on others, attempting to determine their color visualization.

In 1794, Dalton published a paper entitled "Extraordinary Facts Relating to the Vision of Colors with Observations." He believed that his color blindness was caused by a blue discoloration of his aqueous humour filtering color incorrectly. This theory was eventually proven wrong, but at the time, nothing was known about genetics or genetic mutations.

Even now, color blindness is sometimes referred to as "Daltonism" in honor of John Dalton's groundbreaking work, and International Color Blind Awareness Day is celebrated on his birthday.

Acknowledgments

THERE ARE SO MANY REMARKABLE people who work behind the scenes at
Covenant with very little public recognition. Thank you—each of you—for
all you do to help me and my books succeed.

My editor, Samantha Millburn, is incomparable. I'm so thankful for her.
The marketing and sales teams, particularly Amy Parker and Jessica Bybee,
work tirelessly to share my books with readers. I'm grateful for their friendship
and support.

Special thanks also to Lara Abramson for using her extraordinary proofing
skills to help make this story more accurate, to Tyler Sommer for sharing his
professional and personal experience with color blindness, and to my family
members for offering me so much encouragement.

I'm very grateful for my wonderful readers who write to tell me how
much they enjoy my books. I hope Emily and Henry's story brings you much
pleasure and that those of you who have come to love the characters featured
in earlier Georgian Gentlemen books relish another moment with Aunt
Millward.

ABOUT THE AUTHOR

SIAN ANN BESSEY WAS BORN in Cambridge, England, and grew up on the island of Anglesey off the coast of North Wales. She left her homeland to attend university in the U.S., where she earned a bachelor's degree in communications, with a minor in English.

She began her writing career as a student, publishing several articles in magazines while still in college. Since then, she has published historical romance and romantic suspense novels, along with a variety of children's books. She is a *USA Today* best-selling author, a *Foreword Reviews* Book of the Year finalist, and a Whitney Award finalist.

Sian and her husband, Kent, are the parents of five children and the grandparents of three beautiful girls and two handsome boys. They currently live in southeast Idaho, and although Sian doesn't have the opportunity to speak Welsh very often anymore, *Llanfairpwllgwyngyllgogerychwyrndrobwllllantysiliogogogoch* still rolls off her tongue.

Traveling, reading, cooking, and being with her grandchildren are some of Sian's favorite activities. She also loves hearing from her readers. If you would like to contact her, she can be reached through her website at www.siannanbessey.com, her Facebook group, Author Sian Ann Bessey's Corner, and on Instagram, @sian_bessey.